DEAD MOON

/ / / /

J.R. RAIN
MATTHEW S. COX

THE VAMPIRE FOR HIRE SERIES

Moon Dance
Vampire Moon
American Vampire
Moon Child
Christmas Moon
Vampire Dawn
Vampire Games
Moon Island
Moon River
Vampire Sun
Moon Dragon
Moon Shadow
Vampire Fire
Midnight Moon
Moon Angel
Vampire Sire
Moon Master
Dead Moon
Dragon World

Published by
Crop Circle Books
212 Third Crater, Moon

Copyright © 2019 by J.R. Rain

All rights reserved.

Printed in the United States of America.

ISBN: 9781095076347

Chapter One
Burning the Candle

Exhausted, I melt into the couch, dimly aware of a chorus of wretched moans around me.

No, it's not my kids reacting to me telling them to clean their rooms—they've got some show on with a bunch of zombies staggering around an old train yard.

"Not funny, Mom," mutters Tammy. "And my room's clean. Mostly."

I'd chide her for eavesdropping telepathically again, but some battles are, in fact, pointless. Every now and then I have a day that leaves me thinking it would be easier to kill the Devil again than be the mother of a seventeen-year-old girl. But, as Tammy often reminds me, she really is on the good end of the scale. I mean, she *could* be running around with a bad crowd, stealing, doing drugs, or drinking, that sort of thing. As teens go, I've been blessed. Some amount of attitude is to be expected. I can't exactly ask Dr. Phil how to cope with the world's most powerful telepath. Though, ever since the fairy, Maple, gave her an amulet that blocks out the constant chaos of hearing all thoughts for several miles, her attitude has done an almost 180-degree flip.

She suppresses a laugh and playfully punches me in the shoulder. "Geez, Mom. I don't have *that* much of an attitude."

Anthony gives her a 'you don't?' glance, but doesn't say anything.

"Don't say it," mutters Tammy.

I raise an eyebrow, confused.

"Not you. Him." She blushes.

"She was on the phone with her new boyfriend... again," says Anthony with a big, cheesy smile.

"Stop looking in my room!" yells Tammy.

He laughs. "I don't have to. You aren't exactly a quiet talker."

"You heard them, too?" I ask.

"Yeah. Don't need to be a vampire to hear through the walls of this house." Anthony grins.

Anthony and I both make kissy sounds.

"Oh, my God! Shut up, you guys!" Tammy buries her face in one of the little throw pillows on the sofa.

I may not be able to read my kid's minds—or even be a bloodsucking fiend any more—but my supernatural hearing is as strong as ever.

"So gross, you guys. And I do not sound like that. And, yes, Anthony was spying. And so were you, Mom. I hate you two."

"No you don't," I say, while hugging myself and making more kissing sounds.

"Grow up," moans Tammy into the pillow.

"I can't." I fuss at her hair. "I'm kind of stuck like this."

"In ten years, you're both gonna look the same age." Anthony pointed at us. "More like sisters."

"That's not funny!" Tammy snapped her head up from the pillow and glared at him. "It's gonna be real weird, actually."

"We'll talk about all that later," I say. "Can we go back to talking about Tammy's new *boooooy-friend*?"

"Gawd!" Tammy throws the little pillow at me before unloading the mother of all eye rolls. I catch it and throw it at Anthony, who snags it out of the air, and throws it back at Tammy... except my superhero son threw it a bit too hard and nearly knocks her off the end of the couch.

"Ow! Butthead!"

"Anthony," I say. "No throwing things at your sister... or at anyone."

"Sorry."

"Say sorry to her."

"Sorry to her," deadpans Anthony.

"Such a butthead," mumbles Tammy.

"A butthead who has your back," he says. "Remember that when this new boyfriend of yours turns out to be a jerk."

"He's not a jerk. He's... sweet."

I examine my—no longer pointy—fingernails. This change I've been through is still a bit strange getting used to. "When are we going to meet this boyfriend of yours?"

"I don't know. He's shy."

"I want to meet him," I say. "And soon. I want to know who's on the other end of all those kissy sounds."

"Ugh. Mom!" She grabs another pillow and covers her face with it. At a flurry of gunfire from the TV, she pulls it down to keep watching, emitting faint squeals as the character she's dubbed 'super hot' runs for his life through a field of tall grass.

Whatever the allure of that show is, I'm missing it, albeit I'm a little distracted at present with all this new boyfriend talk. Still, it's not a bad show, just not my thing. Seems like the writers are going out of their way to make it as tragic/depressing as possible. I've had plenty of that in reality, thank you very much. But the kids can't get enough of it, and to hear them talk, it's like some kind of big time hit.

My mind bounces from the show to her boyfriend. Truth is, it's not a big deal if she's got a boyfriend. Not that I'm upset or anything. No, it's more that her having a boyfriend is tangible proof that she's no longer my *little* girl and she's growing up. Heck, next year, she'll be eighteen and a senior. I don't know if I'm ready to face that. I'd rather deal with the Red Rider again.

Okay, maybe not.

"Aww, Mom." Tammy leans against me, obviously reading my thoughts. "Don't be like that. I'm growing up, not dying."

"Growing up *is* dying," says Anthony before singing something about every step being one less until the last one.

I blink.

Tammy whistles and says, "Wow, that's morbid."

"No, it's Dream Theater." He smiles.

"Um, what?" I say.

"A song, Mom." Anthony chuckles.

I shrug, lost once again, and put my arm around Tammy. These past couple of years… more than once, I've worried her making it to eighteen would be an *if* more than a *when*. Our lives have been far from ordinary. And how messed up is it that my fifteen-year-old son feels like he's capable of protecting both of us? The same way I shapeshift into Talos to fly, he's got this giant fire warrior… *thing* he can transform into. Ever since I made him a vampire for a few minutes to cure him of a terminal illness, his guardian angel has gone off duty. I guess it's kind of like the way a blind person develops better hearing and touch or something. In the absence of having a guardian angel, he's developed powers of his own.

And, yeah, my *very* dead ex-husband has taken up residence inside him in somewhat the same way

I used to be stuck with Elizabeth. After learning the truth of what she did with me, I've had new fears about Danny, but my ex couldn't mastermind a trip to the grocery store much less pull off the kind of next-level twenty-moves-ahead-at-chess shit Elizabeth did. Whether or not Danny's presence is going to be a problem, I don't know. Toward the end of his life, he'd been a complete bastard to me, but other than using the kids to hurt me, I don't believe he'd have harmed them. He also didn't think of me as *me,* more like something impersonating his dead wife.

Joke's on him. I'm not dead anymore. In fact, I couldn't be more alive, now that I know my soul is fully contained in this flesh and blood shell of mine... and now that I know Elizabeth is gone, along with all of the dark baggage she brought with her. Like those creepy ass nails.

"And he's not really my *boyfriend*," says Tammy. "He's just this boy I'm friends with."

The girl blushes rather hard for that to be a true statement. Naturally, she responds to my thought by blushing even more.

"A friend you make kissy sounds with?" I ask. Like a true partner in crime, Anthony makes the special effect for us.

"I swear to God, if I ever hear the word 'kissy' again, I am going freak the eff out."

"Like now?" asks Anthony, laughing.

"Tammy, watch your language. Anthony, don't be mean."

"But I didn't say it. I just said the first letter."

"No one's ever seen this guy, Mom," says Anthony, leaning forward to glance past her at me. "Couple people at school think she's really dating a girl in secret."

"A couple of your creepy friends, you mean!" she snaps. "And Kai's not a girl! He's just… umm, well… pretty. And stop eavesdropping on me. And so what if I was dating a girl."

He shakes his head. "I'm not eavesdropping. People at school are saying someone saw you kissing a girl behind the gym. And, it's not eavesdropping if I'm sitting in my room reading. You're not at all quiet on the phone."

She sighs. "Well, he's *not* a girl."

"Have you checked?" asks Anthony.

She grabs a pillow and starts beating him over the head with it. He puts on this stupid grin and just sits there tolerating the assault. The two of them wind up laughing after a while.

Okay, so my seventeen-year-old daughter may or may not have kissed a boy at school. Of all the things she could've done, that's barely even a blip on the list of stuff to be concerned about. And a girl she insists is a guy? What was the deal with that? Anyway, the kids settle down and get caught up in another battle scene on the television where a whole mass of greyish zombies surround the major characters in an alley, trapping them at a dead end.

I smell a cliffhanger ending.

Right as I smirk at the oh-so-predictable setup to

make viewers scream and spend a whole week agonizing over what's going to happen next, this young female zombie with long, light brown hair turns and stares at the screen. While the other undead continue moaning and grasping for the characters, the young zombie woman stops shambling and continues staring at the screen. I'm expecting a fade-to-black any second, but the scene pauses—except for that one woman. She steps forward from the throng, raising one arm. She points a crooked finger... at me. Or, well, whoever is watching the show. Except this show never breaks the fourth wall, as far as I recall, with characters addressing the viewers—

"Samantha… help me."

I lean back into the sofa cushions, expecting this creature is about to crawl straight out of my TV like the girl from *The Ring*. She's wearing jeans and a dusty, ripped up sweatshirt in dark blue with a red-white-and-blue 'A' over the chest. Her nails look a bit too clean to be a zombie's nails. Guess the makeup people didn't expect anyone to DVR the show, freeze-frame it, and stare at fingernails. Then again, why *did* the show pause? Also, I don't recall a character named Samantha. I do, after all, remember the characters on TV shows with *cool* names.

Except... yes, except I am pretty sure she was addressing me. Like... *me*. I could almost hear Allison say, "Narcissistic much, Sam? The whole world doesn't revolve around you."

The exact second that thought hits me, the scene comes to life (metaphorically speaking) and the zombies collectively converge on the camera until the screen blacks out.

Whoa. That was trippy. Do people still use 'trippy'?

"Hey," I mutter. "Did you guys see that one zombie?"

"Which one?" asks Anthony while chewing on pretzels. "There's like a shitload."

I open my mouth to harp on the swearing thing, but… I'm totally weirded out. "The one that pointed at... the screen, and said, 'Samantha, help me.'"

"He thinks swearing makes him sound cooler than he is," says Tammy, sitting upright again. "I didn't see… holy shit." She snaps her head around and stares at me. "No way!"

"Stop cursing," deadpans Anthony.

"Mom, you're hallucinating." Tammy puts a hand on my forehead. "Are you feeling normal?"

"Since when does Mom *ever* feel normal?" Anthony asks, raising an eyebrow. "Sorry, Ma. Just playing. Love ya. Mean it."

I rub the bridge of my nose, eyes closed. "Right. I had a feeling that didn't really happen."

"You look exhausted," says Tammy.

"Well, yeah." I emit a sleepy chuckle. "I haven't exactly been sleeping well after what happened a few weeks ago." Elizabeth is out there who-knows-where doing who-knows-what. Maximus thinks she'll lay low and gather power for a few years, but

I don't trust her enough to let my guard down.

I also don't trust Tammy's new boyfriend. Then again, maybe it's Tammy I shouldn't trust.

She emits a squeak, and promptly bounces a pillow off my head. I could've caught it or moved away, but A: I'm too damn tired, and B: That show still weirded me out.

That said, can vampires—or whatever I am now—suffer sleep deprivation? It's been a bit of a challenge trying to sleep at night now that my brain doesn't automatically shut down at sunrise or refuse to accept sleep during the dark. For so many years, I've hated having the daytime stolen from me… how much time had I lost where I could've been with my children? They've almost grown up, and I feel as though I've missed half their lives. At random, the thought of four-year-old Tammy curling up beside me when I'd been mortal and took a bullet while working for HUD hits me.

"Aww, Mom," says Tammy, before flopping against my side and doing her best to make the same face she just saw herself make in my memories. "Don't be sad. Get some sleep. It will all be better tomorrow."

I put an arm around her, about to say something sappy when another episode of that zombie show starts.

"Ooh! A two-fer," chirps Tammy.

"That's my cue," I say, standing.

"For what?" asks Anthony.

"To read a book."

Chapter Two
An Easy Five-Hundred

Mindy Hogan gnawed at her lip while walking along a street in southwest Tucson.

She glanced down at the basic white flyer she'd plucked off a tree on campus. Large black letters promised $500 cash for a few hours of her time as a guinea pig. While the idea of 'medical testing' sounded rather terrifying, the fine print only mentioned skin cream, no actual drugs or invasive procedures.

She stopped in front of a nondescript grey building that looked more like a small shipping warehouse than a medical testing company, or even a cosmetics factory. She glanced at the flyer again, and checked the maps app on her phone. The address appeared to match.

A sudden fit of nerves welled up and made her take a step back, on the verge of chickening out for the fifth time. But $500 for an hour or two of not-work was hard to resist. Her parents barely managed to help out with school fees, textbooks, food, and such. Bad enough she'd be paying student loans back until she hit forty.

Three steps later, Mindy stopped and stared again at the giant $500 printed on the paper in her hands. Boy, that spoke volumes to a gal in need, and yet...

"This doesn't feel right," she mumbled into hair that had fallen forward. "But it's an easy couple hundred bucks if it's legit."

Legit being the operative word here.

She pulled her hair off her eyes and glanced around. This street had the look of something post-apocalyptic that hadn't seen people for thirty years —only in somewhat better condition. All the buildings appeared commercial, boards over their windows, not a car or truck anywhere in sight, except for the plain white van parked beside the one in front of her. She'd never been to this street before, or even this part of town. Now she knew why. Nothing here to see or do.

"Okay. If it looks shady inside, I'll leave." She chuckled to herself, wondering why she suddenly had a need to talk out loud. Maybe she needed the comfort of her own voice... or any voice. "Yeah, right. It already looks shady on the outside. Make that, if it looks shady-*er* inside, I'm out."

Mindy walked up a short driveway but cut left before it led around back to a bunch of big garage doors meant for tractor-trailers to back up against. The front door had no bell or button, so she tried pulling the handle. Much to her surprise, it opened, releasing a blast of air conditioning and a clean hospital-like smell.

"Hello?" whispered Mindy while leaning in.

The room resembled the waiting area of a dentist's office. Thin chairs lined three walls around a glass-top coffee table covered in magazines. Another door stood to the left of a reception counter behind a tall, probably bulletproof, window with a small slot to pass paperwork back and forth. Confused at the discrepancy between clean, modern interior and abandoned-looking outside, she hovered in the door for almost a minute until a fiftyish man with neatly trimmed black hair appeared behind the glass.

"Hello," he said with a welcoming smile. "Can I help you?"

Mindy let the door shut behind her, caught off guard by a faint whiff of something like rotten eggs. As soon as she noticed it, it disappeared. She turned in place, looking over the pleasant but super-generic décor on the way to the counter. The man appeared to be a doctor, or at least an actor hired to play one. His neat, white lab coat had a medical caduceus above the pocket, but she couldn't make out the name embroidered in cursive beneath it. "Umm. Hi. I found this flyer at school, and I had some questions."

"Oh, wonderful. You're here for the testing?"

She fidgeted at the paper. "I was considering it, but it's kinda scary. What's involved?"

"Well," said the man, "it's technically two different projects going on at the same time. We're working with a leading cosmetics company to test a new moisturizing cream. While you're doing that, we're also performing a study on brain activity in response to various external stimuli."

"Umm." She leaned back, uneasy. The flyer hadn't said anything about the brain thing.

"Oh, it's harmless." The man smiled. "You'll be comfortable on a reclining chair and looking at a screen that displays either images or simple mathematical problems. A headset will pick up your mental activity. It's a data analysis project to map brain function."

"That doesn't sound too bad. So, you're seriously offering $500 to people to lie there and look at pictures?"

"With a little skin cream dabbed on your arm, yes." He chuckled. "We'll also need to take a small blood sample."

Mindy cringed. "I hate needles. Is that really necessary?"

"In the extremely rare event that you have a reaction to the cream, it's for analytical purposes. We've had almost two hundred people come through here so far and not one of them has experienced any adverse side effects. Once we confirm you don't have a reaction to the cream, the blood samples are incinerated."

"How long does it take?"

"The whole process? About an hour." He smiled.

Mindy folded the flyer up into a small square and stuffed it in her left pocket. "Okay. Do I have to like fill something out?"

"Yes, there's a short medical form." He grabbed a clipboard from the desk and pushed it out via the slot at the bottom of the window. "Have a seat and answer to the best of your ability."

"Thanks."

Still uneasy about the idea, she took the clipboard and sat in a coral-orange chair on the right side of the waiting area. As if volunteering to test an experimental skin cream didn't scare her enough… needles. Ugh. Then again, it wasn't like she'd have to take pills or be exposed to any drugs. For five hundred bucks, tolerating a potential sore spot on her arm for a little while seemed a small price.

Mindy looked over the form on the clipboard. Basic questions about her age, family medical history, was she taking any prescription drugs, any diagnosed conditions or mental illness, and so on. She filled in 'too darn many' in the spot for job. Trying to keep herself afloat while attending U of A had required about a dozen part time jobs, half of which paid her under the table, and most of which only lasted a couple weeks. She'd done just about everything from running photocopies around an office to waiting tables to retail. She refused to do the stripper thing, though she did pose naked for a figure drawing class two months ago. That had been an easy $100, but suffering the intense stares of twenty people for forty-five minutes exceeded her tolerance for embarrassment, so that wouldn't be happening again.

Nothing that sounds too good to be true is ever true. She bit her lip, eyeing the waiting area while envisioning some mysterious green goo dissolving the skin over her arms. *This feels like a giant mistake.* She drummed her fingers along the arm of the chair. She huffed, blowing her hair away from her eyes. *Can't be a chicken all your life, right?*

So, she answered most of the questions except for blood type, having no idea. Over-cranked air conditioning kept her shivering. The form reminded her of the one she had to fill out at the dentist office near the school when she'd gone for a checkup freshman year. Nothing in the questionnaire struck her as bizarre or shady, so she stood and approached the glass.

The man looked up from the desk, smiled, and took the clipboard, leafing page to page. "Sorry, I can't quite make out what you filled in for age. Is that twenty or twenty-six?"

"Twenty. Sorry. I don't actually write with a pen too much." Mindy air-typed. "Everything's on keyboard."

"Okay, okay." He skim-read. "No major history of disease in your family."

"Nope."

"Wow." He smiled up at her. "Not even glasses?"

"Nope."

"Okay, let's get started."

He left the clipboard on the desk and walked out of sight to the left. Seconds later, the door beside the reinforced glass window opened. The man waited for her to enter, then led her deeper into the building. She followed him down a plain teal-green corridor with a growing sense of trepidation to the third room on the right.

Why, oh why, did I not tell anyone I was coming here? She vaguely recalled being embarrassed, and/or worried someone might talk her out of an easy $500.

She repeated the number over and over as he led her to a dentist-type chair in the middle of the room that faced a big TV screen. Beside it, a wheeled cart held a few pieces of computer equipment and a cloth cap studded with wires. A big box of blue exam gloves sat on the counter, white Formica cabinets on the right.

"Please, have a seat and make yourself comfortable." He handed her a teal towel. "If you don't mind, please remove your sweatshirt and shirt. I'll need to put some sensors on your chest to monitor heart rate. For the duration of the test, you can cover yourself with this."

She glanced around, not liking the idea of being alone in a room with a guy with only a bra on above the waist. "Umm." *Well, he is a doctor…* "Okay."

The doctor—or whatever he was—smiled and

went over to a computer workstation sitting on a shelf at standing height beside the door. She stared at his back for a few seconds before she worked up the nerve to pull off her sweatshirt and tee. Again, she caught a faint whiff of bad eggs, looked around, but the smell vanished before she could figure out where it came from or if her overactive imagination had decided to play tricks on her. After setting the removed clothing on the nearby counter, she sat in the chair and pulled the towel up like a blanket to cover her top.

If he asks me to take the bra off, I'm outta here.

A dark-haired woman of Middle Eastern descent walked in, also wearing a white lab coat. "Hello, Miss Hogan."

"Hi," she muttered, reassured somewhat at seeing more people working here than one possibly-shifty guy.

The woman picked up a TV remote from the cart, turned the screen on, and plunked it back down. She next proceeded to affix a series of round sticky pads to Mindy's shoulders, chest, and sides. The doctor approached on her left. Mindy glanced at him only until she noticed a syringe, and shied away, gritting her teeth in anticipation. The nurse, tech, or whatever she was, grasped Mindy's right arm and rolled it over to expose the underside. There, she drew a rectangular box with a felt-tip marker before dividing it into sections and labelling them 1-6.

"There are a few creams here," said the woman.

"One is a currently-on-the-market lotion as a control. One is completely inert, and the other four are various potencies of the item we're testing. To prevent any sort of bias on your part, I can't tell you which sample is which."

Mindy nodded.

Alcohol fumes wafted by a few seconds before cold smeared across her left arm inside the elbow. Mindy kept staring at the grid, watching the woman pull out and open six small white plastic bottles. Each one contained a mostly-identical beige cream. A needle pierced Mindy's left arm while the woman squeezed small lines of cream from each bottle into different numbered sections on her other arm.

A second needle jabbed her in the arm. By the time she made herself look, the doctor withdrew it, but the syringe appeared empty, the plunger all the way down.

"What's that?"

"Oh, I had an issue with the first needle," said the doctor, smiling. "Didn't get a good vein." He held up a small phial three-quarters full of blood. "All set. Sorry for having to stick you twice."

Wait, where did that vial come from? It hadn't been there before, right? It had been empty...

She frowned, picking at the armrest, certain he'd injected something *into* her rather than took blood, but not confident enough in what she thought she saw to open her mouth. *My brain's playing tricks on me. I'm so convinced this is something shady I'm imagining it.*

"Your heart rate is going up," said the doctor. "Is everything okay?"

"Needles," muttered Mindy. "I hate needles."

"Ahh. Don't we all." The woman smiled, squirting the sixth and final sample into place. She put on a pair of blue gloves and used a different finger for each sample to rub them in a little. "All right. We'll just leave that sit there for about an hour and then you're done."

"Okay."

"Lay your head back, please," said the doctor from behind the chair.

Mindy obliged.

He tugged a cloth cap bedecked with wires down snug over her skull. "All right. Bear with me a moment here…"

She tried not to blush too hard while he lifted the towel to connect thin wires to the various pads stuck to her.

"For the next hour, look at the television screen. You'll see a series of images. If it's a picture, just say the first word or feeling that comes to mind. If it's a question or a problem, say the answer. It doesn't matter if you're correct. There's no time limit. The next slide will come up as soon as you answer."

"Okay."

The doctor and the woman left the room, nudging the door closed. A few seconds later, the black-on-grey 'target' image disappeared, replaced with a picture of a lake and a group of ducks swimming.

"Nature," said Mindy.

A broken-down windmill appeared.

"Umm. Holland?"

'25+35' appeared on the screen.

"Sixty."

The image of a scowling old man in a yellow raincoat followed.

"Angry."

After a few landscapes and animal pictures that made her say things like 'peaceful' or 'aww,' a photo of a nude woman casually walking down a city street while no one around her appeared to notice came on the screen.

"Umm. Embarrassing."

Baby goats.

"Aww. Cute!"

A dark dirt road in the forest at night.

"Scary."

Mindy glanced at her right arm, mildly annoyed that the woman wrote on her with a marker. *That'll take days to go away. Still... $500.* A dull ache started in her left elbow, creeping up to her shoulder. *Crap. He did inject something. Or I'm driving myself crazy.* Soft beeping behind her picked up speed—it had to be her heart rate.

A mixture of cute animals and simple math problems appeared one after the next on the screen. A few minutes later, a man's body, nude and burst open evidently as the result of a fall from great height made her gag.

"Eww. Disgusting."

Steak appeared in the following image.

"Poor cow," said Mindy.

The dull ache in her shoulder spread into her chest.

She squirmed, picking at the towel, which started to feel as heavy as a lead apron.

"Which arrives first: a car driving at 50 MPH going 100 miles, or a car driving 100 MPH going fifty miles?"

"The second car, duh," said Mindy.

Beach scene with three small children digging in the sand.

"Sandcastles."

"138 – 27" appeared on the screen.

"111," muttered Mindy after a few seconds to think.

The Eiffel Tower appeared.

"France."

A brain in a jar, an old timey photo like from the 1950s came up.

"Eww." She cringed. "You should've told me there'd be so many disgusting pictures before we started."

The towel became heavier, almost pinning her down to the chair. She tried to lift her left arm to pick at it, but couldn't move. Her right arm responded sluggishly, but moved; she tugged at the towel. The fabric moved as it should; it didn't feel heavy, her chest did. What had been a dull ache in her left arm grew painful.

"Umm, something's wrong," said Mindy.

Another nude woman, middle-aged, standing in front of a white background appeared on the TV.

"Weird," said Mindy.

The next image showed a big salad in a bowl.

That looks good. "Hungry," said Mindy.

Crushing pressure squeezed at her chest, making it hard to breathe. She writhed in the chair, feeling as if the towel made her burn up. A sharp burning ache spread down her abdomen into her thighs. Spikes of pain stabbed her in the heart. She tried to scream, but couldn't make a noise.

The TV switched to show a city street at night.

"H-help… me," wheezed Mindy.

Another forest scene.

"N-no. That wasn't an answer." She groaned in agony. "Seriously, help me!"

Sweat ran into her eyes. Her heart hammered at her breastbone. The beeping from behind her had increased in tempo so fast it had become a steady tone. Another image, the same exploded man appeared from a different angle, showing his head cracked open on the sidewalk and brain splattered out.

She barely noticed it, overwhelmed with panic at being unable to breathe or move. Her head lolled to the right, forcing her to stare at the swaths of cream on her forearm. None of them looked odd. No rash, no pain. She couldn't feel anything at all. Her entire body had gone numb except for faint tingling at her fingers and toes. The screen flashed back and forth from images of brains to hamburgers, fried chicken, salads, steak…

I can't feel my heart pounding anymore.

Mindy tried to scream 'Daddy!' but nothing came out. Her lips didn't even part. The door flew open as the doctor ran in. He flung the towel away and pressed a stethoscope to her chest. A rush of awesome cool air blew over her mostly bare skin, as if she'd been stuck wearing a parka in the middle of an Arizona summer.

Minutes passed in a blur of activity, yet she couldn't even find the energy to blink her eyes. Motion by the window caught her attention. A sheet of inky, black smoke fell from the sill, blanketing the floor like dry ice fog. It gathered itself into a mass and drifted toward her. Terror burst out as a bloodcurdling scream, but only in her mind—she couldn't even twitch a finger. The mass of vapor rose up over the chair, but neither the doctor nor the woman appeared to notice it at all. She recoiled in dread from an indefinable sense of *presence* within the inky fog, as if it looked at her. It hung there for a few seconds, seemingly assessing her, before collapsing forward and washing over her.

She mentally braced for agony, but felt nothing. As randomly as the black smoke had appeared, it vanished.

I'm seeing things.

An unidentifiable sound emanated from the void near her head on the left. It repeated, again and again, gradually clarifying into the doctor's voice calling her name.

"Mindy?"

Perhaps the fifteenth time he said it, the heaviness pervading her body lifted away. She lurched upright, flailing and screaming. All the terror at being immobile exploded in a fit of struggling that took both the doctor and the woman to hold her down.

"Please, calm down," shouted the woman. "You're fine."

Pinned to the chair, Mindy stared between them at the screen, still showing the brain matter dashed across the sidewalk. It still horrified her, but not because it looked disgusting.

Because it didn't.

In fact, she stared at it, fixated, fascinated.

A series of sharp pains in her chest snapped her out of her mental fog. She looked down at the doctor hastily removing the electrodes while the woman wiped her arm off, removing all traces of the skin cream.

"What happened?" stammered Mindy. "I couldn't breathe or move."

"You fell asleep." The doctor rushed a false smile. "You did well. The test is over."

The woman removed the electrode cap then pulled Mindy's T-shirt on over her head, dressing her like a toddler before adding the sweatshirt. "All set, hon."

Mindy gazed around at the room, though she couldn't quite remember how she'd wound up in a dentist's office.

"Thank you for your help." The doctor put an arm around her back, easing her out of the chair.

The two of them half carried her as they walked her out, down the hall, and to the waiting room.

"Who are you?" asked Mindy.

"You're a volunteer. Helped us test out some skin cream," said the man in the white coat. He handed her an envelope. "Here you go. $500 under the table."

She stared dumbfounded, offering little resistance as he more or less shoved her out the door into the not-quite-cold Arizona November. Mindy squinted at the sun, gazing around at the abandoned warehouses. Her legs barely listened to her desire to walk. She staggered forward, stumbling worse than the time she'd woken up with a hangover at Trent's place last month.

Where am I?

Nothing about her surroundings appeared at all familiar. She stopped and turned in place, having the vague idea she should go *somewhere*, but couldn't pull the 'where' out of her head. For that matter, she couldn't much remember anything.

Who am I?

The dull ache returned to her chest, falling far short of pain... just mild discomfort.

I need help.

One hand pressed to her chest, she staggered onward.

Mostly because she already faced that way.

Chapter Three
New Day, New Vampire

There's nothing quite like a good night's sleep.

It feels strange even thinking that now. It's been my routine for almost as long as I've been a vampire to force myself awake against my nature during the day. I mean, small children don't look after themselves, right? And I wasn't about to let something as trivial as being dead stop me from caring for my kids. But now... sleep at night is almost weirder than the idea of regaining my magical, witchy power. Alas, I haven't done much with it yet. I've been waiting for Allison to have time to hang out and show me the ropes.

Turns out, the fairies Tammy thought she'd been hearing outside our house all these years now had been real. In fact, they have apparently sensed the change in me too and risked coming closer; that is, if the lights I see out of the corner of my eye in my backyard are any indication. After what we saw at the tree behind that little girl's house, my daughter no longer thinks she'd been hearing fairies due to insanity.

As far as I'm concerned though, hallucinating a TV show character talking directly to me provided the inspiration to do something I haven't done in years: I slept for a full eight hours. They say a person can acclimate to anything given enough time. My vampiric nature initially made me pretty damn groggy when the sun was up, but over the years, I've grown accustomed to dealing with only like half the sleep a person usually needs. Though, with my kids being fifteen and seventeen, it's not quite so important that I watch over them 24/7.

Lately, Anthony has even been making breakfast for the two of them while I usually slept in. He's become oddly fascinated with cooking actually. Two days ago, he made dinner. His spaghetti sauce smelled so much like Danny's that I wound up half wanting to kill Danny all over again. No doubt exists in my mind that the vaporous essence of my ex-husband had coached our son through the process.

A *long* time ago, I loved that man… but he gave up on me the moment he accepted I had died. Well, that's not completely accurate. He truly believed Samantha Moon had died and I was some creature impersonating his wife. I suppose in some way he continued to love me, given that he'd been tinkering around with dark magic behind my back, presumably in an effort to 'save' me. Though, as much of a bastard as he'd been to me, I can't really pity him for his mental breakdown. That's the thing about fanatics. Once they make up their mind about something, they refuse to consider any information that contradicts what they want to believe. I'd never have been able to convince him that I'm still me inside. He thought he had to protect the kids from the creature pretending to be his wife, and then find a way to change me back.

Even without Elizabeth inside me, I've gone through so much shit in these past thirteen years since becoming a vampire that the Samantha Moon I used to be is basically gone. It's almost laughable how naïve I was. I mean, about stuff like vampires, devils, demons, witchcraft. Another time, another life, I would've laughed and thought people who believed any of that were crazier than someone who goes to Walmart on Black Friday.

These days, I feel pretty good, though I can't tell if it's due to my sleeping all night or if I'm enjoying having a span of like two whole weeks where nothing freaky has tried to kill us. Maybe it's the general nicety of it being Saturday.

Time to get up, Sammy.

Still in the thigh-length T-shirt I'd slept in, I wobble down the hall and check on the kids. Anthony's in his room on the computer, headphones on, playing that online game he's usually attached to when nothing more pressing demands his attention. It's some manner of sword and sorcery fantasy game with millions of players. He's told me all about his 'guild' and how they all group up to do 'raids' or something, but it went straight over my head. Amazingly, he never shirks his schoolwork... and only plays video games after his homework is done. I'm not sure what younger me would've had more trouble believing: that vampires exist or that I'd have a son who's *this* responsible. Anthony's remark about Tammy and I looking the same age pretty soon gets me thinking… I look far too young to have kids this age. Vampirism has been good to me.

When I catch sight of his video game character, a giant of a man with a massive, fiery sword, I'm not sure if I should laugh or worry. Did he pick that guy on purpose to kinda look like his alternate self or did he do it subconsciously?

"Oh, hey, Mom." Anthony twists his head around to smile at me. "Good, uhh, morning. Wow. It's weird seeing you up in the daylight. Still not used to it."

I yawn. It had been, what, two weeks since our fight with the Red Rider? Two weeks since Elizabeth had been blasted out of me. And two weeks of sleeping through the night. Yeah, I was still getting used to it, too... all of it. "Join the club, sweetie. Did you eat?"

"Yup. I made pancakes. Already cleaned up, too. Tams said they were pretty good, maybe even better than Dad's." Anthony chuckles. "Dad didn't like hearing that!"

My body flash froze for a brief second. Ugh. There he was again... Danny. Injecting himself into our lives, via his possession of our son. I told myself we would take care of Danny someday. The problem was... yes, the problem was Anthony liked having his dad near. And by near, I meant, inside him.

"You're not going to play video games all day, are you?"

"No, ma. Sheesh. I'm all caught up on homework. Well, mostly. I'll do it later, or maybe tomorrow. Right now, we're about to take on Magmatus."

"We?"

"Me and my team. It's a group quest."

"Oh, right. You do realize that we had a real group quest not too long ago, right?"

"I know, Mom. In the higher frequencies, whatever that means. Your point?"

I smile. Truth is, these group quests were a lot safer. I wonder how many of his online friends knew they were playing make believe with a real-life hero. "No point. Enjoy your game."

I walk in long enough to hug him, then head for Tammy's room.

She's gone. I'm not entirely surprised. Kid's gotta have a social life... and everything. The everything part being a potential new boyfriend. She responds to my text in a moment with an 'Out w friends, back by eleven tonight. And he's not my boyfriend.'

Sweet mama, that kid's mind reading powers are incredible. I start typing 'try ten' but stop myself. She's almost eighteen. I should consider myself lucky she's self-curfewing at eleven and not begging for midnight. Instead, I send back an 'Okay. Be safe. Lmk if you need anything.'

I nearly wrote 'use protection,' but I knew I didn't have to. Thinking it was, of course, enough.

'Mom! Sheesh! We haven't even kissed yet!'

Just saying... or thinking. Be smart, kiddo. Love you.

If she could read my mind, she wasn't too terribly far... maybe within five miles.

After a slight delay, her text came back. 'Love u 2.'

Mary Lou said the hardest part of loving your kids is letting them stretch their wings. But for Tammy, it's so damn hard. I want to suffocate her with love and protection, but she's getting to that age now where I do need to start letting her have some independence. As long as she doesn't go crazy. If I overprotect, she might wind up resenting me and that would kill me inside.

Not that worry isn't already gnawing away at me.

'No need 2 worry, Mom. We R at Sam2s.'

I laugh. She knows me too well. And, irony is a bitch. There are six girls named Samantha in her junior class. Guess names go in cycles. When I was in high school, I had a math class junior year with seven boys named Mike in it. The teacher just called them by numbers. Not even Mike1, Mike2. Just One, Two, and so on.

Like some California version of a hillbilly, I trudge outside to the detached garage in my night T-shirt and pull open the mini-fridge… and catch myself. It's been more than a week since we emptied this thing out and cleaned it. After my change, I nearly threw up at the smell of blood. In fact, the fridge isn't even plugged in at the moment… and it kinda stinks like dead stuff. Guess storing blood in a fridge seeped into the plastic. I should bleach the crap out of this thing. I've come a long way from slurping down hemoglobin from packets like a frat boy chugging beers then belching loud enough to scare cows.

Ugh. Cows.

I shudder, flashing back to being stuck in 1862 and having to bite the furry necks of animals to sustain myself. Yes, those memories are coming back and more, strange as they are. And, yes, it really does appear I had traveled back in time, Anyway, my fangs—which I'd mostly forgotten about for years—are well and truly gone now. I'm still a vampire, but rather than blood, I consume mental energy. Allison called me a 'psychic vampire.' The best part about this, other than no longer having to deal with blood, is I can have Starbucks again. And, while I'm waiting for my drink, I can feed on everyone in the coffee shop without them noticing.

Turns out, I have a feeding 'range' of about

twenty feet. As soon as I concentrate on wanting to draw nourishment, a stream of phantasmal energy emerges from the target, which I breathe in. The more people around, the less my feeding affects them. I can even draw from animals or even plants—as Allison suggested and we tested on trees. The downside with plants is that it takes for-damn-ever to get full. Slight feeding (such as one person among a crowd of a dozen) might make someone yawn or feel a momentary bit of tiredness. More severe draining can leave a victim listless or wanting a nap. Worst case scenario—like if I'm starving and there's only one person anywhere near me—I could leave someone in a permanent vegetative state, consuming their consciousness to a point where I damn near destroy them.

It's tempting to go to Starbucks right now, but I'm only wearing a T-shirt. You know what? Screw it. They have a drive-thru. There's no reason for me to even get out of the Momvan. Wait… if I tempt fate by leaving home with only a T-shirt on, my bare ass is going to wind up making the news somehow. Besides, I need more than a latte, don't I? Yup, a lot more. Yeah, I'll need to go inside to feed. Hunger trumps laziness. I run to my room and throw on a basic outfit, look at my son who's focused entirely on his game and talking in his headphones, and head out.

***

DEAD MOON

Nine people wait in line at Starbucks. The mocha latte is for me—since I can once again enjoy them... like really enjoy them without alchemical shenanigans. Anthony's a fan of caramel, so I order one of those for him as well as a big cookie. While waiting for the drinks to come out, I draw energy from everyone in the room except the baristas. This job is already enough of a drain on them mentally, no point being cruel.

Fed, I drive home again. It's really weird driving anywhere without a great sense of urgency or the sun making it hard to see. I feel like one of those people in the ads for the colorblind glasses looking at the world for the first time. It's been years since I've truly been able to open my eyes all the way during the day, and it still feels amazing. Once home, I head back inside and set Anthony's coffee/cookie on the desk beside him.

"Thanks, Mom!" He grins at me. "It's almost like you read my mind."

Laughing, I pat him on the head. "You're not that hard to figure out, kiddo."

I return to the living room where I flop on the couch to let the DVR cure my Judge Judy addiction. One curse of having so much time on my hands is I'm almost out of episodes I haven't seen yet. I've started watching other 'judge' type shows, but they all feel like pale imitations. They also don't do much for my faith in humanity. Are people *really* this stupid? Then again, the producers probably cherry pick the most boneheaded cases for better ratings. Or they're actors. Wait, they're probably not actors. I doubt any actor could keep a straight face through half this material if it wasn't true.

Much of the afternoon is sacrificed on the altar of housework. The sale of that mansion to Fang hasn't closed yet, so I still can't afford a housekeeper here. Not sure I'd bother anyway. I'd feel too weird having an employee or a maid. Some part of me feels a touch of regret at giving up that giant house, but it's super creepy, plus those property taxes would be a burden.

Tammy calls at 10:55 p.m. "Hey, Mom. Dana's car took a dump. I'm gonna be late."

The sound of traffic in the background unsettles me a little, but at least I know she's not giving me a lame excuse. "Do you need me to pick you up?"

"Umm. I can't just ditch my friends and leave them stranded. Would you mind giving the guys a ride, too?"

"I got nothing but time." I chuckle. "Where are you?"

"On La Mirada, near the Korean place. Umm, right by the Super 1 Mart."

"Okay. Be right there."

After trading my nine-year-old housecleaning clothes for a plum babydoll top and jeans without holes, I head out and hop in the Momvan. A few minutes later, I pull up behind a police car which has stopped behind Dana's beat-up silver Camry. A pack of six girls congregates on the sidewalk by a female officer while her partner has his head under the Toyota's hood. The female cop looks my way and starts waving at me to go around. When I get out, she puts on an 'oh, here we go' face, probably expecting me to start complaining or something.

"That's my Mom," says Tammy. "I called her for a ride before you guys pulled up."

A random barrage of "Hi Miss Moon" comes from her friends as I walk over.

Realizing why I'm there, the officer relaxes and smiles at me.

"Ugh. This is a bit more serious than a loose wire," says the male cop.

"My Dad's gonna kill me," mutters Dana, a short redhead with big, round glasses that Archimedes would've killed for.

"Not your fault," says Ankita. "It just died."

Tammy kicks the tire. "This thing's older than my mom."

The kids, and cops, chuckle.

"Hey now," I say in mock offense.

"That's your mother?" asks the female cop, eyeing me suspiciously.

"Yeah," I say. "Good genes I guess. I'm older than I look."

"Oh, hi, Sam," says the other cop. Officer Wilmott. I've run into him a few times around here. "It's cool, Rivera. I know her."

The woman nods. "Okay."

"Yeah, Tam's mom is a total milf," says Renee, the only blonde among my daughter's friends. For California, that's an achievement.

The girls all stare at her. Tammy's face goes as red as a fire truck. The cops find interesting places to look that don't involve eye contact with me or any of the kids.

"Renee?" I ask in a sweet tone. "Do you know what that means?"

Her clueless stare answers without words. Not that she's an airhead, but she evidently doesn't understand this particular word.

"Where did you hear it?" I ask.

"Umm. My dad and brother use it all the time."

Oh. Right. Her mom's out of the picture. Single dad and two brothers. Ugh. Poor girl dealing with an overload of testosterone at home. "It's not really a nice thing to call someone." I smile.

"Sorry," she says in a small voice. "I thought it just meant someone who's like not a kid anymore, but pretty."

The other girls burst into laughter, except Tammy who's too mortified.

"Whaaat?" asks Renee, staring at them, turning.

"So, yeah." The male cop walks over to me. "Gonna call for a tow. Since the girl's not eighteen yet, she can't accompany it to the shop. I take it you're going to give them all a ride?"

I nod.

Awkward tittering comes from the girls over the next ten minutes. Eventually, a tow truck shows up. I take a business card from the driver so I can give the info to Dana's parents, then herd the girls into the Momvan.

Tammy flops in the passenger seat, still blushing. I clasp her hand. When she looks up at me, I think, *Thank you for being responsible.*

Her embarrassment lessens a little.

And away we go...

Chapter Four
Referral Business

The next afternoon around four, my phone rings. Based on the caller ID, it's a forwarded call from my 'private investigator' business number.

"Moon Investigations," I say by way of answering.

"Hi. Is this Samantha Moon?"

"You found her."

"My name's Amy Rios. I got your number from a Detective Sherbet as a referral."

"Yeah." I chuckle. "He's got enough referral credit with me to track down six cheating spouses." Though, the last I heard, he's happily married, with a son who's growing into his own... a son who had challenged Sherbet's surprisingly narrow view of sexuality. When I first met him, the guy almost seemed offended to have been saddled with a son who might be gay. Well, there was no 'might' about it now. Luckily, the old bugger—who's had his son late in life—was coming around... if not slower than most.

Amy emits a nervous laugh, then sniffles. "He said you can help me."

Clear desperation and worry in her voice drains my humor. "What can I help you with?" Truth is, it must have been important if Sherbet sent her to me.

"Yes. I'm about to divorce my husband, Walter. He's... abusive. But, I think he figured out I was gonna leave him, because he..." She falters to crying for a few seconds before pulling herself together. "He took my son and disappeared. Joey's only four. I'm terrified he's going to hurt him to get back at me."

Shit with a capital S. "All right. I know it's hard. But please try to stay calm at least until we're off the phone, okay? Tell me as much as you can about him."

"I don't have a lot of money, but Detective—"

"We can worry about money and such once your son is safe. Right now, all I care about is finding your boy." I hurry over to my desk, flop in the chair, and grab a pen. "Give me as much information as you can about this guy."

"Umm. Okay." She sniffles. "We met in high school, married after graduation. He's real possessive. Used to yell at me all the time if I spoke to other men, like even at work to do work stuff. I got fired from my job because he kept showing up and being a pain."

As she rambles about her soon-to-be ex, Walter Rios, age twenty-seven, electrician, employed by a contracting company that does mostly construction site work, big drinker but not to the point of stumbling drunk, and so on, I jot everything down on a notepad. From the sound of it, the guy's got a bad case of what I call Chihuahua syndrome. Little dude with a big chip on his shoulder, a hair-trigger temper, and absolutely enraged by anything that threatens his dominance. She mentions he has a couple friends, but she's only ever seen them in passing. He wouldn't even allow her out of the bedroom when he had them over, as if she'd seduce one and leave him. Ugh. It's not too often I hate someone before ever meeting them, but this guy might be the exception.

"Does he have any guns?" I ask. "And how long has it been since your son disappeared?"

"I don't think so. I've never seen him with any guns or anything. Joey disappeared yesterday morning. I went to his room to wake him up and he was gone." She breaks down in sobs. "I found a printout on his bed from our phone account. Walter circled the number for the domestic violence support place I called. And he spelled out 'bye mommy' with magnet letters on the fridge." Again, Amy devolves into sobbing.

I almost spear the pen into my desk, but I manage to hold myself back. Okay, it's been a full day since the bastard disappeared with the boy.

Sherbet's aware of the case, which means the police are, too. If he sent her to me, that's a pretty good sign the cops haven't found a tiny body yet. Usually rage-punishment murders like this don't try to hide the remains, opting for murder-suicide in a conspicuous place to hurt the ex-wife. Maybe he's thinking more beyond blinding anger and he's planning to disappear with the kid or hide the body so she never knows for years what happened. Ugh.

Before I drive myself crazy with speculated grief, I ask, "Has Walter ever been violent with Joey?"

"No. Not that I saw. The worst he's done is taught him to call women 'bitches.'"

Grr. Okay. Maybe he's not an imminent threat to the kid's life, but he's going to raise him to be a true gentleman—not.

"Are you safe now? Do you have a number where I can reach you?"

"I'm at a women's shelter right now." She gives me the phone number. "Once Joey's safe, I'm going to move back with my parents."

"Okay. I'm on it. I'll call you as soon as I have any information."

"Thank you," she says in a teary voice before muttering in Spanish, asking God to lead me to her son.

Not sure if He's paying attention, but I'll take any help I can get for something like this. And yeah, I kinda met God, too. I think. Long story. I give her my email and ask her to send me a laundry list of info, including his social security number and phone records, if she has them.

Now, let's find this bastard...

***

When her email arrives, I hit the usuals: Facebook, Linkedin, Instagram, criminal records search, as much as I can get in various database services, both public and proprietary. Amy was able to forward me their phone bill, and phone records. Ha, the bastard wouldn't be the only one going through phone numbers.

The guy's FB page is practically a misogynist's user's manual. This (possible) woman named Andrea Richards shows up a lot, commenting on his posts. I hit her page, and can't quite tell if it's a real person or some overseas scammer pretending to be an available young woman. The photos this woman's shared look staged to the point of feeling scammy. Most of her recent posts are 'look at me' type images. She practically has a selfie-stick surgically attached to her hand.

Hmm. Walter possibly has a side girl, but this one looks too confident to put up with being treated poorly. But… pictures can be deceiving. Unfortunately, there's not a damn thing about where this woman might live. For all I know, this really is someone from overseas—maybe even a guy using fake photos—trying to take advantage of horny men.

Anyway...

Between his phone records and Facebook, I notice a match. This guy has routine phone contact with a number that matches a name with one of his frequent Facebook commenters: Mike Helford. A few minutes later, I discover Helford also works for the same electrical contracting company. Bingo. Co-worker or possible friend. Since a kid's life may be in the balance here, I'm less averse to pushing the boundaries, so a face-to-face meeting is preferable. It's hard to poke people in the brain over the phone.

I luck out on Searchbug—one of the information search engines I use—and find a physical address for the friend. He lives a bit south of here in Santa Ana. A brief phone call to Sherbet tells me he didn't find any unusual activity on Walter's bank account or credit cards other than a stop for gas in Irvine.

"Some of the guys think he might be headed for Mexico," says Sherbet, laughing. "I don't think the guy's got that much forethought."

"What's he driving?"

"Hang on. Hmm. Okay, a 2013 Ford 250, navy blue." He shares the tag number. "Already sent out an Amber alert, though nothing promising has come in. If he spends any significant time on the road, someone will report him. Oh, and the little boy's face is gonna be going up on electronic billboards any minute now. The bastard has nowhere to hide."

"Because I'm on the case?"

"You're my insurance policy. Never hurts to add a little woo-woo to the mix."

"I'll take that as a compliment."

"It's something."

"Great. Okay, I got a potential lead on a friend from his Facebook. Going to check that out."

"Sounds good. Thanks for helpin' her out, Sam."

"Anytime."

I toss on a T-shirt and jeans, add a black pullover sweater and my low-top hiking boots. Need something a little beefier than sneakers in the event I have to apply boot-to-head—or wind up tromping through who-knows-where searching for a child. Damn, I hope this doesn't turn into another one of those bunker-in-the-middle-of-nowhere cases.

***

Rolling up on a place in the Momvan isn't exactly intimidating.

Fortunately, Mike Helford lives in a reasonably average slice of suburbia where I don't stand out. Okay, well, maybe the van does—for being a bit old. I start to have the somewhat maudlin thought that I don't need to taxi a pair of children back and forth from school anymore. Anthony rides his bike or walks with his friends, and Tammy's friends all seem to drive now, although she herself doesn't yet have a license... and no car to drive either; however, I can't dwell on that now. There's a four-year-old boy out there in the company of a man who'd likely snap the kid's neck purely to hurt his wife.

That, of course, makes me think of Tammy as a four-year-old the day I came home from the hospital as a vampire. The first—and last—time her blood smelled appetizing to me. She had such a look of total innocence on her face, not the faintest clue that she stared up at a monster—no. Stop. Focus. Besides, I don't drink blood anymore.

Never again.

Fists balled, I storm up the little walkway to Mr. Helford's house, and ring the bell.

The door swings open after a short wait, revealing a late-twenties guy with fluffy brown hair, a tank top, red shorts, and a cast on his left leg up to the knee. Air blowing out from inside carries a hint of warmth and more than a hint of beer. The guy doesn't appear drunk, but he's clearly self-medicating.

"Hello. Are you Mike Helford?" I ask.

"Yeah." He raises a bushy eyebrow. "You from the insurance place?"

"No. I'm a private investigator."

Mike blinks, stares at me a few seconds, then cracks up laughing. "Seriously?"

"Yes. Seriously."

My tone stalls his humor to intermittent chuckles. "Wow. I didn't think that private eye shit was like real, yanno? Just stuff for movies. So, seein' as how I ain't never been married, why's a PI looking for me?"

"We do more than investigate cheating spouses… like hunt for abducted children."

"Wait, what? I didn't grab no one's kid. Been stuck here last two weeks on account of a damn transformer slipping off its foundation and smashing the piss out of my foot."

"Sorry." I cringe at the cast. "I didn't mean to imply you're involved. Do you know a man named Walter Rios?"

"Oh, Walt? Yeah. No way he kidnapped anyone. I know the guy since high school. He'd never hurt a kid."

"What about his wife?"

Mike fidgets and glances away. Pretty sure he knows exactly how Walter treats Amy, but also can't quite bring himself to say it. "Ehh. He and his ol' lady have some issues. Not my business."

"You know he hits her. Pretty bad, too. She planned to leave him, but he disappeared with their son. Amy's afraid he might harm the boy to get back at her."

"Aww, shit." Mike sets his hands on his hips, shaking his head, looking down. "Nah, yanno, I know Walt. I don't see him hurting his son. He's so proud of the little dude."

"Mike, people do strange things when they become highly emotional. In the heat of the moment…"

"Yeah." He rakes a hand up over his head, and sighs.

"You know something. Spill." He seemed

cooperative enough, so I didn't bother coercing him mentally or dipping into his thoughts. But unless he talked fast, all bets were off. Including another stomp on that foot of his.

He might have seen the look in my eye. "Okay, yeah. He came by here yesterday, said the wife left him and the kid. Wanted to borrow some money."

"The boy wasn't with him? What time did he show up here?"

"Oh, 'bout eight in the morning or so. I remember 'cause he woke my ass up. Painkillers have been brutal. I honestly didn't look at his truck. Kid could've been in there, but he said Amy took the boy and ran off. I had no reason to believe he wasn't alone."

"Did he tell you why he wanted money?"

"Nah. Just said he needed it since she'd siphoned the bank account empty. I figured general stuff, yanno. I didn't have much on hand but I loaned him like ninety bucks."

"Do you have any idea where he went? Are his parents still around? Any other friends he might've wanted to crash with?"

"Not sure exactly, but... he had a side girl. I promised I wouldn't say anything about her... but if what you're saying about his kid is true, then that's pretty messed up. Anyway, his girlfriend—or whatever you call her—lives in Mission Viejo. Hang on. I got the address in my Garmin."

I blink. "Do I want to know why you've got the address to his mistress in *your* GPS?"

Mike laughs. "I picked him up there once. Drove him back to his car at this night club a couple miles from her place. Hang on a sec." He limps out onto the porch and wobbles over to a black Nissan pickup in the driveway. After pulling a Garmin out of the console, he fiddles with it for a little while and holds it up to show me an address in Mission Viejo.

"That's the 'side girl's' place," says Mike. "Umm, Andrea something."

The maybe-fake girl from his Facebook page. "Oh wow. Andrea... Richards?"

"Sounds about right."

"Hey, no problem. For the kid, right? Wow. I really don't think Walt would hurt the boy, but… I guess it's better not to take any chances."

"Yeah. I'm definitely not taking any chances. No, not at all."

Chapter Five
The Side Girl

The address in Mission Viejo leads me to a five-story building that kinda looks like a sponge cake of pale stucco separated by layers of glass 'filling.' Open patios jut out the right side, and a glass-enclosed lobby offers a view of a central elevator shaft.

Crap. It's an apartment. Nice one though... probably can't be cheap to live here. Based on the layout of the decks, I figure each story has four apartments, so they're a decent size. The problem being, of course, the GPS address didn't come with a suite number.

I draw in a breath to curse again, but really... twenty apartments to check isn't *that* bad. So, stifling the giant F-bomb that I almost screamed, I pull into the attached parking lot and... stare straight at a giant dark blue Ford. Considering every other vehicle in this lot is something small, sporty, and overpriced, I'm pretty sure I won the lottery.

Walter is here.

My Momvan's engine protests as I race to a parking spot. "Geez, come on girl, don't quit on me yet. I swear I'll bring you in for service first thing after I get home."

Ready to race from door to door, I hop out of the van and start for the lobby, but catch the sound of screaming coming from overhead. It's muted too much to make out anything more than a man and a woman raging at each other. My supernatural ears are probably the only reason I can even hear them at all.

Wow, this place has thick walls. The rent has to be astronomical.

I can, however, pick up that it's coming from maybe the fourth floor. Probably one of the two apartments facing the parking lot. Forty feet is a bit too much to ask of my legs for a vertical leap, and using Talos would actually take longer than the stairs, unless I want to barge in on them bare-assed. So, I race inside and up four flights of switchback stairs.

Fatigue is only in the mind. I am a vampire... or something close to it. Still, I do not get tired.

At least, not from running up flights of stairs.

Four jet-black doors with silver numbers stand back in small alcoves from the hallway, with an elevator at the middle. Blue-grey carpeting keeps my boots silent as I run straight to the door from whence the screaming originates. Being in the hallway makes it beyond obvious where I need to go as the doors don't do as good a job at holding back sound as the exterior wall.

I head straight to apartment 4-3.

The woman sounds like she's upset at him for bringing a kid there. He's mostly stumbling with his replies saying he has no other choice. While it sounds like he's attempting to rein in his temper, the way that woman's refusing to back down, I give him maybe another three minutes before he snaps and the beating commences.

I ring the bell.

The shouting match cuts off.

"Goddammit, Walter. Now the cops are here."

A man's incomprehensible murmuring follows.

The peephole's dot of light cuts off to black.

"The hell is that?" mutters a woman. Andrea's door opens an inch, still secured by a chain. One eye peers through the gap at me. "Who are you?"

"Miss Richards," I say. "Why don't you open the door so we can talk?"

I lean on her mentally just enough that she obliges without question. Walter paces around behind a giant leather sectional, the heels of his hands pressed into his eyes. He's practically shaking with rage. This dude's little, but he's got thick arms and shoulders. One look at him and I know he'd been inches from losing control and getting physical with this woman.

"You still didn't tell me who you are," says Andrea.

"My name is Samantha Moon. I'm a private investigator."

Andrea frowns at Walter. "Your wife sent a PI."

Walter lowers his hands from his face and smirks at me. "Bullshit. She ain't got the money for that. You tryin' ta catch me cheating or somethin'?" He tries to 'roll up' on me, but he's only like an inch taller than me, and I'm five-foot-three. Heh. I was right. Chihuahua. At my complete lack of fear, his face reddens.

"No, Walter. I'm here because you've kidnapped your son."

"What?" screams Andrea. "No wonder you're being weird. You really stole him? Go. Get the fuck out of here right now."

Walter glares at me for a second before whirling on her. "Babe, calm down. I can't kidnap my own son. I'm his father. We ain't divorced."

I step forward, and say, "Your wife planned to file for divorce, Walter. You took the boy from his bed yesterday morning and disappeared without a word, leaving a phone bill with the number of a domestic violence support group circled. That's a clear message that suggests you meant to hurt her by abducting and/or harming the boy. The police are looking for you. Now, where's your son?"

"I can't believe you," shrieks Andrea. "You think you're gonna hit her 'til she can't take it anymore? Then just show up on my doorstep with that kid and move on in? That ain't how this works."

"I want to take us to the next level," says Walter.

"There ain't no next level, babe. We're a hook up. That's all."

Walter's eyes nearly bulge out of their sockets. He takes a fast step toward her. She flinches. I zip in between them fast enough to make her yelp in surprise and Walter's anger melt into a gawk of WTF.

"Where. Is. The. Boy?" I ask, staring into his eyes.

"Back room," mutters Walter like a zombie. He blinks off the mild compulsion. His features twist into an irrational rage a second before he reaches for my throat.

I grab his arm, flip him around, and drive him face first into the top of Andrea's glass coffee table. His skull makes a loud *pank* noise when it hits the surface, the impact is hard enough to knock over a pair of slim vases. He slumps off to the side and collapses unconscious on the floor.

"Wow. Table didn't break. That's some serious glass." I squat to appraise the table. Yeah… it's almost an inch thick.

"Holy shit." She gasps, staring at Walter. "How did you do that?"

I turn toward her, smiling. "I'm a retired federal agent."

"Mommy?" asks a tiny voice.

A shirtless, pale Hispanic kid in cartoon pajama pants stands halfway around the arch to a back hallway. Dribbles of brownish sauce stain his chest, by smell, I guess McDonalds BBQ. His hair's on the long side, almost touching his shoulders. Watching his hope crash and burn, giant brown eyes welling with tears when he sees I'm not his mother hurts more than demon's claws ripping down my back.

"Hey, Joey," I say. "Your mother sent me to find you. Do you want to go see her?"

Hope returns. He nods, but continues clinging to the wall. "What happened to Daddy?"

"He's tired."

Andrea looks away.

I glance at her. "Did he get physical with you, too?"

She fidgets, still staring at the floor.

"I'll take that as a yes."

"Okay, once," whispers Andrea. "My brother got involved. Scared him enough to back off."

"Your brother?" I ask.

She points at a photo on the wall. I gawk. Whoa. The dude's arms are bigger around than my thighs. Andrea's standing next to him in the photo. I figure this girl's about twenty-five or so, and next to this monster, she looks more like eleven. Well, that certainly explains why Walter was trying so hard to behave himself. Andrea's brother would've twisted his head off.

"I not s'posed ta talk to strangers," whispers

Joey.

"You're right. Hang on a sec, okay?" I take out my phone and call the number Amy gave me. It rings a few times.

"Hello?" says a woman with a voice on the deeper end.

"Hi. My name is Samantha Moon. I'm trying to reach Amy Rios?"

"The name doesn't sound familiar."

I grumble to myself. "Look, I know this is a women's shelter, and you're all about their confidentiality, which is cool. I'm a private investigator that Amy sent to find her boy. I found him. I need her to tell him it's okay to go with me."

"Hang on a sec," says the woman.

Meanwhile, Andrea walks around Walter's unconscious body. "Shit. What am I going to do with him?"

"He's currently wanted. Just call the police."

She nods, and hurries off to grab a phone from her purse on the kitchen counter.

"I'd also suggest you avoid him in the future."

"No shit," echoes from the kitchen.

"H-hello?" asks a sniffling Amy over the phone.

"Hey. It's Sam. Great news. We got phenomenally lucky. Someone wants to talk to you. Can you tell him I'm safe and he should go with me?"

Amy cries something back that I can't make out.

I wave at Joey. "C'mere, Joey. Your mother's on the phone."

When he un-clings from the side of the archway, four clear fingerprint bruises on his right side catch my eye and boil my blood. He creeps out into the room approaching me like an apprentice lion tamer on his first day. I take a knee, holding out the phone.

"What happened?" I point at the marks.

"Daddy got mad 'cause I said I wanted ta go home. I miss Mommy."

The same mental voodoo that stunned cows long enough for me to feed from them works wonders on a four-year-old so he doesn't see me kicking his bastard of a father in the side hard enough to break a few ribs. Once done, I hand him the phone.

"Joey?" calls Amy from the phone, easy enough for me to hear.

I again sit on the floor in front of the kid and back off the mental fog.

"Mommy?" asks Joey.

They talk for a few minutes, and I pick up snatches, but mostly give them some privacy. The boy eventually looks up at me. "Umm, she's got lots of hair. Yeah, it's dark. Uh-huh. Yeah. Okay, Mommy. I miss you. I wanna go home." He offers me the phone.

Amy sobs a few thank-yous before explaining that she can't give me the shelter's address. The deep-voiced woman mutters something in the background.

"Oh. Paula says it's okay." She recites an address.

"Great. I'll be there as soon as I can."

"Thank you so much." Amy sniffles some more.

Andrea walks out of the kitchen. "Police are on the way."

"Good." I nod at her then look back to Joey. "Go get dressed so we can get you back to your mom."

He flaps his arms. "I don't have anything else."

"You went out in November in just PJ bottoms?"

"Yeah. Daddy said we hadda go fast."

Ugh, that man. Granted, it's not brutally cold here, but still. The boy needs more than PJ pants. Not like I can get frostbite. I may not be a bloodsucking fiend anymore, but this body of mine—and my fully-contained soul—was still damn near indestructible. Anyway, I remove my sweater and pull it over his head. It's way too big, but it'll work.

I wait for the cops to arrive, just in case this idiot wakes up and takes it out on Andrea. While waiting, I help myself to his car keys so I can borrow the car seat. Naturally, they're not terribly keen on letting me walk off with the boy, but it doesn't take much mental poking to convince them not to worry about it. Once they've hauled Walter out of the apartment, I carry Joey downstairs to the van, keeping him as bundled as possible until I get him inside and the engine running. With Joey in one arm, I one-handedly open Walter's truck, remove the car seat, and leave his keys on the front seat. There's a real good chance someone might steal it, but with cops here already, more likely they'll tow it.

Back at the van, I set up the car seat like an old pro and buckle Joey in.

"Are you taking me home?"

"Your mom isn't at your house right now. She's with some people who are helping her. I'm taking you to your mom."

"Okay." He smiles. "Where's Daddy going?"

"He's got a few things he needs to do."

The boy shrugs. "Mommy's scared of Daddy 'cause she's a bitch."

Oh, hell no.

I lean close, staring into the little angel's eyes. Fortunately, he doesn't understand what he said, only that his father taught him that name for her.

He doesn't need to remember that.

After moving to the driver's seat, I lean my head back, staring at the ceiling. Gee. The fabric looks dingier than I remembered. Well, this Momvan is about fourteen years old. She's starting to show her age, unlike me.

Of course, once the sale of the mansion goes through, I was going to come into a lot of money... all thanks to my one-time father, God bless his sweet soul.

Wherever it is...

So, yeah, maybe it was time for a new ride.

Maybe. We'll see.

Chapter Six
Special

Amy's an absolute mess for the first ten or so minutes.

The rep from the shelter, Paula, is an imposing sort of no-nonsense large-framed woman who'd not hesitate to drag an ex-husband out the door physically. I don't get the sense she distrusts me, but she does hover nearby the whole time. Even the face on her Bob Marley shirt is giving me the suspicious stare.

From the outside, the shelter looks like some nondescript 'professional building.' The kind of place one usually finds chiropractors, dentists, and OB-GYNs... maybe a psychic reader.

Apparently, I have a nametag that reads 'giant sucker' on my chest. Once Amy composes herself, she asks me if I can give her a ride back to their apartment long enough for her to get some clothes and such, since Walter won't be there. Of course, I can't say no, so… yeah.

She trusts Paula enough to leave Joey with her at the shelter. Maybe an hour later, after we've stuffed the ninth garbage bag full of clothing into the back of the Momvan, she hits me with a bigger question.

"Hey, umm. I really hate to ask this, but…"

I chuckle. "It's fine. I was planning to waive the fee anyway. You and Joey need the money more than I do. Not many of my cases are one-day affairs. Happy enough to have found him that fast."

"Oh." She stares at me, crying again. "That's…"

Crap. I see the question she's too choked up to ask in her thoughts. While she *was* dreading what I would charge, she wanted to ask me to give her and Joey a ride to Tucson, Arizona… where her parents live. She can't afford a plane ticket—or even bus fare. Walter had all the money in his name and didn't even let her have an ATM card. That line he gave his friend about her draining the bank account had been total bullcrap. Hmm, that's like a seven or eight hour ride. If I remember right, it's mostly a straight shot east on Route 10. I know the road goes at least to Phoenix. Tammy can watch over things for at least a day. Maybe I'll have Allison swing by. And Kingsley, too. Can't be too safe with Elizabeth out there.

What she is doing out there is another story. I hadn't a clue, though I suspected she was regrouping... and rounding up the other dark masters who'd made it out of the Void, although I wasn't quite sure what was going on with all that, either. Archibald Maximus, alchemist extraordinaire, would know, except he wasn't around these days. Fang had heard the alchemists were having a devil of a time repairing the breached Void. I'd known they banished the dark masters to the Void long ago, but didn't realize the light warriors actually *made* the Void.

Learn something new every day.

"Amy... was there something else?" I prodded.

"Well... I was gonna ask if, umm... is there any way you could drive me to my parents' house? They live in Tucson. I know it's a really long ride. My parents will at least give you gas money."

"Sure, I can do that."

She stares in total shock. "Wow. Really?"

"It's all part of the service."

"No way."

"For you, way. Tomorrow though. I need to get the van checked out. She's overdue for a tune up and routine maintenance."

"Oh. That's fine. I can wait at the shelter."

I close the van's back door. "I'll make an early appointment tomorrow and call you when I'm out. We can probably hit the road around noon if that's okay."

She nods. "That's so awesome of you. I really don't know what to say."

"Hey, it's fine. I know what it's like to have an asshole ex."

***

I arrive back home a little after nine at night.

Tammy, and four of her friends, Dana, Ankita, Paige, and Veronica, are sprawled around the living room abusing the PlayStation. Paige looks like a giant antique doll straight out of a Tim Burton movie. The girl's got less color than I used to have, since I no longer look like a ghoul. That poor kid is whiter than paper with ink-black hair, black frilly dress, black leggings, black lipstick. Veronica is a 'metalhead,' according to Anthony. I'm not entirely sure what that means, but know enough to grasp (or 'grok' as the kids say) it has something to do with music. Her hair's also super-black but she favors the 'T-shirt and jeans' style. Dana and Ankita are dressed like what I'd consider 'normal' kids these days.

"Hey girls," I say, walking over.

"Hey," they chorus back.

Tammy looks at me, hesitates a second as she scans my thoughts, then grins, giving me a thumbs-up. "Good one, Mom. That guy was a real asshole."

Tammy doesn't talk about her telepathic abilities to anyone but me… and Anthony to a point. For that, I don't blame her. Nor do I blame her for using that power to keep herself safe. Pretty sure she dips into the heads of everyone she comes into contact with. While that does step on some ethical toes, it's a rough world out there for a girl. Since that amulet blocks out the constant barrage of *everyone* around her thinking, she's almost a new person. When it hits me how happy I am for her, she blushes in response, probably hoping I don't get all mushy in front of her friends.

She squints at me some more, then gives me an 'oh wow' look, and hands off the controller to Veronica. "Be right back."

Tammy shadows me into the kitchen. Once we're out of earshot of her friends, she whispers, "Tucson? Seriously?"

"Yeah. This woman's in a bad situation. Just driving her to her parents' home. Fifteen hours on the road for maybe twenty minutes unloading stuff from the van. Figured you should be able to watch the house for a day. There's um, a chance Allison and Kingsley will swing by."

"Yeah, no kidding, because you're planning on calling them."

That said, Tammy leans on the counter, smirking at me while poking her toe at the floor. It's a bit of an 'aww, I'm not a little kid anymore' stance.

"Or I could always ask Mary Lou to watch you two."

She starts to roll her eyes, but winds up laughing. "I'll be okay, Mom. Anthony's easy to watch. Just plop him down in front of a computer and change the Dorito bag every two hours."

I snicker. In the back of my mind, I can still hear little Tammy calling him 'Anf'nee.'

Her face goes bright red. "Mom!"

"Well, you shouldn't randomly listen then. And you were adorable at four." I hug her. "So, yeah. As much as I don't want to admit it, you're old enough to be responsible at home and Anthony's not exactly a troublemaker. Pretty much the opposite."

"Ugh. He's abnormal. Boys his age aren't supposed to be so… so… well behaved." She fake sighs.

I'm not sure if it's because he's got that Fire Warrior thing, or if it's having his father constantly privy to his every thought. Whatever the reason, I'm not complaining. I say, "You're not too bad yourself, Tam Tam."

She gasps and shoots a look to the living room to make sure none of her friends heard that. "Do you *have* to call me that? It's so embarrassing. I'm not six anymore."

"Well. If things were different—and I wasn't what I am—I would say there might come a day where you wished you could hear me say that one more time. You know, when I'm dead and gone."

"Except I'm gonna be the little old lady *you* are gonna miss." Her attitude drops dead, and she leans into a hug.

"You'll be back," I say. "It's all just a big ol' circle."

She sniffles. "Yeah. Okay. Geez, Mom. That's a giant guilt hammer. Fine, it's a cute pet name. Just… don't call me that when my friends can hear you."

DEAD MOON

I kiss her on the head. "Deal. So you two are okay with me taking a road trip?"

"Sure, Mom. We'll be fine. You're not expecting any demons or anything on the way?"

"Last I checked, demons want nothing to do with me."

She giggles.

"But Elizabeth is still out there," I say.

"She's nowhere around here."

I nod, knowing I could trust her. "Still, I would feel better if Allison and Kingsley swung by for a few hours. And Mary Lou's always willing to help," I add.

"Fine. So are you like leaving now?"

"No. Tomorrow afternoon. The van needs a trip to the doctor's. Needs to be checked before a long trip."

"That thing's like *old*. Are you gonna get a new car when we're rich?"

"We're not going to be that rich."

"We're going to be millionaires!"

"Just one million."

"And a half."

"Fine, and a half."

"Maybe you should buy us all cars?"

"Or not. If I do get a new car—"

"Oh, no. Don't say it!"

"Yes, the Momvan is going to you."

"I won't drive it. No way."

"Then you can save for your own car."

"This sucks."

"I know. A free car totally sucks."

"But it's not a car. It's a minivan."

"Even better... and safer."

"Gah!"

"Dude, that was epic!" shouts Veronica from the living room.

"Well, I'm keeping you from your friends. Guess I'll be in my room reading or something to stay out of your hair. And remember, no boys over tomorrow. I'm pretty sure the sight of Kingsley would scare the life out of your... friend."

"My... friend is special, ma. He doesn't scare easy."

I narrow my eyes. "How special?"

Tammy hooks her thumbs in her pockets and smiles. Her black jeans make her bare feet almost corpse-white. Guess she's going for the goth look, too. At least she's got naturally black hair and doesn't have to dye it. "Just is. And I'm really glad you found that little boy. He sounds adorable."

I grin. "He is."

She puts her hand over my mouth before I can say she was cuter at that age. We both crack up and walk to our respective timekills: Tammy to her friends and the PlayStation, me to my bedroom and a Kindle.

All the while I mull her words... 'My friend is... special.'

Now, what the hell could that mean?

Chapter Seven
Mom's Taxi

You there, Fang?

Sometimes I think AOL chat stayed in service just for me and Fang. Honestly, I haven't heard of anyone using it in years. Sure, we had contemplated using Whatsapp, or even good old-fashioned texting. But we both agreed that, well, we kind of liked using a real keyboard, and we kind of liked the AOL chime. And we were both oddly nostalgic about it all.

I knew he was at work, but he kept his laptop on behind the counter, where he served booze to the living, and hemoglobin to the not-living. Turned out, after our own version of the Snap, a ton of vampires elected to stay in their hosts... and many more couldn't find a way out. As Fang had explained it to me a few weeks ago, for a vampire to escape the host, they had to kill their host. Much the same way the Devil had killed his host when he had stepped in front of a train a few years ago. Indeed, there had been reports of strange suicides across the nation, and it had led to report after report, but the craze had faded almost to a non-story. Fang had explained it this way... those dark masters who had been able to exert some sort of control over their hosts, had promptly killed off their hosts, to be free again. Those who did not have much control of their hosts—or none at all—were left trapped within.

The good news for Fang and his business... there were, apparently, a large number of vampires who either couldn't escape... or had elected to stay, as was the case with both Fang and Kingsley. Fang was a new vampire, and had promptly made an agreement with his dark master to often give up control to him. The agreement worked, as Fang was alive to this day to talk about it. I didn't want to point out that I still feared for him. Last I heard, the Void was still wide open, which meant his dark master might decide to ditch their agreement, kill Fang, and escape.

But yeah, some of these facts remained sketchy to me, which is why I was hailing my pal, since the Alchemist had temporally flown the coop. At least, I hoped his absence would only be temporary.

Hey, Moon Dance. Busy tonight. Sorry.
That many vampires are around?
Enough, certainly. But no, I'm busy with mortals and their damned chicken wings. I swear I have

buffalo sauce in my hair.

I'm laughing over here.

I'm sure you are. What can I do for you, my friend?

I need to know more about the Void.

It's presently still open, according to Edward, but emptying fast.

Edward was, of course, Fang's dark master. Each day while a vampire sleeps, their bodies—as mine used to do—entered a semi-death. As such, the trap-ped souls of their dark masters could temporarily leave and rejoin their brothers and sisters in the Void, where, I assumed, much planning and strat-egizing ensued.

How, exactly, is it emptying?

Hang on, Moon Dance. I got a guy here being an asshole...

Hanging...

Okay, back, appears a minute or two later in the chat window. *Said asshole has realized the error of his ways and has apologized to each and every one of my customers.*

With a mental prompting? I ask.

But of course. And to answer your question... those without earthly hosts have all fled the Void.

Fled to Earth?

Yes. Remember, dark masters are outside of the reincarnation loop, having long ago bypassed the natural cycle of life and death and life again.

With black magic.

But of course, writes Fang.

Then why don't they get re-absorbed back into the Origin, like my father had?

In fact, I had personally witnessed it... and it was a sight I would not soon forget, if ever.

Their souls are free, Sam. They are not chained to a physical body. It is why they need a host. The host can die, but they themselves will not. In the past, they returned to the Void.

Then why, when I die, do I get returned to the Origin?

Ah, I am in the same boat, Sam. It is because our souls have been summoned from heaven—or, more accurately, from the world of the energetic. We have no anchor, and thus have been cut off from the reincarnation loop. Our souls are completely at the mercy of these physical bodies. Once the physical body perishes, we are adrift until we return home with the Origin.

I recalled those feelings of being adrift, and I didn't much like it.

The dark masters are different? But have they not also been removed from the reincarnation circle? Are they also not without physical bodies? Why are they not re-absorbed? Let me guess... black magic.

The blackest and most vile of magics, Sam. It is how they roam free, bodiless. It is why they need hosts.

Fine, and now that the Void has been removed... where do they find their bodies? How do they exist without a host?

DEAD MOON

Aw, Sam. Now that the Void is down, and the dark masters have returned, you will see just how cunning and clever they are. Now, they do not need the living to project themselves into the physical. They can summon physical material—similar to ectoplasm, but far superior—to live again. The bodies they choose can shift and change at will. One moment they will appear as one thing, and the next another.

Great.

It is why they are so deadly, so powerful, and so elusive. It is why the alchemists work so hard to repair the Void even now, and to make it stronger still.

But the dark masters have escaped already.

True, but others can be returned to the Void, perhaps one at a time... or perhaps in a great battle, which had been the case 500 years ago.

So, a dark master could literally be anyone?

True, but you will sense them, Sam. The wave of vileness cannot be hidden. They will not have auras, nor can you read their minds.

Like any other vampire, then?

In many ways, yes. But killing them won't happen.

Because they can't die.

This is true.

Not even with silver?

Oh, silver would extinguish their temporary form. But the dark master will not be returned to the Void.

I thought about this crazy turn of events. I knew in the past that when a vampire was killed, its human host would return to the Origin, while the dark master returned to the Void. This prison the alchemists had created worked out well enough, but the dark masters had figured out a loophole... which had been possession of mortals. But the dark masters themselves were ultimately still bound to the Void, and would return there when their human hosts perished. Now, apparently, this no longer worked. Whatever Elizabeth did in the higher dimension tore a rip in the fabric of the universe.

So, their temporary physical forms perish... and then what?

They can create another form, over and over again, without end.

Mercy. How can they be stopped?

You will have to ask your light warrior friend.

I would, except he's been gone.

They're all gone, Sam. It is a group effort to repair the Void. The complexity and power behind its creation is mind boggling. I imagine this is not a quick fix.

Meanwhile, the dark masters are regrouping, I wrote.

True, but according to Edward, they are not in a great rush. Most are reveling in their freedom.

How do the dark masters sustain themselves?

Blood, Sam. Always blood. Some human sacrifices work too. In a pinch, an animal sacrifice.

Okay, here's a hypothetical... if and when the

Void gets repaired, will it be empty?

Doubtful. Those dark masters who did not escape their hosts would still be bound to it.

Like Edward? I wrote. *And the dark master in Kingsley.*

Yes, and others like them.

Why would they choose this over complete freedom?

Hard to say, Sam. But I am glad Edward and myself have an agreement.

I nodded to myself. I knew why. Otherwise, Fang would be dead. And so would Kingsley.

Remember, not all dark masters gain control of their hosts. Elizabeth never got control over you. She manipulated you the old fashioned way until she escaped through other means.

The other means had been, of course, the destruction of the Red Rider. His death had released a God-awful explosion that had rocked my world in more ways than one... and promptly freed Elizabeth. All part of her crazy master plan.

Truly, an evil genius.

The good news is, I hadn't died in the process. After all, had I died, she would have been returned to the Void. Instead, the walls of the Void had come undone... and life as I know it would be forever changed.

Fang wrote: *The dark masters who chose to stay in their hosts... or weren't able to escape... don't have it so bad, Sam. Each day they live side by side with their hosts. Some have become friends even.*

Others enjoy the ride, I suspect. Still, others are not very motivated for more.

Which had been the case of the dark masters inhabiting my one-time father. JC had mentioned his dark master had basically checked out. And Kingsley told me his one-time wife (so weird to think that), the mermaid up in Seattle, was, like, actually best friends with her dark master. He described it as living with his wife and mother-in-law constantly.

Moon Dance, I gotta jet. No rest for the wicked.

Wait... quick question.

Fire away.

I've been so used to thinking of myself as a vampire that I'm left without... identity, if that makes sense. Fang, what am I, exactly?

I'm not sure that qualifies as a quick question, Moonie.

Can you give me the condensed version?

A slight pause, then a rapid succession of short messages streamed in, rather than one long one. *You are an immortal, because your soul is fully contained within your physical form. You are a kind of vampire because you feed off the energy of others. Apparently, immortals—all immortals—need an energy source. This is new to me, too. I assumed blood was simply a byproduct of the dark masters— and in a way it is. But I'm also seeing that immortals, in general, need some type of fuel. In your case, it's psychic energy. Is this helping?*

Yes. Well, everything needs food.

Moon Dance... do you want to think of yourself as a vampire?

I don't know. I just need to think of myself as something... feels weird being a big question mark.

By its very definition, you are a vampire. Maybe not the bloodsucking variety, but you are certainly a kind of leech.

So says the actual bloodsucker.

The irony is not lost on me.

I crack my longish fingers, wiggle them, then type: *It's hard for me to think of myself as a vampire when I can go out into the sun and eat whatever I want without the use of magical rings.*

It's okay, Sam. You are something new... or perhaps something very old. Perhaps you are the base model immortal... and the dark masters simply added their own take on it. You are as strong as ever. Your mind control is as sharp as ever. You are a vampire in every sense of the word... minus any of the darkness. And you have wings, to boot! And last I heard you were a budding witch.

Maybe, I write.

Truth be told, the witchcraft came along slower than I expected. Nothing sparkly or powerful shot from my fingertips, not like Allison. In fact, the only magical thing that Allison and I could find about me is that I can see fairies. She couldn't. She guessed that might be some aspect of my immortality... until Kingsley pointed out that he couldn't see them either. But then again, he didn't have witch magic. Millicent chimed in that not all witches are the same. Where some can throw spells like weapons others are... sensitive. Seers, for example. Who knows?

Would I still die by silver? I asked via chat.

I assume so.

I nod to myself, and type: *I think so, too. Still can't go near the stuff.*

So, Moon Dance... identity crisis averted?

For now, I wrote.

He signs off by sending me a vampire emoji... along with a little lightning bolt.

I giggle and send him a clown face. He hates clowns. He sends me a final "bitch" before we both log off.

Chapter Eight
Fundamental Laws

I suppose it's one of the fundamental laws of the universe that a car will be a financial albatross.

At least for us normal people. Well, okay. I'm quite far from normal, but I mean the non-rich. Probably should say 'us little people' then. Damn. I can't even say that anymore. Once the sale of that house goes through, I won't exactly be poor. One of the mysteries of being immortal I have yet to unlock is money. Kingsley's rolling in cash, though I don't sponge off him. I mean, hell, the man could buy me four new cars without batting an eyelash, but that's not me. Detective Hanner, my one-time friend and later nemesis had been rolling in the dough, too. Same with Jeffcock, my vampire sire and one-time father with the terrible name, which is why I preferred to refer to him as JC.

Anyway, my point is that as soon as a person finishes with car payments, the mechanic payments start. They're more sporadic and often more painful due to being unexpected. Case in point: $1,032.98 for the Momvan's check-up. Why is there always a .98? I guess that's one of life's great mysteries, too, along the lines of why do drive-up ATMs have braille on their keys?

Six new spark plugs, air filter, new oil, wheel lubricant, and four basic new tires later… the Momvan's back to fighting trim as Jacky would say. And, I manage to get out of the place about ten minutes to noon. So, I'll only be a little late.

And speaking of Jacky, I really need to hit the gym when I get back. I'm damn curious if I've maintained my strength and speed. Plus, I need to see how the little old Irishman is doing. He wasn't looking so good last time I worked out. Plus, I love that feisty bugger.

Amy and Joey are waiting for me at the women's shelter when I pull up, along with the bags of stuff we transported last night and a couple suitcases. The boy clings to his mother's side, gazing into space with a nervous, forlorn expression. I imagine she's told him his father won't be around much.

After I help load their things in the back, we hop in. Amy straps Joey in the car seat, which I left in place from last night. This triggers a casual conversation about kids in general, so I spend a while talking about Tammy and Anthony while we swing by a drive-through Starbucks for some coffee and breakfast sandwiches.

Of course, Amy is likely going to have to return to the area to testify if/when Walter's case goes to trial, but her parents can worry about getting her here and back at that point. As it turns out, Route 10 goes straight to Tucson by way of Phoenix... so yeah, the ride is going to be pretty damn mindless. She's originally from that area, so once we get *to* Tucson, she'll be able to tell me how to get to her parents' place easy enough. I may or may not need my GPS to find my way back to Route 10 afterward.

Too much thinking, Sam... chillax and enjoy the ride...

Right about now, I seriously expected Elizabeth to say something demeaning, snotty, weird, dark, or all of the above. Perhaps remind me that I'm above such mortals, and why would I waste my time. Or that within their warm bodies flows a life force that would make me oh so strong. That if I pulled off on a side road and fed, and erased their memories, no one would be the wiser. Or that, if I felt inclined, I could leave their drained, lifeless bodies for the buzzards.

Yeah, that kind of bullshit. Except, of course... I heard nothing.

Nothing at all... except for the chatter of my own thoughts.

In a very, very, very strange way that I haven't yet put my finger on, I missed the crazy old bat.

Despite her being twisted and evil, it still had been kind of nice to always have someone there, listening and analyzing, and, rarely, offering me advice. Mostly, I kept her hidden as deep as I could in my thoughts. But the wily bitch always found a way out... always crept closer and closer to my frontal lobe. Sometimes I let her hang around 'up top.' Sometimes I didn't mind her crazed opinions. Mostly, she scared the crap out of me. Often, I worried she might figure out a way to take me over. But she never had. And I had kept her at bay. And much to my surprise, her absence left me feeling a bit... empty.

I spend the next hour or two trying to convince Amy that Walter turning abusive wasn't her fault. Evidently, they had a fairly typical high school romance and decided to get married on the one-year anniversary of their graduation. Considering she's twenty-one, that means they've probably been married about two years... and she had Joey to deal with while going to high school. When I try to convince her she's going to be okay by saying she managed to take care of Joey while still in school, I get the whole story about how Walter's parents basically took her in at that point and now she feels guilty about 'doing this' to them.

A rest stop (mostly for the boy) comes and goes while I backpedal and reinforce the idea that Walter's parents are not Walter and if they can't realize she doesn't deserve to be mistreated, she shouldn't feel any sympathy for them.

Five hours into the ride, Joey becomes fidgety and cranky—so I do what any self-respecting immortal who values their sanity on a long road trip would do: I compel him to nap. Of course, I try not to be *too* obvious about it. The process is pretty simple really. Pull over, twist around into the back seat, and make soothing noises and silly faces to cover up mentally influencing a four-year-old.

When Joey passes out for a nap in twenty seconds, Amy's convinced I'm like the 'toddler whisperer' or something.

One thing about this ride? There's a *lot* of wide open nothing on both sides. Route 10 is mostly a pair of two-lane highways going in opposite directions, separated by maybe a thirty-foot swath of dirt that's occasionally a gully. I *thought* I was driving a little on the fast side until a tractor-trailer shot past us so fast the wind nearly sucked us into the left lane. That guy's gotta be going over a hundred.

When we reach the mountains, the scenery becomes slightly more interesting. Hilly brown nothingness instead of flat brown nothingness. Around 6:18 p.m., we arrive in Phoenix and I stop for gas as well as food at an IHOP close to Route 10. Amy walks with Joey to the bathroom after we order, so I take advantage of not driving and being alone for a while to call home and check up on the kids.

They're fine. No otherworldly shenanigans have occurred. Anthony's in the middle of a 'raid' on his game, so he chats for a few minutes while still playing and randomly complaining to someone on his headset about not getting enough healing.

"So, how's the trip?" asks Tammy after taking the phone back.

"Oh, it's *exhilarating*," I say. "Six hours or so of mostly desert."

"Sounds like you're having a blast, Mom," she says, somewhat distractedly.

"Totally. But it's for a good cause. All right, I can hear your friends giggling in the background. I'll let you get back to them. If you need anything, just call. You know I'm a couple seconds away if need be."

"Yeah. I'm totes jealous. If I could teleport, I'd sleep an extra forty-five minutes and just pop to school in the morning. Guess I'll settle for reading test answers out of the teacher's head."

I sputter and cough.

"Oh, come on, Mom. Joke."

She had to have picked up on me wondering about that at some point in the past. "You better hope so," I say in my fake-scolding tone, before chuckling. "Honestly, at seventeen, I'd have been exploiting the hell out of mind reading."

"Is that permission?"

"No. It's me being proud that you're a bit nobler than I would've been in your position."

She fakes an annoyed sigh. "Don't get sappy on me."

"It's hard not to. I just—"

"Oh, no. Here it comes."

"Love you two so much."

"I know. You tell us, like, all the time. Plus, I see it in your thoughts."

"This... change that has come over me... it's ummm..."

"It's allowed you to feel real emotions again. I know, Mom. Everyone in crying range knows."

It was true, of course. I've broken down in sobs more than I cared to admit these past few weeks, The absence of something so dark, angry and vengeful in my head did wonders for me. Though the woman hadn't succeeded in taking me over, her presence had stained my life in ways I hadn't fully appreciated. I was no longer fascinated about death. I found the feeling of love and compassion faster. Most important, I found my empathy... which had been slipping, faster than I'd let on. I cared again. I cared about my friends and family and about myself. It was undoubtedly why I had leaped at helping Amy and her son. I cared, dammit. I cared a lot about what happened to her and her boy.

"Okay, gotta go," said Tammy.

"Stay safe, sweetie."

"You too, Mom. Try not to like kill Odin, huh?"

"Odin?"

"You know, a god? You seem to be on a roll, killing the devil and the Red Rider. I figure Odin is next."

I grin, glancing up as Amy sets Joey into the high chair. "Okay, deal. I promise not to kill any more entities of great power... unless they attack me first."

Amy quirks an eyebrow.

"Video game," I whisper, while covering the phone.

To Tammy, I say, "Where did you inherit that imagination, young lady?"

"Dunno."

"Have you ever considered writing... stories?"

"Like books?"

"Yeah."

"Maybe," she answers.

Wow, she didn't flat-out deny it. Interesting. "Okay, we can talk about it later."

"Sure, whatever," But I hear it in her voice. She *had* been thinking of writing. Well, who better to write stories than a kid who'd lived through it all... and pretty much knew everything that went on in the minds of everyone, mortal or immortal.

Grinning to myself, I say, "Night, Tam Tam."

"Night," she chirps, and hangs up.

I get a chicken-bacon-cheddar sandwich. Sweet mama, it tastes even better than it smells, which is startling and awesome all at the same time. My body's not exactly meant to have real food anymore, but it's a lot more amenable to it now that I'm technically alive. While we eat, I feed on the mental energy of everyone around us. When we finish, Amy snags the receipt after I hand the waiter my credit card, insisting that her parents will reimburse me.

The trip to Tucson from Phoenix is about two

hours between traffic and meandering the neighborhood streets to Amy's childhood home. I park in the driveway of a nice one-story sky blue ranch house at 8:12 p.m. Her parents emerge from the front door and I initially mistake them for older siblings. They have to be in their forties but they don't look much older than thirty. She's got a younger brother who's fifteen, same age as Anthony, only he appears closer to twelve: lanky and wearing glasses.

Joey zooms off to hug his grandmother while her dad and brother help the two of us unload her stuff from the Momvan. I work together with the li'l bro to undo the car seat, and pretend not to notice Amy talking to her parents about money. Next, I busy myself tidying up the Momvan's cargo area. Eventually, her father, Nick, walks up to me.

"Miss Moon?"

I lean out of the van and face him. "That's me."

"I wanted to thank you for going out of your way to help Amy." He smiles. "We're so grateful you were able to locate our grandson before that man hurt him. Umm, Amy tells me you waived your usual fee for taking on a case like that?"

"She doesn't have any income. The man wouldn't let her out of the house." I shake my head. "It's likely she could use some counseling."

"What's your normal fee? Least I can do is cover that, plus your gas for coming out here."

"Don't worry about it. I'll take the gas money, but I don't want to cause any undue hardship."

He raises a hand. "It's fine. You saved my

grandson's life."

"Well, if you insist." I quote him my usual rate for a one-day case and hand over the gas receipts.

"No problem." He smiles. "Why don't you come on inside for a bit, relax. Stretch your legs?"

"Oh, it's okay. I was going to just head right on home."

He blinks. "You drove out here from Fullerton and plan to go back the same day?"

"More or less, yeah. I've got kids at home, too. But they're older."

"Ahh. Well, at least let me give you some coffee."

"You twisted my arm." I smile.

The house is pleasant, the coffee weaker than I like, but not bad. Joey zips around the place, repeatedly shouting "It's so big!" The apartment Amy and Walter shared in Fullerton would probably fit in her parents' living room.

Over coffee, her mother, Annette, gives me the whole 'I always knew that boy was bad news' routine, as well as thanking me for bringing her baby home. Nick hands me a check for enough to cover my fee as well as the gas money both ways.

I again make a polite gesture of protest, but cave in without much of a fight. I mean, the Momvan just took her blood tax this morning so I really *could* use the money. Before I leave, I give Amy the tiniest of mental prods to convince her nothing Walter did to her was in any way her fault. Maybe I can save them a couple thousand in therapist bills.

DEAD MOON

Citing the time, I head out the door around 9:40. I may need to drive a little fast to make it home by sunrise—duh. Nevermind. That's not a problem for me anymore. Neither is instant-unconsciousness as soon as the sun comes up. We haven't tested what happens if I go more than twenty-four hours without sleep, but Allison's theory is I'd burn vast amounts of energy to keep going that would start forcing me to feed more and more and more until people merely dropped unconscious as soon as I came within twenty feet of them. My real dad—as in, my hippy dad from *this* life—had a similar effect, but it came from his paranoia that the aluminum in deodorant would give him cancer.

Not wanting to risk the time loss on a wrong turn, I crank on the Garmin and hit the 'go home' button. I only really need it to get back on Route 10 going west. Then it's eight-ish hours of straight line.

I don't have the first clue where to go, but the purple line on the little screen points the way. While looking back and forth between the road and the GPS, I get the Momvan up to about fifty—perhaps a bit much for city streets, but they're pretty deserted (pun intended) and if I draw the attention of a cop, I can always encourage him to let me off with a warning.

My anxiety at being in unfamiliar surroundings starts to wane when I spot a sign indicating the on-ramp for Route 10 is a half mile away. I start to smile at the GPS, but a blur of pale skin and dark blue comes out of nowhere in front of me.

Screaming, I stomp on the brakes, but there's no possible way I can stop in time. While *I* may have super reflexes, the Momvan does not. In a two-second span that feels like ten to me, the screech of tires pitch-shifts into a demonic roar. Time seems to stop as I stare in horror at the face of a young woman gradually mushing against the hood. And—bam! Time speeds up again. Her hands strike the windshield, but don't break it. A cascading series of *thumps* comes from her body, head, arms, legs, all hitting the grille split-seconds apart.

She flies up and away, blood spraying out of her face, and sails off the road into the scrub.

I lurch forward in my seat as the Momvan finally slides to a stop, slightly twisted to the left compared to the road. The entire world falls silent around me. For another few seconds that feel like an eternity, I stare aghast at dribbles of blood rolling down my windshield.

My mind races to process what happened.

Holy shit. I just killed someone.

What do I do? Despite the sudden, instinctive temptation, I can't simply take off and pretend it didn't happen. No way. Not with this newfound sense of compassion having taken hold. Elizabeth would have found this funny... or merely a nuisance. Worse, her influence on me might have gotten me to agree. Now... horror filled me.

Maybe I could run over there and turn her... into what? A vampire? Could I even do that now? I didn't know, but I could try. Existing like that might be better than death—no, what am I thinking! I can't do that to someone, pull them off the cycle of reincarnation. And I don't even have fangs anymore. And I'm pretty sure there aren't any available dark masters to possess her anyway. The bastards are all free.

Shit. I really killed someone.

I bonk my head on the steering wheel. My thoughts leap to my kids, and I start shaking. It was an accident. Okay, I shouldn't have been looking at the Garmin so much, or doing fifty in a thirty-five, but still. Accident. Crap. I'm going to get the hell sued out of me, but I deserve it. That was someone's daughter.

A knot of grief twists in my stomach. Shock. I'm in shock. Nothing feels real anymore. I should've spent the night at Amy's house. What was I thinking trying to drive so much in one day? No, I'm not tired. But I'm also not nocturnal. I sleep at night now. I get tired at night. Well, kind of.

Shit! I just fucking killed someone.

A pale hand spears up into the blackness in front of my eyes, practically glowing in the glare of my headlights.

What. The. Hell?

Chapter Nine
Not a Scratch

The hand grabs the hood. I sit there staring dumbfounded.

Another hand rises up and grabs hold. Part of me doesn't want to see what I know is coming, some poor girl with a mangled face. The steering wheel starts to bend under my anxious grip, but the visage that creeps up into view is way worse than I imagined.

That is to say, unhurt.

Bloody as heck, but… unhurt.

The young woman braces herself on the hood and drags herself up onto her feet. Her head tilts to one side, draping her long brown hair half over her face. Greying eyes don't quite focus on me. She's wearing a navy blue sweatshirt with a red-white-and-blue A in the middle of the chest. My heart stops when I lock stares with her.

I'm staring at the same girl I saw on TV two days ago, the one who said 'Samantha, help me.'

At least... I think it's her.

And... she pretty much looks like a zombie. Well, I mean posture, bloody, dirty, that sort of thing. She's not rotting or anything, though her eyes don't look too good.

Curiosity holds down my shock while relief at seeing her not dead punches it in the head a few times. The war within me is enough to let my brain re-engage. I hop out and run around the front to her.

"Holy crap! I'm *so* sorry. You just came out of nowhere, walked onto the road." I grasp her arm. "Let me take you to the hospital."

The woman pivots toward me in a jerky not-quite-human way and emits a low moan. I try to get a better look at her face past her matted hair. She's gotta be somewhere between eighteen and twenty-two, about my height. Based on the condition of her sweatshirt and jeans—covered in dust and dirt—she's recently homeless, or she's been living outside a while.

"Sweetie, hey... look at me. Did you take something?"

She moans again.

Oh, shit. Something's clearly not right here. What's that stuff called? Bath salts? Some guy in Florida tried to eat people if I remember right. Why is it always Florida Man in the news doing bizarre—and often stupid—things? This girl seriously looks like a zombie with a killer skin care regimen. As if she literally just got up off the slab ten seconds ago, no sign of rot or even smell, except for her eyes, which look like she's wearing some serious smoky-lens contacts. Glaucoma from hell.

"What's your name?" I ask, grasping her cheek and forcing her head up to look me in the eye. And… her skin's corpse cold.

The instant I look into her gaze, I can tell she's like me. Well, not exactly like me. She's got a dark master inside her, or at least similar energy. Are the dark masters still jumping into people or is the Void empty now? Or had this happened before the collapse of the Void, thanks to yours truly? I don't know, but she's … something. I glance at the dent in the hood and broken grille. Great. More money. And no, it's not shallow of me to think that. This girl's fine. I didn't kill her. Something tells me I didn't even injure her. Whatever killed her happened way before I met her.

"Model," says the girl, in a slow, half-moany voice.

"What?" I ask. "You're a model?"

She looks at the Momvan. "Family car."

"Are you okay?" And yes, the dumbest question of the year award goes to *moi*. This girl is clearly *not* okay.

She pivots back toward me in another jerky, sudden swivel. "Target."

"What? Target? Is someone hunting you?"

The girl points at my sweater. "Tar… get."

"Oh. No. This came from Macy's thank you very much."

She grabs me by the chest. My supernatural reflexes kick in as she swings me around and slams me down on my back in the middle of the road. Apparently, I was the target. Boy, I must be dense tonight. I get my hands up to catch her by the shoulders as she lunges, mouth open, trying like hell to bite me in the face. All while I try like hell to keep my face intact. Wow, this bitch is strong! Right before I teleport out of there, she stops, tilting her head at me in the manner of a confused dog.

"Not... food." She clicks her teeth, biting air twice before standing up.

"No. I'm not." I spring to my feet. "And what the hell is going on?"

Shit. This girl's a damn zombie. Has to be. Kingsley never mentioned anything about zombies existing for real. Lichtenstein monsters—aka Frankenstein's monster—sure, but they don't really count as zombies. Though, zombies aren't usually much for conversation. The collective consciousness is all about zombies these days. Can't turn on prime time television without at least one show featuring them.

"Come on, sweetie." She doesn't put up any resistance as I usher her into the passenger seat and close the door. I hop in and pull the van over to the side of the road as if parked. Leaving it sitting in the middle of the lane *will* eventually attract a cop—or at least an idiot who wants to show me his middle finger.

The girl sits there staring into space, moaning her heart out, often, and loudly, extensively, and embarrassingly. She rocks and crosses her arms over her chest. After a few minutes, she bursts into tears. I wait, highly aware I can't read her mind or see her aura, a sure indication she is a freak like me. Maybe even freakier. She moans again, her mouth only partially open, her lips trembling. Blue veins appear in her cheek, pulsating. Definitely freakier.

The moaning-rocking-crying stuff goes on for at least ten minutes. So much for making it home in one night. I check my cell phone and see a text from Anthony lights up the screen with 'Hi mom!' Only two words, but it's enough to bring a tear to my eye. Nearly killing this young woman next to me makes me want to teleport home and squeeze Anthony until he turns into the Fire Warrior to be strong enough to peel me away. Not that he'd do that. He wouldn't want to burn me. Somehow, I manage to push my family-clinginess aside and give my full attention to the sloppopotamus—as Tammy would call her—sitting next to me.

"You're sick," I say.

The girl moans.

"Can you talk? You spoke before."

She starts to turn toward me, spots the Garmin, and says "Map." Then, shudders, holding her head in both hands. There is an odd rectangle drawn on her right forearm, spaces numbered from one to six but it doesn't click with me as anything ritualistic.

"Yes," she says slowly. "Speaking is... hard.

Everything is... foggy. I think I'm dying." She shakes her head side to side and emits another loud moan.

"How long have you been this way?" I asked.

"Three days." The girl rocks for a few seconds, then snaps her teeth at nothing. "So hungry."

I find myself narrowing my eyes and studying her some more. Three days was about how long it had taken me to become the thing I am today, or at least, version 1.0. If I had to guess, I would say I'm on version 6.0 and counting.

"What's your name?"

"Mindy. Umm. Mindy Hogan." The girl looks up at me again. "Model."

"Hi, Mindy. I'm Sam. Sorry again for hitting you with my van."

"It's okay. It didn't hurt." She stares at me with those eerie milked-over eyes. "That's bad right? That should've hurt?"

I don't bother saying I saw her face smush on my hood. "It looked like it probably should have hurt, but maybe it looked worse than it was." Understatement of the year.

Mindy doesn't have an aura and her mind is closed off to me. I note again the profuse sweating and the huddling and rocking. The moaning is new, though. That didn't happen to me. And the appearing-and-disappearing blue veins in her face. Then again, within days, my reflection had disappeared entirely, so if that vein-thing had happened to me I never would've known it. The door mirror tells me this girl still has a reflection, too… so she's not a vampire.

Wait a second…

I shift my gaze to the center mirror and squeak with surprise. Holy shit! I have a reflection again. How did I not notice that over the past two weeks? Maybe I'd grown so accustomed to avoiding mirrors out of shame I just never thought to look?

Wow... just wow.

I watch myself smile. And holy crap! I do look like I'm in my mid-twenties. No wonder people make weird faces at me whenever I say Tammy's my daughter.

Okay... back to the girl. I can stare into mirrors later. And I will... *hard*.

Mindy seems more disoriented than anything else. I endured real changes, real pain, real confusion. I'd had my husband by my side, helping me through what would ultimately destroy us. But back then, he'd been a saint, and been there every step of the way. For that, I thanked him. His later choices in life were all on him. Although maybe a little on me, too.

Might it have been better if I'd gone away? I think that over as I watch the girl swipe at bangs stuck to her sweaty forehead. Maybe I should have gone away, faked my death, and watched my children from afar. They might've had a relatively normal life that way, even if it would've gutted me to let them believe me dead.

A lone green car rolls by us.

"Toyota," says Mindy.

I made the choice I'd made, and shit went down, and I would live with that forever. My son still loves me, and my daughter does as well, even if we butt heads sometimes. What more could a mother of two superhero teens expect?

Then again, they wouldn't have been superheroes if I hadn't been around. Anthony would have been dead when he got sick so young, and Tammy would have been, well, Tammy, minus all the crazy mind reading. She might have gone down a dark road with the loss of her mother and brother. I could see that happening with her.

Now… well, now she only has to deal with the loss of her father—sort of. Danny's hiding inside Anthony, so deep that even she can't detect him. My ex-husband had been fleeing his personal version of hell that had been awaiting him. Danny, of course, had just enough dark master training, thanks to my now-dead vampire frenemy, Detective Hanner, to know how to run and hide from the Devil. And run and hide he did—inside my son.

Little had I known that the two of them had formed a blood bond; after all, most dark masters—even wannabe dark masters like Danny—can't possess the living without a physical bloodletting. An initiate like Danny could foreseeably create such a bond while still living, which is exactly what he did. The bloodletting had been a small cut and an incantation, all done without my knowledge. He'd sworn my son to silence. Maybe that's why he tries so hard to be a perfect angel these days? My son didn't have a clue what his father did and only wanted to help his daddy any way he could. Danny couldn't possibly have known he would die so soon, killed by his co-conspirator. But he'd been suspicious enough to plan his escape from hell. Most of this I'd learned from my late-night talks with him while he took brief possession of Anthony. We often talked for hours, and it usually left me furious at him all over again.

My life, I thought. Talking to my dead, cheating, wannabe dark master husband through my superhuman son, a son who literally went toe-to-toe with the Devil a few months ago. The ultimate irony in all that was, Danny had gone into dark magic looking for a way to 'kill the thing that replaced his wife' and bring me back, but in becoming a dark master himself, he'd wound up coming to understand that I'd been me all along. Though, I'm not sure Danny counts as a dark *master*. Dark journeyman perhaps? Dark apprentice? Meh.

My life… and, strangely, I wouldn't change a thing. No, really, I wouldn't. Even what I was. Even what I am and what I had been. Even what my kids had become. We are making the most of it. It's all pretty fantastic and wild—that is, when we're not being hunted by demons, or werewolf packs, or dark masters. Or worse. Yes, amazingly, worse was out there.

Anyway, my past gives me some insight into the young lady rocking in her seat next to me, a young lady who, I am certain, is going through 'the change.' As in, the supernatural change.

"If I try real hard, I can still think. But... I'm *so* hungry. I've been picking at food left behind in trash cans, but no matter how much I eat, I'm still hungry. I even stole a hot dog from a little girl. It kinda made me sick. Lately, the more I eat, the sicker I get."

Made sense. Her body had no more need for regular food. Just as mine had rejected that Ding Dong so many years ago. Now, not so much. Now, I could eat to my heart's content... even if it did little by way of sustaining me. Still, a minor miracle. Trust me, I'm not complaining.

"Mindy, this is going to be difficult for you to process, but you're not entirely... human anymore."

She twitches like a drunken marionette. The way she rolls her head to look at me, I half expect it to fall off and land in my lap. "I got that feeling when I bounced off your van and got up."

I hand her a tissue.

Mindy wipes blood from her face... a face that had already healed from its introduction to my hood. "Thanks."

Of course, now the biggest question on my mind is—what the hell did I see on television? Did this girl send me a call for help or did I see the future? Or did some external force send me a message? Ugh. Well, one thing's for certain: I'm going to be late going home.

I text the kids and Mary Lou that something

unusual happened and I would probably be home a day later than expected.

Tammy responds with, 'Vegas here I come!' Then 'LOLJK' a few seconds later.

My son sends a 'U ok?'

Saying 'yeah, no worries' isn't a complete lie, but it's also not the complete truth. My heart is still racing from hitting Mindy. Which, in and of itself, is an interesting feeling, considering my heart hasn't raced in over a decade. And I suppose sometimes I do have *good* luck. I mean, the first time I've ever run over a pedestrian while driving and she turns out to be a near-indestructible zombie. But hang on, zombies don't usually talk. She's got the moaning thing and the rickety not-right posture down, but this girl sounds way too intelligent to be a zombie.

Oh, hang on.

"Mindy?"

"Van," she says, pointing at the dashboard.

"Yes. Why do you keep doing that?"

She looks at me. "Macy's. Umm. Doing what?"

"Saying random phrases whenever you look at something?"

Mindy groans again, curling fetal-like in the chair, grabbing two fistfuls of hair. Thankfully, she doesn't rip her scalp off. Though, the girl doesn't appear to be rotting. Perhaps she's too new at the zombie thing and still—I shudder—retains her human memories and appearance. Oh, this poor kid.

"I…" She twitches back and forth a few times, like she's attempting to physically shake a bad idea out of her ear. "Stupid word association test. It's the last thing I remember… the only thing I remember about anything that happened before."

"Word association test?"

"These people." She presses her face against her knees, shaking. "I went to this place. They did something to me. There was a television screen and I had to say whatever popped into my head when I looked at the image. One slide had this guy who like fell off a skyscraper or something and burst all over the sidewalk."

I cringe.

She lifts her head and fixes me with a ravening stare. "The first time I saw it, I thought *eww!* But, the second time it came up, it made me hungry. I think I know what they were doing. They kept showing me pictures of people, then food. People, then food. Back and forth. When I look at people, I get hungry now. I'm scared. I guess it's good I'm going blind."

"Wait. You're going blind?" Well, I think to myself, that explains why she stumbled out onto the road.

"Not entirely. My vision is getting crappier and crappier like I'm walking in a cloud. I can only see a couple feet in front of me now. And sometimes, I think there's something alive in my gut moving around."

"Ick."

"Yeah. Ick." She starts to salivate looking at me, but catches herself. "You don't smell like food."

"Yeah. We have something in common, kid."

"I'm not a kid. I'm twenty."

"You're a kid to me," I say, chuckling.

Mindy lifts her head and looks at me. "Model."

"Oh… Thank you. You're too kind."

She biffs herself in the side of the head a few times. "Sorry. I gotta stop blurting like that."

"I… umm… think I might have an idea what could help you."

Mindy tilts her head again, like a bewildered golden retriever.

"Sit tight."

I drop the Momvan in gear, and pull away from the curb.

Chapter Ten
Brain Food

I whip out my phone and swipe it on after using my thumbprint to unlock it.

That I still have a thumbprint tickles me to no end. Anything that keeps me grounded on this earth and makes me feel human again, is always a relief. I used to take delight in happy moments because they made the fiend inside me squirm… but Elizabeth is gone.

Still not sure how to feel about that. Instinctively I'm overjoyed, but despite knowing I'd been played and I really hadn't been cosmically fated to contain her, it's difficult to give up on guilt like I somehow failed.

I shouldn't really be texting while driving, even with vampire-like reflexes. Especially not after running Mindy over. But then again, she did leap in front of the van.

Also, I'm not texting. I'm trying to find an authentic Mexican restaurant, preferably taco trucks. These days, even taco trucks have websites and Twitter followers. My luck holds out, and I get a hit on one, supposedly set up only a quarter mile from here.

I hang a right and narrowly miss a jaywalker laughing into his phone. The narrowly-missed jaywalker casually raises his middle finger, turns in the street, and pauses long enough for me to catch a glimpse of him in my side mirror. He's still laughing into his phone. Multi-tasking at its best.

"Where… where are you taking me?" asks Mindy. She shakes her head and runs her hands continuously through her hair.

"We're getting tacos," I say.

"I-I don't want tacos. Please pull over, I just want to leave…"

"And go where?"

"I dunno. I just wanna walk."

I picture what she would look like walking, and it would undoubtedly match what I'd seen on TV the other day, something that, I think, many believe is on its way to all of us. As I've been hearing now for some years, when enough people believe, the Universe answers that call. Zombies are everywhere —on TV and in the movies, on bumper stickers and Facebook posts—and it seems that the power of Creation has finally gotten around to them.

"Please trust me, Mindy," I say. "I think I know

what you need, and that taco truck just up ahead will probably have it."

She lets out a long, low, plaintive moan, and stares at me with eyes far more milked over than they had been just ten minutes ago when I'd first met her. Lucky me, she had been going through 'the change' during our meeting.

"Not tacos, per se," I say, realizing the young lady had retreated back into her void-like mind. What little bit of her personality came through before seems to have faded. Hunger does that to most supernatural beings with a connection to the Void, especially the kind of hunger that only feeds the darkness within. I've been there before. After my attack thirteen years ago, and another time, too… a time when I'd been surrounded by scores of wounded soldiers and looking at brutal surgeries. I can't quite remember if I had an extremely vivid dream of the Civil War or somehow actually wound up there. But I'm certain, although I can't quite put together the specifics, that I have a connection with the Civil War.

Not just a connection, but a memory. And within that memory, I had been nearly comatose with my need for blood. I shrug it off. Now, of course, I had more pressing matters, like stopping Mindy from going full zombie on me.

"Aha!" I say, spotting the taco truck parked in the glare of streetlights near a civic building. At this hour, nearly ten at night, they're probably about to pack up and go. Made it just in time.

I find a spot. Granted, it's not so much a spot as an empty space of asphalt next to the taco truck.

"Wait here, okay?" I say to Mindy.

She rocks in the seat, moaning. I shrug. Good enough.

***

The truck has a line. Oh, shit. Maybe not quite ready to go.

And not any old line, but a giant line of semi-drunk people fresh out of the nearby watering holes. By their dress, I'm sure most went straight from the various downtown government buildings to the bars, and now they're here. Every last one of them has security badges hanging from neck lanyards. Neck lanyards after dark? Don't all of them know they look like dorks? I mean, they have to, right?

I bypass the line while drawing small amounts of mental energy from everyone. Hey, the smell of food made me hungry. A few look at me, but no one says a word as I step straight up into the open side door of the food truck, filled with sizzling food, rapid Spanish chatter and gringos trying to order in Spanish via the propped-open side panel. The interior is spacious yet oddly cozy, and for a brief moment, I feel like I want to buy a food truck and travel from city to city, serving delicacies and feeding the masses.

Hello, Sam. Reality check. 'Vampire Taco' sounds like a cheesy movie you'd find on cable at three in the morning—probably directed by Uwe Boll.

The scene is one of barely controlled chaos, so much so that no one notices me—for a heartbeat or two. Finally, a short order cook looks up from his steaming griddle where he's busily working over something meaty and sautéed, possibly beef or chicken. Both of which sound good to me. Then again, these days, I'm not exactly picky. I adore any chance to eat things-other-than-blood, even if they happen to be offal. It's useless for me from a nutrition standpoint, but now that I can have real food without magical cheating, I'm never going to take it for granted again.

The cook is surprisingly shorter than me, covered in sweat, and works faster than I think I'd ever moved in my life. He blinks and stares at me brazenly walking into their truck. He blinks again, then turns back to the griddle. I guess I don't look threatening. The truck did have a rather big line, and I'm sure the people running it don't want to be here until midnight.

"Who are you?" asks a woman with a thick accent. She fires me an irritated-as-hell glare from behind the short refrigerator she'd been rummaging through.

"My name's Sam, and I need you to want to help me."

She opens her mouth to speak, and the irritated crease in her forehead slackens. After a momentary foggy stare, she smiles. "Sure, anything. What can I help you with?"

"You serve *tacos de sesos*?" I ask.

"Of course, *señora*. How many would you like?"

I count mentally, then on my fingers, basing the equation on Mindy's size, age, and weight, F.O.M. (frequency of moaning), D.S.T. (days since turning), and, finally, L.O.C.R.H.B. (likeliness of consuming real human brains), and come up with 'shitloads.' Let's see Young Sheldon figure out *that* equation. Since I'm sure this woman can't translate 'a shitload' into literal numbers, I say, "Ten. No, Twelve. No, fifteen."

"Fifteen, *señora*?"

"*Si*. Er, yes."

She glances at the fridge. "I may not have fifteen."

"Then give me whatever you have."

"Of course. Would you like cilantro with those?"

"No," I say. "And the answer to that is always, 'no cilantro.'"

"Excuse me?"

"Never mind," I say. Back in the day, I'd been part of the 14% who couldn't stand the taste of cilantro. As my friend-in-arms used to say, "It tastes like mummy wrappings." I couldn't agree more.

"Very well, give me ten minutes—"

"I need them now."

"But *señora*, we need to cook—"

"No," I say. "Raw is fine. And, come to think of

it, hold the tortillas, hot sauce, and lettuce too." As I say this, I instill within her the idea that my request is very normal—and very forgettable.

"Of course, *señora*, I will be happy to give you all the *cerebros de carne* we have, raw."

"*Gracias*," I say, and try like hell not to sound like the gringo I am.

She smiles and returns to the freezer in the center of the truck; meanwhile, the young chef is watching me with wide eyes. I dip into his thoughts while I wait, and, yes, he can understand English. He heard every word and is wondering why I need raw cow brains. He starts to think about zombies, merely a fleeting thought from watching that same TV show. But, he winds up having no thoughts of zombies, as I alter his memory of my request, replacing it with a simple notion that I'm merely a county inspector and he needs to be on his best behavior.

Yeah, I always feel like crap stealing someone's memory. I mean, it's their memory after all. But such a memory serves no one, least of all my new client, currently sitting in the Momvan and, for all I know, chewing on my steering wheel. Better that than shambling after pedestrians.

And yeah, she's a client now. Or maybe a friend. I dunno. Thirteen years ago, it would've been nice if I had a friend on the other side to help me adjust to the change. Maybe I can do that for her, even if I don't have the first damn clue what the hell to do with a zombie. It would be like I'm a bald eagle trying to raise a puppy. Flight lessons are probably a bad idea.

The woman hands me a heavy plastic bag of cold meat. Then again, is brain considered meat? I don't really know, but I also don't have time to split hairs over that. I hand her a $20 bill—hey I'm no thief—and dash back around to the Momvan in time to stop Mindy from opening the passenger side door. Her eyes are even milkier, her face raked with scratches from her fingernails, and the veins stand out on her like fat, blue earthworms.

I shove the passenger side door shut with my hip. Oops, I might have crushed her hand. Oh, well. Can't have a zombie running loose on the streets.

Back in my front seat, with a confused, angry, and hungry Mindy reaching for me, I bat her surprisingly strong arms aside, open the plastic bag, and set it in her lap.

She continues reaching for me for a few seconds until the smell hits her, and she looks down. Mindy sniffs once, twice, and her hazy eyes clear briefly. I watch with sick fascination as the young woman scoops brains out by the handful, shoveling them into her mouth as fast as she can swallow. She practically inhales the cow brains until the bag is empty. She picks at the meat (I'm going to call it meat… even if brains are organs) at the front of her shirt, as well as a few stray bits in her lap and on the floor between her feet.

Once she can't find any more chunks, she licks the bag clean, too. I figure Mindy ate the equivalent of two whole cow brains. Certainly enough, you would think—

Mindy looks up at me, a manic gleam in her eyes—which have become clear again, mostly. At least far more human than they were five minutes ago. And, the blue veins are gone. Aside from her weird posture and herky-jerky movements, she looks pretty close to human.

"More," she groans. "Please, I need more."

"Well, okay, then," I say, and start the minivan, while simultaneously grabbing my phone and opening Google.

At least she's stopped moaning.

I'll call that progress.

Chapter Eleven
A Bad Idea

I don't expect the local Von's—or whatever supermarkets they have around here—to offer what we need.

So, my Google search brings me to the best choice: a Mexican grocery. Mindy seems lucid enough that I trust leaving her out in the Momvan while I run inside. Near the back of the store, I find a cold case with more cow brains in those foam-and-shrink wrap packages like from a butcher counter. I gotta say, they look *disgusting.*

Then again, to that poor girl waiting for me outside, these probably look amazing.

I grab four packs, about six pounds, and head for the register. On the way, I catch a whiff from a prepared food counter where the guy's wrapping it up for the night. Smelling burritos after being around that food truck is too much for me. I grab a giant chicken burrito for myself, purely because I've developed a hell of a craving for the taste—and he's probably going to throw it out anyway.

A few minutes later, I'm back in the minivan. Hey, one advantage to shopping five minutes before a place closes is no lines.

I hand Mindy the bag with the brains in it and do my damndest not to look at her while devouring my burrito. Yeah, it tastes like it's been sitting under heat lamps for an hour or three, but it's authentic enough to still be pretty awesome. It's somewhat difficult to enjoy it with all the slurping and squishing in my right ear, but I persevere.

Much to my amazement, I finish first.

A minute or two later, Mindy finally drops the fourth Styrofoam tray back in the bag, gasping for breath. Grease smears her face. Bits of brain cling to her hair. But at least the dark circles have gone and her eyes are no longer milky. In fact, she almost looks like a normal twenty-year-old woman, except for being pale enough to appear as an extra in a Marilyn Manson video.

"Are you okay?" I ask.

"Yes, thank you. I feel so much better." She thuds a fist into her chest twice and belches. "Almost… good enough to think I'm dreaming and I just woke up."

I hand her a wet wipe from the box I keep in the console. She opens it with hands that aren't shaking anymore. In fact, her motions have lost all jerkiness.

The girl's even holding her head up straight. She proceeds to clean the grease and brain juice from between her fingers and under her nails.

"Did I just eat brains?" she asks.

"You did. Copious amounts."

"Copious?" she asks.

"Means you ate a lot of brains."

"Raw?"

"Yes. The rawer, the better would be my guess."

Everything about her seems to have settled down, although I'm not one hundred percent sure I can see her breathing. No surprise there. I also suspect her heart isn't beating very hard either, if at all. Before, when I'd been an undead, I had a ring that allowed me to tolerate normal food. Even though I got no benefit from it, whenever I ate, the inevitable aftereffect occurred. I catch myself starting to wonder if zombies have to deal with that, too... and decide my thoughts are better occupied elsewhere.

So anyway, sitting next to me is a full-blown high-functioning zombie.

Go figure.

"Is it wrong that I want to suck this wet-nap dry?" she asks.

I shrug. "Knock yourself out."

She looks at the dirty thing, then shakes her head with a nauseated expression. I hold up a plastic bag that I keep between the seats and she deposits the tempting piece of soiled napkinry into it. I seal the bag and toss it over the back seat.

"You wanna talk now?" I ask.

She starts to nod, but winds up staring blankly forward. And damn this girl has a hell of a blank stare. "Did that really happen, Susan?"

"Samantha," I say. "And yes it did."

"Did I really eat all those brains?"

"You did." I say. "And with gusto."

"I wanted to kill you, and everyone around me."

"I'm sure you did."

"But you stayed, helped me."

"I bought more brains today than I ever have." I chuckle.

"Weren't you afraid?"

I smile at her. "No."

"Why not? My memory is hazy… but I was out of control, like going crazy. Holy crap, was I moaning?"

"Like a nor'easter off the south Irish Sea."

She blinks. "Is that nor'easter business a real thing?"

"I have no idea. I've never been to the East coast."

Mindy giggles, and I do too, and soon her giggles turn to soft crying, then full-blown tears, and I find myself leaning across the seat and hugging a woman who just might be one of the world's first zombies.

Once the tears run their course, I get the full scoop—and what a scoop it is.

Mindy's a student at the University of Arizona, and like most kids in college these days, she's pretty hard up for money, despite working nearly full-time as a waitress. So, when she spotted a flyer on a post advertising a $500 payout to anyone who volunteered for some medical testing, she figured she was young, strong, and healthy enough.

"Who pays for your college?" I ask. "You're not affording that off waiting tables."

She emits a sad laugh. "No… My parents are paying for the tuition, and Dad sends me like $300 a month for food and stuff, but it's never enough."

"So, that's why you decided to do the thing? Five hundred bucks is a really tempting number."

"Yeah. I was scared. For good reason!" She balls her fists. "I *knew* something was wrong with it. I had the *worst* feeling before I went into the place. I knew something bad was gonna happen to me."

"What did they do? Where is this place?"

"Umm. Somewhere in southwest Tucson, some abandoned-looking warehouse district. I don't remember the address. The place looked empty, but inside it was like a nice dentist office."

"Okay, go on…"

She explains that once there, some guy in a doctor's coat had her fill out some paperwork, and then he brought her to a room deeper in the building that looked, again, a lot like a dentist's office, complete with chair and a big TV screen.

"Felt like I was descending through the seven gates of hell."

I chuckle. "Are you a lit major?"

"No, a Dan Brown reader."

I blink at her.

"His novel, *Inferno*, is based on *Dante's Divine Comedy*."

"Ahh." I smile and nod, and decide to keep to myself that I might have vanquished the Dark Prince himself, and that hell itself wasn't just one place—let alone merely seven levels—but many hundreds of thousands of places, personalized for each soul. Of course, with the destruction of the Devil, I've often wondered what happened to those personalized versions of hell. My gut tells me they remain in existence—and would continue to do so—until the souls themselves had enough and moved on. Though, the new Devil might keep them or remodel them, and wow, is that fascinating to contemplate. After all, with enough belief, the Universe provides. There have to be more people who believe in Satan than think zombies might be real, and here Mindy is. Sigh. Poor kid.

And the vast majority of the world believes in the Devil. Had people known I killed the Dark Lord, they could, officially, stop believing in the bastard. But they didn't—and wouldn't—know such a thing. Nor would anyone believe me if I tried to tell them. Unless, of course, I sprouted my wings on live TV and flew around on stage at like the Ellen show. Alas, the world at large would assume it to be only special effects. Besides, I'm fairly certain the world needs a Devil. Heck, it needed something, anything, to provide balance to the light.

Of course, I hadn't had a problem with the son of a bitch until he went after my daughter. He'd come looking for trouble, but he picked the wrong Mom to mess with.

And now he's no more. Well, that version of him. I'm pretty sure another has replaced him.

So, yeah, I keep all of that—and more—to myself. Especially the two wing tattoos under my T-shirt, tattoos that are oh-so-much-more than tattoos. Or that, from a secret pouch, I could produce a sword that could kill just about anything, the Devil and his demons included. On a far less interesting note, I also keep to myself that my son's underwear often looks like the pavement at the starting line of a dragstrip.

Mindy tells me that she stumbled down the street from the place, not knowing who she was, where she wanted to go, or much of anything more than having a bizarre need to wander around. She didn't sleep; however, she did fall over several times and it took her a long while to find the urge to get back up. A few people had seen her, and she tried to chase them, moaning, but they all ran away. She lived in a dorm at college... and with it being the weekend, no one had come looking for her. At one point, she had managed to send her mother a smiley emoji text. It seemed to work. Her mother hadn't tried to contact her since.

"Ugh. Those people on the street probably think I was high on something super nasty." She rubs her eyes.

"At least they probably wouldn't recognize you now. I think we can safely conclude that starving causes you to lose both muscle coordination and mental faculties."

"I guess. I still feel a little stiff, but not *too* out of sorts."

She describes a heaviness in her bones, like weights in her feet when she'd attempted to walk. In fact, she almost had to re-learn how. The leaden feeling remained until moments ago when she'd eaten those brains.

"I still feel kinda sluggish, but it's more like I stayed up a little too late now. I've always been kinda hyperkinetic, restless, and fidgety. Could never talk without waving my hands. Whenever I'm bored or waiting for something, I bounce around. It's kinda freaking me out that I don't really wanna move much. Just like, sit here, yanno? Mom always said I had 'ants in my pants.' I haven't had to go to the bathroom once since leaving that place." She glances at me and folds her arms. "A few minutes after I left that place, I got so damn hungry."

"Are you hungry now?" I ask.

"No, not really. I mean, I feel like I *could* eat, sure. But I'm not ravenous like I'd been for the past few days."

"Since your visit to the clinic."

"Yes," she says, nodding.

"And that was three days ago?"

"Yes."

"Have you contacted the clinic about your

concerns?"

"I tried. Once, like an hour after I left before I couldn't think anymore."

"What did they say?"

"No one answered."

"Do you know what kind of drug they tested on you?"

"They said it was a skin ointment, and that I had responded nicely to it." She holds up her arm to show off the marker-drawn rectangle. "Nothing happened."

We sit in the minivan for another few long seconds before I ask, "What do you think happened to you?"

"I think they turned me into a fucking zombie. Or something real close to one."

I nod. "How does that make you feel?"

"Pissed. Like I legit want to kill someone. They ruined my life." After a few seconds of staring into space, she whips her head toward me, sudden hope in her eyes. "Maybe it's not permanent. What if they like gave me a drug that makes me into a zombie for a little while? The doctor said he needed to take a blood sample in case I had a reaction to the cream, but he stuck me with a second needle, and I'm sure he injected something into me instead of drawing blood. I bet that's what did this to me."

"Maybe," I say.

But she caught my tone. "You don't think so? Maybe it was something subliminal in the TV, you think?"

"Hmm…" I pause and try to scan her thoughts. Her mind is blocked to me as surely as if, well, as if she were a fellow immortal. "I think… I don't know."

"You're holding something back."

"I don't have enough information yet."

"I think you do. Tell me what you know, please." She gestures at herself "Look at me! Look at what I just ate. I *know* something happened to me. I can feel it. You don't have to sugar coat it."

I consider her words and remember back to when I changed. Of course, I became a very different animal, though my confusion, pain, and suffering could be similar. It didn't have to go on as long as it had for me, but I had no one else to turn to. I look at Mindy again and it doesn't surprise me to find her gazing at me unblinkingly. Her eyes, of course, are the key here. I lean closer, almost nose to nose.

"Why are you staring at me like that?" asks Mindy a moment later.

"I'm looking for something."

"What?" she asks, with a blink slow enough that I'm not sure 'blink' is the right word for it.

"Keep looking at me," I say.

She obliges. "What are you trying to see?"

I peer deep into her dark brown eyes, which have only the faintest hint of haze to them, looking for that thing I knew had to be there… or at least, suspect like crazy is there. All supernatural entities have it. Well, at least the entities I'm familiar with do. Zombies—or whatever it is she's become—are certainly new to me. That said, all other creatures have one thing in common: possession. And not just possession by any ol' being. But possession of a dark master, even the lesser ones. Or as in the case of Danny with my son, possession by a dark master-in-training.

Then again, with Elizabeth working to free them from the Void, would any of them even want to possess humans again? They only did that to escape, to get back into the world. With them now having the power to physically enter the world on their own, they have no need for possession. Maybe that's why this girl turned into a zombie? Those things are typically depicted as mindless—even more so than marketing executives. Could this be what happens when there is no dark master, merely Void energy? Either way, there has to be some manner of dark presence in her.

And the surest way to spot such a presence is… there.

Yup, I spot it as plain as day, perhaps even easier thanks to the distinctly dead look in her eyes.

It is, of course, the flame, flickering way back in the darkness of her pupils.

"Mindy, I hate to tell you this, but… you're dead. And, you're probably a zombie."

Chapter Twelve
In Morte Veritas

"I don't wanna be a zombie," says Mindy in a small voice.

Okay, that might have been the saddest thing I'd ever heard. "Sorry. I didn't ask for this either."

"Am I gonna get all like rotting and stuff?" She sniffles. "I don't wanna."

"Well, when I think of zombie, I don't picture someone who's able to carry on a conversation. And, if you've been dead for three days out in the sun—even in November—you should look a lot worse than you do."

"So what does that mean?" She blinks, again super slow. "And what did you mean by you not asking for it? Me stumbling into the road?"

"No. Crap. One sec."

I pull the hood release and hop outside. One

thing about being supernaturally strong… I more or less fix the dent Mindy's face left in the hood with my bare hands. She stares at me the whole time, mouth slightly agape. Once I'm back in the driver's seat, she gestures at the hood.

"You're stronger than a person should be."

"So are you." I wink. "And pretty damn tough."

"What did you mean by 'dark master'?"

Our conversation goes off the rails a few times as I try to explain. For now, I leave out that Elizabeth got free and dark masters may or may not still want to possess people. Baby steps.

We fall silent once or twice for long periods of staring, while the almost-eleven-at-night world passes us by. Then the denial begins, followed by the usual questions, and finally a little hint of acceptance. With the acceptance comes more silence.

"I'm really possessed?" Mindy asks for the fifth time.

"Yes. Well, most likely. If not a dark master, you have Void energy in there."

"Because you can see a flame in my eyes?"

"Yes."

"This is hard for me to believe."

"I know," I say.

"Then again, none of this makes sense. You don't have a flame in your eyes."

"No," I said, and nearly tried to send her a suggestion to let it drop, and remembered she couldn't be influenced. "It's a long story, but my dark master is gone. But she had been there. And the flame had been there, too. At least, that's what I was told, since I couldn't see myself in mirrors back then."

I next have her look in the mirror... and really look into her eyes. As deep as she can see, until she finally gasps.

"Shit! There's fire in my eye."

"A flame."

She continues staring, then snaps her head to look at me. "Wait, are you like me?"

"A zombie?" I ask.

"If that's what I am… or turning into, or whatever."

"No, I'm not a zombie."

"But you had the flame. Wait, did you say you couldn't see yourself?"

I nod once, and wait for it.

"No way!"

There it is. I smile and say, "Way."

"You're seriously a…" She gawks.

"Kardashian?" I ask, eyebrow up.

She continues staring at me for a few more seconds before she giggles. "No, not a Kardashian. Wait, are they also?"

"No," I say. "At least, I don't think so."

"Well, I wouldn't be surprised if they were."

"Me either."

"So, you're telling me you really are a…"

She waits. I wait.

"Someone has to say it," I finally say. "And it ain't gonna be me."

"A vampire?"

"There it is."

"For realz?"

"For realz," I say. "But I'm not the garden variety of vampire. I no longer drink blood."

"But I thought all vampires drank blood. Well, that's what the stories all say."

"I used to. I drink—or feed—on something else."

"Please don't say zombies."

I laugh. "No. Mental energy."

"OMG. I heard about your type!"

"My type?"

"Psychic vampires."

"That's me," I said.

"But you used to drink blood."

"I did."

"And you're different now... because your dark master no longer possesses you."

I nod, impressed. Her mental faculties are as sharp as ever. After sending my kids an 'I'm definitely going to be a day or two late' text, I tell her about this new world of supernatural beasties she's been baptized into... my world. Far more, in fact, than I'd expected to. Turns out, zombies make for an ideal audience.

"But I'm not a vampire, right? I mean, I'm barely accepting that I might be that... other thing."

"Right," I say. "But most things that go bump in the night—"

"Bump in the night?"

"Monsters," I say, remembering she's young

and, undoubtedly, addicted to her phone—and not in the good way. Meaning, she probably makes liberal use of Snapchat and Instagram, and not so much her Kindle app or, say, Wikipedia. "You know, scary things."

"Yeah, okay. Go on."

I nod. "Most of us share something similar."

"The possession thing you mentioned."

"Yes. But it goes deeper than that."

"I'm not sure I can handle deeper, Sam. You're laying a lot of information on me. I mean, before I met you only a few hours ago, I wasn't even thinking zom—well, you know."

"Right, sorry," I say. "It's a lot, I know."

She stares at me for a while in silence. "Basically, you're saying we sort of operate the same way."

I nod. "Yes."

"But some of us are vampires and others are…"

"Other things," I say.

"What kind of other things?"

"Are you sure you want to know?" I ask.

"No. Yes. Wait. Maybe not." She grabs her hair in two hands and lets out an *Argh!* "At least, not right now."

"Okay."

She breathes deep a few times, holding it for a long, long time. "I really have dark energy inside me?"

"Yes."

"And that flame in my eye is the proof."

"Yes."

"Is there a way to be un-possessed?" she asks.

"Not really," I say. "Well... in my case, it was a really long, drawn out, involved process that probably had less chance of working than winning the lottery. I've found one other way, but you won't like it."

"What is it?"

I offer a wan smile. "Final death. Complete oblivion."

"So I'm stuck like this."

"I think so, yes."

"A fucking zombie?"

"Yes... or at least something kinda close to one."

"For how long?" she asks.

I hesitate, not knowing thing-one about zombies. Although I suspect they're a new entity that came about due to the public's fascination with the creatures. How many times had I heard people talking about 'when the zombie apocalypse happens?' A dozen. Many dozens. It's everywhere. I think even my sister said it the other day. Be careful what you wish for folks, or what you kid about. The zombies are here. Our recent zombie fascination provides a perfect confluence for a bunch of dark energy seeping into the world. Naturally, humans' interest in the reanimated dead aligns with some undoubtedly nefarious scientists. Lichtenstein had been one such scientist, using the methods of his day to patch together creatures made from body parts. Science had progressed since those days, and Mindy is likely the result of it. At least she's stopped word-associating, probably because she's returned to full consciousness.

"I suspect you will never be the same again," I say.

"Ever?" She sniffles.

"Ever. But maybe there's still hope for a relatively normal life."

We sit in my van and stare at each other again. She doesn't bother looking anywhere but right at me the whole time. "Do you really think that, Sam?"

"I do, yes."

"But I'm a *freak*. You can see that. Anyone who looks at me for longer than ten seconds will see that."

"Actually, you're not that obvious now that you've had some brains to eat. Some people are naturally as pale as you. I have a feeling that the longer you go without eating, the more zombie-like you'll become. When I first saw you, you pretty much shambled around like one of those TV zombies, couldn't talk, moaned a lot. But now, you're pretty normal. I think if you can keep yourself fed, you should be able to fake it as a live person. And, don't give up, okay? You're not the first freak I've come across, nor will you be the last. We all adapt. We all figure a way to blend in."

She stares down at her hands, fidgeting with a charm bracelet on her left wrist. "I don't know what to do."

"One day at a time," I say. "First things first, we should probably get you some colored contact lenses to hide the fog in your eyes when you're getting hungry. They kinda milk over and get all grey and hazy. At the moment, they don't look unusual but I don't know how long you have to stay hungry in order to begin appearing strange."

She buries her face in her hands and has a good cry. "I'm going to be wearing shitty contacts and eating brains for the rest of my life. This sucks."

"Tell me about it."

"I know, I know. I sound like a big baby. You had kids and a family. I'm just, well, me. But this is a lot for me to wrap my brain around. Ah, shit."

"What?"

"Every time I say the word 'brain,' my stomach growls."

Despite myself, I laugh. And so does she.

"What now, Sam?"

"I'm going to find some answers."

"Answers from who?"

"The clinic who did this to you."

Mindy scowls. "But why bother if there's no fixing me?"

"Because, honey, I need to stop them from turning other people."

"But it's too late for me."

I say nothing. And while I sit there saying nothing, she stares at me. Her eyes are unnerving, to say the least. And that's coming from someone who has looked into the eyes of the Devil himself. "Maybe I will find a cure."

"You don't sound very positive, Sam."

"No, I don't. Dark energy tends to be a bit stubborn."

"So, it really is too late for me."

"Yes and no. Maybe there really is a cure. You are the first 'zombie' I've ever seen, so anything's possible. However, don't hold your breath."

"Not funny." She smirks.

I rub her shoulder. "Hey, you can adapt. You can still have a normal life. I did… mostly."

"Do others like you have a normal life?"

"Many do."

"Some don't." She tilts her head.

"Some… succumb."

"What does that mean?"

"It means they give themselves to the darkness within. They enjoy it. It means they feel they are given a license to kill, to maim, to destroy." Or, at least, they did before the Void prison broke. Still, some dark masters couldn't break out... and still others were perfectly happy possessing their hosts. So, yeah, this still applied to those vampires and werewolves... and whatever else was out there.

"I don't want to kill, Sam." She fidgets at her sweatshirt.

"I'm happy to hear that."

"Are you going to try to stop them, I mean the people who did this to me?"

"Yes."

"Is that, like, what you do? Go around stopping people from hurting other people?"

"It's part of the job."

"But I don't have much money."

"You didn't hire me, honey. I'm going after them because I don't want them to hurt anyone else."

"Oh. Right. So, what do I owe you for the cow brains?"

"How much money do you have on you?"

"The five hundred from that shitty place, plus the nine bucks I had before that."

"Okay. You owe me nine bucks."

"For realz?"

"For realz."

She fishes out a fiver and a couple of singles so battered I'm sure they saw action on the beaches of Normandy.

"Wow, so brains. They weren't that bad really. I ate some stuff outta the trash, but it wasn't anywhere near as good as those brains. But, even those cow brains kinda left me feeling like I was settling for cheap ramen or something." She gives me a sidelong glance. "Am I supposed to eat human brains?"

"That's probably a bad idea."

She looks down in her lap. "Yeah." After another long pause, she adds, "Why?"

"Supernatural entities possessed by dark masters have a particular thing they need to consume. The dark masters grow in power if you give them what they crave most. For vampires, it's human blood. Subsisting on animal blood keeps them alive while preventing the dark master from growing in power. For you, the same thing applies—only with brains instead of blood."

She nodded. "Yeah. Is it wrong that the idea of eating people-brains doesn't make me wanna throw up?"

"You're not a normal human anymore, Mindy. What you are—and I'm still trying to work out what—craves brains. You might have a dark master—or something close to it—inside you, and it will grow stronger if you give it *exactly* what it wants. Fortunately, there are alternate options."

"Why is it bad to feed it what it wants?"

I shrug. "Do you like being Mindy… what's your last name?"

"Hogan," she says.

"Do you like being Mindy Hogan?"

"Yeah, but am I still me?"

"For now. But if you keep feeding it what it craves, it will eventually become powerful enough to take over, and you'll cease existing as you."

She shivers. "Ooo-kay. Cow brains it is. Uhh, how often do I need to eat?"

"No idea. You're the first of your kind as far as I know."

She nods. "I don't know either. So, what now?"

I look at the plastic bag on the floor between her feet. "We need to get you stockpiled with food for starters."

"Brains?" She picks the wrapper up off the floor.

"Yes," I say. "And lots of them. Meanwhile, we need to keep what happened to you on the down-low."

"My parents will ask me all sorts of questions. I won't be able to hide this from them."

I mull, biting my lower lip. "You could fool them. Tell them you're sick, moody. That you already ate. Or, hmm, maybe you don't throw food up, but simply gain no benefit from anything but brains. You say you ate something else recently?"

"Yeah. Some stuff out of a dumpster."

"Did you throw it up?"

She shakes her head. "No, but I didn't get any less hungry."

"This is good. It means you can eat and, you know, act normal around people."

She nods. "Okay. Say, do your kids know you're a vampire?"

"Yeah, I told them. But not right away. You might want to keep this a secret for as long as you can."

She nods... and idly licks the wrapper in her hand.

Chapter Thirteen
Depends on the Movie

"Can you do me a favor?" Mindy asks suddenly.
"Sure. What—?"
For an answer, Mindy climbs into the back of the van, strips down to her underwear, then proceeds to twist around like she's searching for fleas.
"Um, something wrong?"
"Do I look okay? Like, am I turning purple or decaying? Any like bruises, rotting, holes?"
Right. Guess it's 'mom' time. I head back there and examine her without being too invasive. Kinda reminds me of checking Tammy and Anthony over for ticks whenever they played outside. Other than allowing Irish girls to feel like they've got some color, she looks fine. Well, that, and in serious need of a bath... and a few seconds of ear-to-chest con-

firms no heartbeat. At least I have one again. Apparently, not all immortals are created equal.

"I don't think I'm gonna be able to handle it if I start falling apart." She folds her arms across her chest and shivers.

"Not too sure that's going to be an issue." I head back to the driver's seat. "If the change happened to you three days ago, and you're supposed to decay, signs of rot should already be there." Okay, I didn't know that for sure, but it seemed right. "Maybe the universe chewed on all the different concepts of a zombie and came up with something different... something that worked within its framework, so to speak."

"Huh?" asks Mindy, while getting dressed. "Kinda like how you're not an 'everyday' vampire?"

"I used to be… but yeah, like that. Real life rules are a little different than books and movies."

"What do you mean something different for zombie?"

"Well, some are slow, non-verbal types, right? Other movies have them being super-fast and climbing up walls and stuff. Most zombies are kinda on the mindless side, but I can't imagine a dark master really wanting to do that to themselves." I rub my chin, thinking. Zombies definitely would be the sort of thing that caused dark masters to make fun of other dark masters. Like 'aww man, Bill got stuck in a damn zombie, hah.' That also makes me wonder if she's absorbed non-sentient

Void energy. As in, mindless energy.

"Do what to themselves?" She hops back in the passenger seat.

"Possess someone to become a creature that's basically unable to do anything but stagger around and moan. Although rules have changed these days... dark masters are driven by a need for power, and I think a creature like the atypical shambling zombie is probably beneath them."

"Oh. Well, that's good, right?"

"I think so, yes."

Wait, hold up. Maybe zombies are the direct result of there not being any available dark masters? Surely all the available ones had fled to join Elizabeth and her ranks... or just got the hell out of the Void to carry on with their own freaky lives. Maybe the displaced Void energy had to find somewhere to go.

Or... or...

Maybe she wasn't possessed by a dark master... but just a run-of-the-mill lost soul, circling the globe. Something to chew on. Maybe it was better to find oneself in a zombie than nothing at all.

I had another thought... wasn't Danny in training to be a dark master? Surely there were others like him, especially over the centuries. And surely some of these others have passed on. If so, perhaps they hadn't gone straight to the Void, which had likely been sealed long ago, if I understood the stories correctly.

Maybe she had nothing do with the Void, and

she entertained an altogether new type of dark master? I didn't know... but maybe. Of course, none of this helped her now.

Mindy nods after a moment or two. "Okay, well that gives me a little hope." She rubs her arms as if for warmth. "Umm. I guess you could take me to my dorm. Well, I mean it's not really a dorm. I'm sharing a rental house with Natalie and Alisha." She sniffs at her arms. "I don't stink, do I?"

"No more than anyone else who spent three days outside in the same clothes." I start the engine and drop the shifter into drive, but don't let off the brake. "Where's the dorm house?"

Mindy points out directions, which I take as a good sign. Evidently, eating brains has given her back the ability to use hers. She asks how I could've been a vampire and not used my fangs, so I wind up explaining on the ride about the time I scared the hell out of some little girl in a supermarket when my teeth came out by accident. Drinking from packets of blood had me living more like a nutrition supplement milkshake addict than a vampire. And now, I feed off mental energy.

"Think your friends would mind if I crash at your place tonight?" I ask.

"They're not really my friends. I mean we're cool, but we don't really know each other. We met the first day of school when we all answered an ad for roommates. The place is pretty small, but... umm. Where's your coffin?"

I laugh. "Don't believe everything you see in

Hollywood, kiddo. A couch works. Even a recliner or something."

"What about the sun?" She gives me this adorable 'OMG you're going to die!' stare.

"The sun's not as much of a problem as it is for most vampires. I'm special." I wink. "Though, I still would prefer a spot out of *direct* sunlight. Bright light in my eyes makes it hard to sleep."

"Same here. Okay, yeah we can work something out. And sure, you're welcome to crash in my room."

We arrive at this small freestanding house in a little suburban neighborhood not too far away from the University of Arizona. It's probably got beige siding, but it's difficult to tell at night. Some of these houses aren't much bigger than double-wide trailers, but they're clearly not trailers. Two small cars sit in the driveway of the place Mindy points at, a RAV4 and a… holy shit is that a Miata? I haven't seen one of those things in years. It's still kinda cute, even if it looks like it drove through a warzone.

I park on the street, cut the engine, and emit a little groan of annoyance at being 'not home.' Then again, I suppose a break from endless miles of desert road is probably good for my sanity. The next person I run over while driving sleep deprived most certainly wouldn't be a zombie… at least, I sure hope there aren't any more. Mindy hops out and I follow her across the dirt lot in front of the house to the front door. No lights are on inside, which is to be expected for around two in the morning.

She pulls out a set of keys, opens the door, and heads inside. I follow, closing and locking the door behind me. I must say, I'm impressed. For a house populated by college-age girls, the place is tidy. Then again, I'm used to Tammy. Although she picks on people who dress shabbily, her room's more often than not a clothes-splosion. How she finds anything cute—or clean—in there, is a mystery to me. Anyway, I follow Mindy across the smallish living room and into a hallway with four doors. Bathroom at the end and three rooms that—regardless of what the builder intended them for—have become bedrooms.

Mindy's room is kinda small. A white Ikea dresser stands at the foot of the bed with about fifteen inches of space to open the drawers. To the left, a cheap particleboard computer desk holds up a laptop and a bunch of textbooks. She's got a stuffed Snoopy and Woodstock on the bed, and a handful of polo shirts with restaurant logos hanging on a chintzy collapsible plastic rack in front of the window.

"Well, here it is. My home away from home." She flaps her arms. "You want the bed?"

"I can't steal your bed." I give her my 'mom smile.'

"We'll figure it out after I shower."

Mindy grabs some clean clothes and heads out.

Alone to my own devices, I flop in the metal folding chair by her desk and flash back to my school days. If the girl had a giant stack of instant ramen on the desk, it would remind me of my time at Cal State Fullerton. Our parents didn't have a lot of money, though at least by the time I was in high school, I no longer needed to steal produce from the farm down the road from us. A good thing, that. Much easier to get away with stealing food as a smaller child than a teen.

Still, this place takes me back. Ahh, the good old days… working two crappy jobs while going to classes all day. The laptop is on, so I take advantage. Floating windows alert of new emails. Some look like her teachers asking about her missing classes on Friday. Mindy told me she'd gone to the medical testing place on a Thursday after school, so she spent Friday and the weekend wandering aimlessly. Wow. It's a real miracle she didn't wind up having the police drag her to a hospital for 'detox' or to a mental ward.

Another line appears to be a worry-gram from the parents since she didn't email or text them on Saturday. I don't pry, only taking a guess based on the subject line in the new message announcement. Leaving the email be, I open a web browser and do some searching for places seeking volunteers for medical testing in the area. It comes back with a few hits, but none say anything about skin creams.

Mindy walks back in wearing a long hot-pink T-shirt and an aura of soapy steam. After hanging her towel on the rickety plastic rack, she collects the dirty clothes she shed earlier, clears out the pockets of the jeans, and stuffs the lot into a laundry bag. She notices me fussing on the computer and tilts her head.

"Was looking for that place you went to. Not finding anything."

"Oh." She sits on the edge of the bed. In the cramped room, her knees almost touch the chair I'm sitting in. "Am I, like, nocturnal?"

I shrug. "Depends on which movies you watch."

"Huh?"

"Some zombies only come out at night, some don't care about daylight."

"Oh. But you said I'm not a Hollywood creation, right?"

"Right. But you have been walking around constantly for three days, dark and light?"

"Yeah."

"Fair bet that sunlight doesn't bother you. Make your own schedule."

Mindy sighs at the window. "That's good, I guess."

We talk a bit more, though I don't provide many answers to her questions. I have no idea if she's immortal like vampires or simply long-lived like werewolves. Taking a stab in the dark, I suggest she's probably immortal like vampires because her heart's not even pretending to beat. Werewolves aren't dead (or undead). Mermaids are similar. I made Kingsley laugh when I quipped that the creating force must've been listening to too many tween girls when mermaids happened, but he seemed to think they were far from 'cute and harmless.' Of course, he would know, having been married to one many years ago. That's Kingsley... if a type of woman exists, he's probably boinked her. At least he's been behaving himself for me lately. Whatever he did romantically before we met, I couldn't care less about.

Since Mindy can't decide if she's nocturnal or should sleep, she winds up deciding to attempt a somewhat normal schedule. I volunteer to crash on the floor, and she shrugs, clearly too distracted to care too much about etiquette. She drops a spare blanket and pillow on the carpet for me, then lies down in her bed. The girl's out in seconds. I'd say I'm jealous, but that would only apply to pre-vampire Sam. Now, when I decide to sleep, I pass right out. As a mortal back in the day, I'd take forever to drift off.

Tammy and Anthony had better be asleep now, so as not to disturb them, I send an email to let them know I 'stumbled on a case' and may be away for a little while. Earlier, both Mary Lou and Kingsley sent me text messages, confirming all is well in the Moon household. Kingsley sent me a heart. So did Allison.

From the floor, and with some time to concentrate, I send Kingsley a thank you, followed by a few sweet nothings and a heart. Despite my better judgment, I send Allison a heart, too.

True to form, she shoots me back a heart almost immediately.

God, so needy. Then again, she would be up hosting her late night talk show. Yeah, crazy as it sounded, my best friend was a minor celebrity these days in Los Angeles. Well, minor to those who worked the late shifts.

Being able to teleport home whenever I need to does wonders to ease my mind. Knowing I can get there if anything goes wrong stops making me feel better the instant it occurs to me that calamity would have to occur in such a way as my kids have the chance to call or text me for help. Anything really dangerous would stop them from calling me.

Okay, relax. It's been quiet for a couple weeks. I'm not sure if I should use my killing the Devil as a reason to feel secure (the universe is reeling from that) or as cause to worry (demons will want revenge). Would the next Devil care or would he be grateful for my creating his job opening?

Ugh.

I arrange myself on the floor under the borrowed blanket and stare at the ceiling for a while. It is *so* nice not to have a worry trap keeping me awake for hours. As soon as I decide to sleep—I'm out.

Chapter Fourteen
Winging It

I have a weird dream, and it makes me nervous.

Before I even open my eyes, I sigh, "Shit."

Me having a sorta-nightmare about being *in* that TV show with zombies means I'm going to wind up armpit-deep in actual zombies at some point. One thing I've learned about being a vampire is that we don't have normal dreams. Everything I've dreamed since the change has been either a literal vision of the future or some kind of cryptic prophetic warning that made no sense until it was too late. I have no reason to think being an energy vampire will be any different. So, for now, I prepare for the worst.

I think back to another dream, one that happened just before my attack over a dozen years ago, a dream that had been prophetic in many ways. I had been sitting in a beach chair during the day, back when Tammy was only four. I'd seen Danny standing off with another woman—who I now recognize as a bimbo from that strip club he briefly managed. And that dark smoke coming out of him and going into Anthony? Yeah. That makes complete sense now. The Universe warned me that my husband would cheat on me and turn himself into a dark master that wound up inside my son.

Stupid me for not understanding that one back then, right?

Ugh. How could I know? My life had been tame up to that point, with barely a whiff of the supernatural.

I sit up. According to Mindy's alarm clock, it's two minutes past noon. Wow, I must have been tired to sleep this long. Then again, I did stay up late. The house is deathly silent save for the distant whirring of a refrigerator motor. Mindy's gone. A scrap of pink catches my eye on the laptop screen where someone has affixed a Post-It note.

'Went to class. Back around one-ish' adorns the paper in flowery handwriting.

Okay. I suppose I should consider it a good thing that she's attempting to be normal. Speaking of normality… the burrito I ate last night is not happy with its current living arrangements and wants to go elsewhere.

I'm still on the toilet when the front door opens and closes. A pocketbook and keys land on—either a kitchen countertop or table—and the crinkle of plastic bags follows. For a few seconds, I'm not entirely sure which housemate is back, until the slurpy 'om-nom-nom' that could only be Mindy munching on raw brains follows.

While I'm finishing up, Mindy jogs down the hallway and goes into her room. I flush, head down the hall, and find her pacing around in circles with mascara running down her face from tears.

"Mindy?"

She spins to look at me. Other than a little bloody smearing around her mouth, she doesn't appear unusual.

"Is something wrong?" I ask.

"I'm a zombie," she says, flailing her arms. "I'd call that pretty fucking wrong."

I stifle the urge to laugh. "I mean… anything more wrong than that."

"No. Just went to class this morning and I kept feeling hungry whenever I looked at people. Not like uncontrollably hungry, just like 'oh, yeah, I could eat him.'" She grabs two handfuls of her hair and screams in frustration.

"That's normal. I mean, before, whenever I saw human blood, it was really tempting. But I didn't want El—I mean my dark master to grow in power."

"El?" Mindy snickers. "You're possessed by that kid from the Upside Down?"

"Huh?" I scratch my head. "No… her name's Elizabeth. And I'm not possessed anymore."

"Wow, do you live in a bubble? You've never watched *Stranger Things?*" She blinks at me.

"Anyway, you could talk to it? Her?"

"I tried not to. The more I engaged with her, the more power she had—or maybe that whole thing was a lie. Pretty sure she's like the quintessence of ultimate evil or some such thing like that, so I wanted to keep her contained."

Mindy stares. "Umm. We're evil?"

I hold my arms out to the sides with a used car saleswoman smile. "Vampires? Zombies? Hi, we're the monsters, sweetie."

She sighs.

"However, it is possible to contain them. And, maybe yours isn't like mine was. But they're still *dark* masters." Truth be told, I didn't know what possessed her... something dark and shitty, of that I had no doubt. "We didn't get possessed by the spirit of Rainbow Brite."

"What the hell is that?"

I wink. "Oh, something from TV when I was a kid. Look, Mindy… Don't freak out. I've managed to have a reasonably normal existence after the change, so you can too. Heck, a friend of mine told me he knew a woman who had actually made friends with her dark master. I'm not sure if I believe that, either." I shake my head. "Mermaids…"

Mindy makes this face like I just showed her a kitten. "Mermaids! Seriously?" she squeals. "Oh, damn. Why couldn't I have been one of those instead of a crappy zombie?"

"Well, you see…" I wander over and put a

conspiratorial arm around her shoulders. "The universe has an extremely complicated method by which it calculates everyone's fate."

"It does?" Her eyebrows go up. "So this was planned?"

"Oh, I dunno about planned. There's a highly complex process involving three gnomes and a carnival wheel... and probably quite a bit of vodka."

Mindy frowns. "That's not funny."

"Okay. So, let me try to look into this while you calm down. Where's the place you went?"

"I don't remember. I kinda lost the flyer. But, they are everywhere at school. Been up for a few weeks now. I saw a bunch of them still up this morning."

Crap. I really don't like that I had a dream about a zombie invasion. Especially at a college. Why do these things always target the young and innocent? It's kinda dark of me to think, but for once, couldn't a monster apocalypse happen at a retirement community? At least the zombies would be really slow and easy to outrun.

"Right," I say. "Wait here, and I'll go check it out."

She nods. "And no more corny jokes."

"That, I can't promise."

I head outside and frown at the Momvan. Bright sunlight makes her look even older than I thought. And Mindy sure did a number on the front end, even with my quick repair work on the hood. I'm going to need a new grille—at least that's plastic.

And she took out a headlight. Crap. Amazing I didn't get pulled over last night. Out of a mixture of sympathy for the van and curiosity, I sneak around between the dorm house and the next one and think about my wing tattoos. A little mental coaxing pulls them out into the real world.

This is *so* weird. Stretching them feels amazing, like I've been sleeping curled up in a ball too long and finally straightened out my legs. Maybe I should take them out more often? Hey, I saw this video go by on Facebook the other day. Some girl makes mechanical wings for geek conventions. If anyone ever catches me with these bad boys out I can just say they're a prop. And if that doesn't work, there's always mind control.

Gee. I really don't need to be as paranoid about 'getting caught' as I have been. Well, then again, I can't mind control someone a hundred feet away with a cell phone camera. So, yeah, best be careful.

I zip straight up and climb to an altitude that gives me a decent vantage point while also hopefully making me hard to see from the ground. Or at least, difficult to recognize as a person. Talos is awesome, but these wings don't require me to pull the old nudist routine, since they hover magically about six inches off my body. So, yeah, not really attached, which makes my life hella easier.

That gets me wondering about the whole clothing thing in regards to angels. Not that I'm any sort of religious scholar or anything, but I do remember something about Adam and Eve not being ashamed of their bodies until after they got kicked out of paradise. Would angels share that shame, or are they only depicted as clothed because puritans didn't want pictures of nude angels all over their cathedrals? The Ancient Greeks sure had no hesitation about depicting their gods in *all* their glory. I know Ishmael and the archangels I'd met had all been robed. But had that been for my benefit? Did they normally walk around 'in the buck,' as my dad would say?

Once my fit of uncontrollable laughter subsides—gee, what am I twelve again?—I fly in circles for a while. It takes a minute or twenty for the novelty of flying to wear off before I orient myself toward the University of Arizona campus (with a little help from my phone) and fly toward it.

I'm alone with the soft flapping noise of my enormous, black feathery wings. I wonder if Azrael knows about the advent of zombies into the world for real. Had she been documented already in the *Book of All Known Beings*, a book presently residing on the shelves of the Occult Reading Library at Cal State Fullerton?

Most important... is Mindy the only one of her kind so far? That's one thing about the shambling undead that seems to be a universal constant: there's never *one* zombie. What they lack in smarts, they make up for in sheer numbers. Though, Mindy *is* smart—reasonably. I mean, for a zombie, she's practically Alberta Einstein. But anyway, I'm sure there are going to be more, *lots* more. Hopefully, I can find this place and shut it down before that happens. Maybe my dream was a warning about what's going to happen if I ignore this situation and go home to my kids like I want to.

Come on, Sam. They're not little anymore. I don't have to watch over them every minute of every day. I really don't, but I want to. Luckily, I had a witch and a werewolf to help out. And a big sister, too, who might be the toughest of them all.

Let's see. If Mindy bites a person, are they going to get up as a zombie? Fingernail scratches? She's clearly aware of herself and only did the stumbling-around-and-moaning deal while she'd basically been starving. Hmm. It's a real pain in the ass dealing with the first of something since there's no information out there to check.

Could this be some major attack from the dark masters? I mean, had they organized the zombies from *this* side of the Void? Back in the day, I might have guessed that a fast-spreading creature type like zombies could usher in a crapload of dark masters... but if they're all non-verbal, stumbling around, and quite obviously dead, what could they accomplish? Plus, that's not the case now. The dark masters once in the Void were already here. And those still trapped in their human hosts were just that... trapped.

Something else hits me... had the dark masters cooked something up whilst in the Void? I wasn't sure how much magic they had access to in there... I once had the Void described to me as a bleak and barren hellscape. But they obviously had access to enough magick to concoct their escape... even if 'escape' back in the day meant one vampire, werewolf, mermaid, or Lichtenstein monster at a time.

I nod as I fly. Perhaps the perfect distraction after their recent escape from the Void was the release of this dark magick... or energy. A release that ultimately manifested as zombies. Like Dr. Lichtenstein and his monsters, a dark master could have been behind the creation of the zombie serum. The timing seems to line up too. The flyers having appeared around campus just a few weeks ago... and the Void walls coming down a few weeks ago, too.

I shrug. We'll call this a working theory.

I next start to worry that this might not be an invasion of dark masters per se as much as some kind of 'weapon' they're using on the mortal world. Maybe Mindy doesn't have a full dark master inside her, but rather a similar energy type to what they're made out of, concocted in the Void to throw mankind into complete disorder. A good plan, for returning dark masters seeking revenge. What better way to ease back into a world overrun by light workers and alchemists? Cause complete disarray.

Shit. I really hope this isn't the universe dealing out payback for me killing the Devil. What if doing that crossed some imaginary line that's got Fate in an 'all right, jackass... you wanna play rough? Here's ten billion zombies. Chew on that' sort of mood?

Or, I could be worrying myself to death for no real reason. The devil had nothing do with this. Nor had the Universe, which I don't think seeks any kind of revenge.

No, there's one set of bastards who do seek revenge... and they were headed by Elizabeth and Cornelius, her one-time lover. Had Cornelius escaped from Dracula? If so, my old and creepy friend was, undoubtedly, dead. Perhaps it's for the best. Lord only knows he was due, having killed an uncountable number of people during his existence.

Hmm. What would Azrael—my kinda sorta angel boss—say about zombies? I'm not *too* worried on a personal level. Pretty sure I can't become infected with zombism and I can kill anything that lives (or doesn't) with this sword. But, if an outbreak kicks off, it could hurt a ton of people, my kids included. Or, at least, Tammy. Since I still don't fully understand what the hell Anthony is.

Argh.

Upon arriving at U of A, I glide down to a reasonably inconspicuous landing in a wooded area along the western side of the campus next to the Arizona State Museum. Alas, it being close to one in the afternoon, a bunch of students are here sitting around in the shade. One skinny dude stares at me as I touch down. Fortunately, he's the only one who saw me... and all he remembers is I came *walking* out of the woods.

As soon as the wings vanish from his memory,

his expression goes from awestruck WTF to 'oh, someone's there' and he promptly ignores me. I wander off to the east, going over the grass to the sidewalk along (what my phone tells me is) East University Boulevard. Rows of palm trees stand on both sides of the street like telephone poles. It doesn't take me long to find a flyer looking for volunteers to donate blood for medical testing and participate in a trial of a new topical skin care cream.

Only, they're offering $50 for one hour, not $500.

That's odd. But then again, the poor girl had been thrown for a loop. She wasn't exactly 'firing on all cylinders' when I found her. I take a photo of the flyer and plug the address into my phone.

Hmm. Grant Road. That's in northeast Tucson. Might as well check it out and see what's going on there. After stuffing my phone back in my pocket, I head across the street and into a thicker patch of trees beside their anthropology building. Good. No one here.

I let my wings back out and take off before anyone comes around the corner.

This time, I do less thinking and more flying.

Chapter Fifteen
The Clinic

My phone's GPS app leads me to the address I found on the tree at the school.

I look down at a series of buildings along a gentle leftward curve in the road. Northeast of them is a wide strip of bare sand, kinda like a river with no water in it... an arroyo, I think they're called. Anyway, it's even got a nice overpass where a six-lane highway spans it. Perfect for swooping under.

A power dive gets me out of sight in the shadow of the highway. Wings away, I trudge along the sand on the north side of the bridge. To my left, a steep stone embankment leads up at about a forty-five degree angle to a railing. It's at least as tall as a one-story building and looks smooth. However, a ways farther north, I spot a ramp. No sense being an idiot.

DEAD MOON

I jog to the ramp, swing around the railing at the bottom, and the soft sound of my shoes on sand becomes the scuff of rubber on stone. As luck would have it, the top of the ramp basically connects straight to the parking lot of where I want to go. There's a Chipotle on the right at the end of a little strip mall, but I'm not feeling terribly hungry at the moment.

Nothing quite like the worry of an impending zombie apocalypse to kill my appetite.

After circling around to the street-facing side, I enter a reasonably normal looking 'medical' facility. It's somewhere between one of those places you go for lab work and a doctor's office in terms of appearance. Pale blue chairs, a table with magazines on it, television tuned to the sort of vacuous daytime talk TV that could dry out a mummy.

Except for two twentysomething women in the office area adjacent to the waiting room, I'm the only one here. A slim dark-haired brunette in a teal smock is sitting at the counter facing me. The other woman would be considered heavyset for a magazine cover, but I think she's 'normal.' Hell, she's got the kind of figure I *should* have at… what am I now… forty-four? Honestly, I've stopped counting. You know how some women 'keep turning twenty-one' every year? Well, yeah, that's me but I'm not being metaphorical about it. I'm going to look twenty-seven forever. At least until I bite the big one. Azrael said it's nothing I should be afraid of. 'Rejoining the Creator' sounds a lot better than being cast out from the cycle of rebirth and hurtled into oblivion. Meh. Now's not the time to waste thinking about that. Plus, I watched my one-time father join the Origin himself... and it looked, well, it didn't look so bad.

I approach the petite woman who's already facing me. She's not wearing any sort of nametag or anything, so I wait a few seconds for her to notice I'm staring at her.

"Hi," she says, finally looking up at me. "Can I help you?"

"Hello." I flash my phone at her like a badge, giving her enough of a poke to think she saw something meaningful, but not exactly what. Hey, it's not impersonating the police if I don't specify which agency I'm pretending to be. "I'm investigating a missing person case. A young woman was last seen going to a site like this for volunteer medical testing. I'm trying to trace her last steps before she vanished."

"Oh." The woman's eyes widen. "Wow, that's so sad."

"Do you have any record of a Mindy Hogan being here? Twenty, brown hair, brown eyes?" I follow up with another little prod that makes her want to help me.

"Umm. Hang on." She attacks the computer in front of her.

The other woman pauses in her rummaging around the large drawers of files and glances over at me.

"Umm. I don't have anyone in the system named Hogan at all," says the small woman. "Got a Mindy Cabrera though."

I peek at her screen courtesy of her thoughts, and the little photo of a college-age Hispanic girl with black hair and brown skin is most definitely not 'my' Mindy. I hold out my phone and pretend to show her an image of Mindy. As I do so, I poke a mental image of my client into this woman's head, and it doesn't trigger any sort of recognition.

"All right. I guess this isn't the right place," I say. "Do you know of any other labs doing medical testing for paid volunteers in the area?"

"There's one or two, but I don't have their info here," says the other woman, shoving a heavy drawer closed. "We're a diagnostic lab, really. Most of our clients come in under doctor's orders to have tests run. The sort of paid thing you're talking about's only a tiny fraction. Maybe one or two a week. People are kinda skittish about volunteering to be guinea pigs."

Gee. Wonder why, I think, then smile. "All right, thanks."

I walk outside and glance down at the phone in my hand. Amid my trying to support Mindy during her change, I had offered a sympathetic ear whenever she wanted, so we traded phone numbers. I'd expected our first phone conversation to be her calling me in the middle of the night with some random zombie-related question, not me calling her for directions... but hey. Life is weird sometimes.

"Hello?" asks Mindy in a hesitant whisper.

"Hi, sweetie. It's me, Sam."

"Oh!" she chirps, back to full volume. "What's up?"

"So I checked out that place on the flyers at the campus, and they have no record of you being here."

She grumbles. "Was that creepy doctor there?"

"Not sure." I twist back to glance at the front of the building. "I met two women working the front desk and they didn't have any record of you in their system or remember seeing you."

"Well, duh! Of course they wouldn't remember me. When I went to the place there was only this creepy ass doctor, and one like assistant. I'm such a dumbass. I should've run out the door. It felt like we were the only three people in the building."

"What did the place look like?"

"Umm. Like a warehouse. Grey. Small black windows. Bunch of other abandoned-like warehouses around it. That whole street was like something out of one of those 'last person left alive on Earth' movies."

I turn in place, eyeing the strip mall with the Chipotle, a Target across the street, plenty of traffic on the giant road in front of me. Yeah… I'm definitely in the wrong spot.

"Where I'm at right now looks nothing like that. Do you still have the address?"

"I lost the flyer. Hang on, I might have another one somewhere. I kept taking them and chickening out for a couple weeks. Argh! Why didn't I *keep* chickening out?"

For the next minute or two, I listen as Mindy rummages her room while simultaneously beating herself up for being a moron, an idiot, a dumbass, and so on. She breaks down to sobs for a little while, then resumes searching. Eventually, she picks the phone up again. Paper crinkles.

"Found one. Wadded up on the floor behind the wastebasket."

"You have a wastebasket?" I blink.

"Yeah. It's small. Under the desk. Anyway…" She reads off an address. "And according to the flyer, the guy's name is Doctor Larry Roberts. I don't remember him mentioning his name when I was there though. He's older, like fifties. Black hair, white guy."

I flick the call to speaker and open a note app to type it in. "Okay. Got it."

"Be careful," says Mindy.

"I'm always careful," I say, practically feeling Tammy glaring at me from home for saying that. "It's not like I'm worried about a little skin cream."

She emits an urgent whine. "No, Sam… if there's something there doing this dark master crap on purpose, they might be a threat to you."

My eyebrows go up. Wow. This girl is not only smart for a zombie, she's smart in general. And when did I get so old that I started assuming everyone in their twenties was clueless? "Okay. Point taken."

Once we hang up, I plug the address she gave me into the map application, and it points to a spot in southwestern Tucson about as far away as possible from where I am without leaving the city limits. Almost as if I'd been sent on a wild goose chase. Was it bad luck that I'd grabbed the wrong flyer? Or had I been set up?

I'm about to look for another place to take flight when my cell phone rings.

A quick glance down both warms my heart... and worries me to no end.

It's Anthony.

Chapter Sixteen
Tracking Ducks

No reason to worry, thank God.
The kids are doing fine.
Mostly.
Anthony called to complain about Tammy 'bossing him around.' Then again, she hadn't asked him to do anything he wouldn't normally do. It's more that she's just saying it to feel in charge. I get it. I try to convince him to let it roll off his back and I'll be home soon. Tammy asks if she can have some friends over. That's fine as long as the house is still standing when I get home. And yeah, Vegas is still a big no.

A quick flight gets me across town in a few minutes, and I land on a street so deserted it really does feel like I've walked onto the set of a movie. Large, one-story, mostly featureless buildings surround me. None of them are damaged or look *too* beat up, but they all have a clearly-abandoned sense about them. Patches of rust on the chain link here and there at some of the properties underscore the sense that no one's bothered with this area in a while.

Another issue is that none of the buildings have numbers on them. Fortunately, her description of plain grey with black windows is close enough for me to pick a likely suspect. I cross a small lot to the front door of a place that probably was, at one point, a warehouse. The door's been jimmied open. Obvious scratches and damage to the aluminum frame says crowbar, as well as amateur. It reminds me of working for HUD and inspecting empty properties where squatters had broken in. That's always fun. Like playing psycho roulette sometimes. Never quite know what to expect with squatters. Might be some crazy-looking guy you think is definitely gonna shoot you, but he turns out to be sweet. Next time, a normal woman with two small kids goes completely apeshit and comes after me with a knife.

Yeah. Fun times.

The door opens without protest and I step into a small office type room with walls covered in Playboy magazine covers, some even framed. Most are thumbtacked to the wood-paneling. Two broken chairs lie on the floor next to a beat-to-hell black steel desk. One chair by the right side wall remains upright.

DEAD MOON

I know it's unbecoming to compare myself to a dog, but vampiric smell is similar to that of a canine. Mindy's scent is in the air here, strongest from that one chair by the wall. She said the place looked like a dentist's office, but... I feel like I'm in the waiting room for a sketchy mechanic shop with all the dirty magazine pages on the walls. I haven't seen this many exposed boobs in one place since visiting that hellhole Danny wound up half-owning.

An interior door opposite the one I came in from leads to a corridor lined with yet more doors. I wander from one to the next peering in on a couple of old conference rooms, a break room with a dead fridge, some small offices, and a closet. It doesn't look like anything's been operational in this place for at least ten years. And, there's a creepy vibe in the air.

Like, real creepy.

Like, 'I'm an immortal and I'm still freaking out' creepy.

When I was ten, Dad got the bright idea to bring us to a haunted house thing for Halloween one year. I hate to admit it, but I was the kid who screamed and begged her parents not to make me go in there. I cried like a baby the whole time, fully expecting to die before reaching the other end. At least I wasn't alone in my shame. Mary Lou wailed right alongside me. I did manage to be brave enough not to demand to leave early or fly into a panic and go off running—though I did cling to my dad and may or may not have buried my face in his shirt so I didn't have to see any of the 'monsters.'

Anyway. That sense of impending doom that hit me as a ten-year-old about to face a bunch of guys wearing costumes… yeah. That's hitting me again. Only, it's not quite as strong. As in, I'm not crying and freaking out. I am on edge though, to the point where I forget I no longer have claws and try to extend them. They say predators instinctively know when they're no longer at the top of the food chain in a given moment. When that little lynx has a giant bear going after it, it senses something wrong even before the bear charges.

But, I don't see anything.

Yet.

Okay, Sam. Get a grip. I shouldn't be this scared. I shouldn't be scared at all. I killed the Devil. A creepy abandoned office shouldn't freak me out. That probably means that something set up some kind of 'fear aura' in this building. Ugh. Magic? Well, if this was a big dark master plan, then magic was a given. How many dark masters had been involved here, I don't know. Maybe dozens, maybe one. Their presence here could've left a mark in the environment.

The last room in the place is about two thirds the size of the entire building and contains several long assembly-line style machines. While I can't tell what those machines used to make, it's quite obviously *not* any sort of medical testing facility, lab, doctor, or even dentist's office. Hell, this place doesn't have a vending machine selling Band Aids.

I backtrack and check each room again, taking care this time to sniff around. Mindy's scent loiters in the air in a small office with a once-nice chair right in the middle. The thing looks like someone took the seat of a high end sports car and put it on wheels for office duty—then let it sit here collecting dust. It's positioned with its back to the door in, facing the innermost wall where a suspiciously-intact flat panel television hangs.

Two other scents briefly cross my nostrils. Cologne gives one away as a man, the other I can't really tell since it's so faint. Since Mindy mentioned a woman, I'll go with that. Whoever these people were, they're long gone. I wonder if something went wrong? Maybe they didn't even do it on purpose, and when Mindy… well… died in here, they freaked out and bailed.

But that doesn't feel right. Not with the vibe I'm getting in this place.

Plus, why does it all look so freakin' old? Wouldn't Mindy have mentioned that part?

This was a bit like trying to track a duck across a pond.

"Dammit." I fold my arms. "Where the hell did these people go?"

Chapter Seventeen
Chocolate Therapy

Frustration is anathema to concentration.

I take a moment to find calm, but fail. Okay, the weird vibe in here is getting to me. A few minutes of standing around outside allows me to calm down. I picture Mindy's bedroom in my mind and call out to the distant, glimmering flame. The safest place is probably a step inside the door where she wouldn't be standing. As always, I feel a sense of moving toward the flame... and it to me.

When I open my eyes, I'm inside her bedroom.

Mindy, sitting on the bed, stares at me like I'd just walked in on her and a boyfriend having an intimate moment. Then she pulls a spoon out of her mouth and is about to scream, when I rush to her side and clamp a hand over her mouth. Her very cold and sticky mouth. Turned out, I'd caught her eating a quart of chocolate ice cream.

"You calm?" I ask. For all I know, there's a house full of people. Always easier for everyone involved if I don't have to go around erasing minds. Plus, I'm not 100% all mind erasing sticks. As in, I'm fairly certain the memories could return over time.

She nods, staring at me with semi-milky eyes.

I release my hand and wipe it on my jeans. I raise an eyebrow. "I've had a few moments in my life where an entire quart of ice cream had to die, too."

"Wait, how did you... what just happened?"

"I have my tricks."

"You just... appeared there."

"That's one of my tricks."

"Are you, like, really fast or something."

"Or something. Do you normally stress eat?"

"A little, but I used to have a really high metabolism, so it never really caught up to me, I guess. It tastes good, but I'm still hungry."

"Something tells me that you're probably always going to experience some degree of hunger." I pull the folding metal chair away from the sorry little computer table and spin it around to sit facing the bed. "Going out on a limb, I'm going to suggest that there's a difference between you feeling hungry and you *needing* to eat."

"But you don't know how much or how often I have to eat brain?"

"Nope. You're new territory. Going to be a lot

of T and E."

"Trial and error?" she says.

"Yup."

Mindy drops the spoon in the carton. "Damn."

"So, anyway. I think someone put up some bogus fliers around the campus," I say. "You happened to pick one of the bad ones."

"Six times?" asks Mindy.

"What?"

She scoots to the edge of the bed and lets her legs dangle. "I took one flyer every other day for two weeks before I was dumb enough to go there. They were all the same. Did I really just get *that* unlucky?"

"Are you sure they were all the same?" I ask.

"Yeah. Five hundred bucks to help them test skin cream."

Okay. Maybe this poor girl really does have epic bad luck. "Hmm."

"So did you find anything there?" she asks.

I swing around and tuck up to the computer desk. "Nope. The building looked abandoned. Like no one had been in it for years."

"Years?"

"Yup."

"So weird," she mutters.

"What's the guy's name again? Larry Roberts?"

She grabs a paper from the tiny nightstand (milk crates) beside her bed. "Yeah."

I settle in at her laptop and start hunting for a Doctor Larry Roberts in the Tucson area. Eventually, I find a hit on *Lawrence* Roberts, courtesy of a couple news websites. From the look of it, he lost his medical license eight years ago due to over-prescribing opiates, probably selling pills, too. Hmm. Shady doctor, check.

"Think I have something. Hey, is this the guy?" I point to one of the articles with a picture of the dude.

Mindy walks up beside me. "Yeah, that's him. Oh... check this out."

I glance at her. She lifts her shirt up to expose her stomach.

"Put your hand on my belly."

I do. It's pretty damn cold.

"Funky, huh? I ate ice cream so now I'm really 'chillin'"

I groan.

"Hey. I'm the zombie. I'm supposed to make those noises." She starts to laugh but it sounds more like crying.

"Aww." I stand and hug her. "Hey. It's okay. You look pretty damn good for a zombie."

She sniffles. "Thanks. This is just so much to handle."

"I think I have an idea what it's like."

"Yeah, but did you worry that you were gonna start rotting and falling apart?" She fidgets. "I mean, I've never been like super obsessed with looking pretty or anything, but I don't want to turn into some hideous thing."

I hold her for a minute or five until she stops

crying, then push her out to arms' length so I can stare into her eyes. "You don't smell dead. Trust me. I have a *really* good sense of smell. If a vampire thinks you smell like a live person, there's nothing to worry about. It's been four days now."

She nods, sniffling back tears.

"Of course, you *did* look a bit more zombie-like when I ran you over." I cringe. "I think if you go too long without eating, you'll start shutting down. That might not mean decaying, but it might look like it. Better to not take the chance."

"Okay." Mindy wipes her eyes.

"And. Weird. You're crying."

"How is that weird? I died. I think I'm allowed a tear or two... or a thousand."

I chuckle. "No I mean, you *can* cry. There are tears on your face. Never did quite understand that one."

"What do you mean?"

"Like with me. Even when I was undead, I could cry, sweat… not sure how that works for the technically dead. At least for me, I figured it was a mechanism to blend in among mortals. For you… maybe it's a sign you're more than a stumbling-around type zombie."

"I guess time will tell."

"That it will," I say. "Okay. I'm going to go check out that doctor. Will you be okay alone for a little while here?"

"Yeah, I think so." She paces. "I got some homework to do. Ought'a keep that up, right?

Though, I dunno what the hell I'm going to do with a degree as a zombie."

"You could go into marketing," I say.

She smirks.

"At least you aren't allergic to sunlight. When I first turned, I had to quit the job I busted my ass for years to get."

"That musta sucked."

"Royally. Okay, be back soon. Hopefully with some answers."

I nearly say, 'And try not to eat your roommates,' but I don't want to put any ideas in her head.

Note to self... buy more cow brains.

Chapter Eighteen
Tainted

Feeling mundane, I decide to *drive* to the address I found for the doctor in question.

It's a little over a twenty-minute ride from Mindy's place to the address in a residential area at the northern part of Tucson. My 'private investigator' mode turns itself on and makes me park a couple houses away on the opposite side of the street.

Doctor Roberts has a relatively large one-story place in a mildly nauseating shade of pale orange with white trim. Basically, he's living in a giant creamsicle. An enormous driveway on the right side of the house has enough space to hold four stretch limousines, one pair parked behind the first. At the moment, only two cars occupy it: a black, sporty-looking thing I don't quite recognize from a distance and a beat-to-heck red Toyota pickup.

I grab the mini-binocs from the glove box and take a closer look around the property. There's a white Toyota minivan in the driveway and a black car that looks suspiciously like a Maserati Ghibli—you know, their 'starter' supercar. I think they go for like eighty grand and up or something 'cheap' like that. Of course, with a looming million and a half pay-off waiting in escrow... I could buy a fleet of these cars. I shake my head. Amazingly, the thought of that much money is overwhelming to think about. Never had more than a few thousand extra in the bank... and even that hadn't lasted for long.

Think about it later, Sammy.

Another car, a gold-ish Nissan, rolls up and parks behind the Maserati. A middle-aged couple who could be Hispanic or Native American hop out and walk over to a side door abutting the driveway. They enter without ringing a bell or knocking.

Okay, that's a little strange. Perhaps friends of his?

The house windows don't have anything interesting going on, at least not the ones facing the street. It's dark inside like no one's home. By the time I pan back to the driveway, a white-haired guy who's gotta be in his eighties emerges from the door and heads for the old Toyota. A few minutes after he drives off, a Honda Civic pulls up carrying a forty-ish woman and four children under ten. The kids, three boys and a girl, are all wearing T-shirts with faded images of 1980s cartoon characters. The boys' jeans are little more than a network of patches holding each other together, and the little girl's wearing this combination skirt-and-leggings hand-me-down deal that might've once been pink. I think it has stains older than Tammy.

Without knocking or ringing a bell, the woman guides her brood through the same side door.

I can think of only one reason that random people would keep showing up at a doctor's house and going inside… the guy's running an illegal practice. Then again, the article I found was a couple years old. I'm not entirely sure how that whole medical license deal works, if losing it is totally permanent or if they can have it reinstated.

My gut tells me he's practicing on the sly—mostly because there are no signs whatsoever pointing this place out as an actual doctor's office.

Not wanting to see four tiny zombies shamble out of there, I toss the binocs to the passenger seat, hop out, and dash across the street. Since everyone else has simply walked in, I follow suit. The door isn't locked, and opens to a short stairway going four steps down into a half-basement done up like a parlor. The woman with the four kids sits on a blue sofa with her daughter on one side, the oldest boy on the other, while the other two boys rummage through a small trunk in the far left corner of the room that contains toys. A corridor leads from the far right corner deeper into the place, decorated as I'd expect a basement to be: bare concrete floor with a long carpet runner.

A woman maybe in her fifties with pewter hair in a bob sits at a wooden desk to my right, two-finger typing on a computer keyboard. Yeah. This is pretty clearly trying to be a doctor's office with a degree of plausible deniability. Really, it's only a study with a bunch of chairs… not a waiting room at all.

"Hello," says the woman at the desk. "Are you here for a tarot reading?"

Every now and then, the tremendous supernatural willpower of being a vampire comes in handy. Like now. I manage not to burst out laughing and approach the desk with a straight face. "Mysticism isn't in the cards for me today, thanks. I need to have a word with Doctor Roberts."

"Oh, I'm afraid my husband's busy at the moment. If you give me your name and number, I can have him call you when he's available."

I glance at the computer. "Maybe you can help me. You're clearly the desk clerk for his medical practice of questionable legality. I need to know what exactly he did to Mindy Hogan."

Evidently, I'm still radiating enough 'federal agent' in my body language and tone of voice to put the woman with the kids on edge. She rasps in hasty Spanish for the two boys to come sit near her. I glance back at her long enough to get the sense from her thoughts that she's worrying about legal trouble for seeing a doctor who lost his license.

"I'm sorry, miss, but I can't simply—"

I lock stares with the 'receptionist.' "Can't simply what?"

"Hogan?" she asks in a somewhat trancelike voice, then spells it.

I smile. "Yes. That's right."

The woman searches the computer, but only comes up with a Floyd Hogan. Wow… people really still name their sons 'Floyd?' I lean around to peek at the screen. Oh, he's like eighty-six. Clearly not my new undead friend.

"Nothing here," she reports.

"Thanks." I narrow my eyes. This house is quite a ways from where Mindy died. I'm betting the 'good' doctor probably set up temporary shop in that abandoned building to distance his 'legit' practice from whatever went on there. "I'll ask him myself then."

She opens her mouth to protest, but I push the thought out of her head. While she stares into the fourteenth dimension, I head down the corridor. Voices emanate from behind a plain white door on the left. The doctor's voice sounds a little deeper than I would've imagined from his picture. He's trying to convince a male patient to go to the hospital for his prostate cancer, saying there's nothing he can do for him here. A woman companion with a mild Spanish accent protests, citing no money or insurance.

My urge to barge in before he turns these people into zombies wanes as the conversation sounds quite normal. So, I wait in the hallway for a while listening while the doctor continues to insist he doesn't have the equipment or facilities necessary to act, and stresses the man should get to the hospital as soon as possible. Evidently, the hospital can't refuse to treat him over money as his condition is life-threatening.

Of course, now I'm awash with contradictions. This guy sounds like he's trying to do the right thing. He's also running an illegal clinic, but his motivation—at least on the surface so far—appears to be catering to the poor. The man also has an expensive car, which raises a red flag. He's not making that much money from these people. Either medical testing pays extremely well or he's scamming insurance somehow.

Eventually, the white door opens and the middle-aged couple steps out. My presence startles gasps out of them, but neither says a single word, hurrying off as fast as they can move without obviously running away from me.

I breathe into my hand and sniff test it. Nope. Not *that* bad. Guess I still give off 'fed vibes.'

Confident my breath won't strip the paint off the walls, I step inside a room that's straight out of Better Doctor's Offices and Gardens. Only, it's missing all the diplomas and such. And, his desk isn't loaded with a bunch of drug company kitsch. More plausible deniability I bet. Just a house with two studies in the basement. Oh, and a medical exam table. I wonder how he plans to explain that if an inspector ever shows up.

The doctor's half out of his chair, stunned by my entrance. For a fifty-one-year old, he's not in bad shape, though he's got an industrial quantity of something in his hair. Bet the dude spends two hours every morning making it perfect. His blue turtleneck, black pants, and hair helmet kinda make him look like Spock and Mitt Romney had a son.

"Who are you?" asks Doctor Roberts, looking down at a clipboard. "I don't see you on my list."

"I'm not on your list. Interesting little operation you've got going here."

His already pasty cheeks pale even more. "How did you get past Nora? Who are you?"

"Well, first, I'm *not* a cop or terribly concerned with you running a general practice with a suspended medical license. That's not why I'm here." I lean on the desk and note a prescription pad with a name that's quite far away from his. "I only have a few questions for Doctor Roberts, or should I call you…" I tilt my head. "Venkatakrish—"

He slaps his hand down on the pad and stuffs it into the top drawer. "If you're not here about that, then what do you want? Are you with... *them*?"

I blink. "Them?" In the confused few seconds of staring at each other that follows, I pick up that he's thinking I'm connected to some local criminals he's become affiliated with and looking to arrange surgery or something for bullet wounds for 'some guy I have out in the car.' Wow. Quite the imagination. "No… nothing like that. I'm here about the zombies."

Doctor Roberts scrunches up his nose. "Zombies? Miss, I think you may have misunderstood. I'm a family doctor, not a psychiatrist."

"I bet you don't believe in vampires either then?"

He folds his arms. "Did you come here to do something more than waste time? I have patients."

"Now that's ironic."

"What?" He raises an eyebrow.

"A doctor losing his patience."

One vein pulses in his forehead. "I really must ask you to leave, miss."

I scan his thoughts. Wow. He really doesn't know anything about zombies. "Did you ever see a patient by the name of Mindy Hogan?"

The instant I say her name, Doctor Roberts' expression goes blank. He looks down and picks at a pile of papers, tugging a silver pen out from under them. He lets out a sudden scream of rage, and comes rushing around the desk at me, brandishing what turns out not to be a pen.

It's a scalpel. And a silver one at that.

I lean back, evading a slice at neck level, then surge forward and punch him with an open palm square in the chest. He flies off his feet, lands on his back, and slides into the wall, legs in the air. Still screaming in anger, he scrambles upright again, but before he can orient himself into another attack, I pounce.

One hand at his neck, the other controlling his wrist, I wheel him around and hammer him face down over the desk, knocking a bunch of papers, pens, books, and some plastic junk crashing to the floor. He struggles, the tone of his shrieking changing to fear once he realizes he can't overpower me. A little squeeze convinces him to drop the scalpel, then I flip him over onto his back, still keeping him bent over the desk.

He grabs my right wrist in a useless attempt to pull my hand off his throat. He might be trying to say something, but my grip isn't letting much air in. Red washes over his face into purple.

"Now, Doctor Roberts," I say in a silky tone. "That wasn't very hospitable of you."

"What's going on?" shouts Nora from the door.

I smile up at her. "Oh, nothing. I was just demonstrating a new chiropractic technique."

She blinks at me. Doctor Roberts gurgles.

"Why don't you head back to your desk and sit quietly," I say with a mental suggestion of the same.

"Yes. I'll do that." Nora hurries away.

I shift my attention back to the doctor and lean down to stare into his eyes. I'm not sure what alarms me more: that I *don't* see any sort of flickering flame, or that he came after me with intent to kill as soon as he heard Mindy's name. *Something* is going on here. He's starting to go full purple so I relax my grip enough so that he can breathe.

He wheezes, but doesn't try to say anything.

"Now, why did you just try to kill me?" I ask, not really concerned with what he's going to say.

One thing about the human mind: ask a question, and the answer slides into the forebrain whether or not the person wants to say it. However, in this case, he's as confused as I am.

"Who… what…?" rasps the doctor.

"Why did you go crazy as soon as I said 'Mindy Hogan?'"

Again, he flies into a thrashing, murderous rage, except he's about as dangerous as an upside-down turtle. While he's in the throes of fury, I dive deep into his consciousness. That same eerie feeling that pervaded the abandoned building where Mindy died comes back to me from inside his head. This man's either carrying or has been touched by a dark energy. A minute or so later, he goes limp and stops trying to fight me. Soon after, I locate a mental trigger. I can't tell if it came from another vampire, but it sorta feels like it. Someone programmed this guy to attack anyone who said Mindy's name.

Maddeningly, I can't find any memory of his meeting the source of that command, nor do I see her in his memories. When I say the address for the place where she swears he injected her with something, there's no recognition at all in his thoughts. This guy's totally clueless. Either that, or he got hit with a mind eraser. I keep pushing deeper into his brain, to the point he grabs the side of his head and wails from the migraine I'm giving him.

Other than a more-than-faint urge to draw the Devil Killer, I feel nothing as I search.

Wait. That's not nothing.

That's something.

That's a *bad* something.
Shit. Tucson has a demon problem.

Chapter Nineteen
Charm

Doctor Roberts, as it turns out, didn't have much to do with the zombification of Mindy Hogan.

As best I can tell, the worst thing he's guilty of is several flavors of medical insurance fraud, plus practicing with a revoked license. I'm not sure how much karmic balance he achieves by providing free help to the poor, but he's still scamming money and increasing the costs on other patients. Mostly because I have bigger (dead) fish to fry right now—and I don't need people asking me how I know all about him—I decide to let fate have its way with him. If he gets caught, he gets caught.

He did, however, evidently have an encounter with a demon. That itch to pull out the sword has to be an instinctive response from whatever power Azrael imbued me with along with those wing tattoos. Or maybe I really have become like a quarter angel. I guess it's kind of like how some dogs always growl at the scent of cats. Whatever 'angelic' side I've inherited reacts to the presence of demons the way Anthony reacts to broccoli. I'm sure if the boy carried a broadsword, he'd smash vegetables whenever possible.

Even when I had him on baby food, he hated it. This one time, I thought he was eating it, but the little bugger had been stuffing his cheeks like a hamster. As soon as he couldn't hold anymore, he spat it back out—mostly all over me.

Anyway, it feels like I'm getting nowhere fast. Maybe if I take Mindy back to that abandoned place, something will happen. With any luck, she might be able to remember a few details. So, I drive back to her place. Except... I'm not entirely ready for the sight that greets me when I walk in.

Mindy's standing in the kitchen, sawing an enormous knife back and forth across her left forearm. Her tongue's even sticking out a little bit like Tom & Jerry when the cat's really concentrating on doing something bad.

"Umm…?" I ask.

She looks up. "Oh, hi."

"What's with the knife?"

"Well I got the munchies, so I was gonna make myself a sandwich. Like once a month, Alisha bakes a whole chicken. The knife slipped and cut my finger, only it didn't. Well, not really. Check this out."

I head around the counter, and almost lean on a plate with her mostly-completed sandwich. It's got tomatoes and lettuce and mayo. Just needs chicken. Meanwhile, Mindy saws at herself again, but not until it looks like she's really bearing down hard does even the smallest cut appear. And, within a second of her pulling the knife away, it heals.

"This is kinda cool. I think I'm like crazy tough or something. Are you? Is this normal for… umm, us?"

"No. I cut as easily as any normal person, but it heals right back up, too."

We fiddle around for a few minutes—okay, I surrender to curiosity—and it looks like the girl *is* extremely resilient to damage. She's also ridiculously strong. Like, I'm sure elder vampires are on par with her, but she's only been a zombie—or whatever she is—for a couple of days and she's already significantly stronger than I am. Our arm-wrestling test nearly breaks the table. Even trying to amp myself up as much as I can, I feel like a seven-year-old arm going up against a pro bodybuilder.

Well, I suppose if she doesn't get to fly, turn into a dragon, or teleport, being stupid strong and as tough as an M1-Abrams tank is probably a fair deal. I bet this girl's bare ass would stop bullets, though I'm not about to suggest we try experimenting with that. Neighbors get kinda testy when guns start going off.

"Okay, enough messing around. I need you to come with me back to the place where you, umm, turned."

She fidgets, staring down. "Do I have to? I'm still hungry."

"Finish making your sandwich. And I think going there might jog your memory."

"For what?"

"I don't know."

"Sam, am I dead?"

I bite my lower lip. "Don't think of it as you dying, kiddo. Think of it as you turning into a superhero or something."

Mindy shrugs. "You're sure I'm not going to start rotting?"

"I'm not sure of anything, but I suspect not. I do have some friends who might be able to help answer those questions, but right now, we need to stop whoever did this from doing it to more people."

She squints. "If I'm a superhero and it's not a bad thing what happened to me, why do you want to stop them from doing it to more people?"

"Because what happened to you may not be 'normal' for this. The goal might've been something way more dangerous and mindless. And, well, it's kinda shitty to just do this to someone without their asking for it. If you could go back a couple days and they asked you if you wanted this, would you?"

Mindy fidgets. "Okay. Good point. Let's go stop the bastard."

***

I park the Momvan at the curb by the suspicious abandoned warehouse.

"Yeah, this is the place." Mindy points at the same building I went into.

We hop out at the same time, and I lead the way across the dirt lot to the door. It's still open, so I go right in. The room's pretty much exactly as I left it except for an empty bottle of bum wine on the floor. Guess some local vagrant found the place unlocked and decided to make it his crash pad. Considering they're not here anymore, I have a feeling the creepy energy in the air chased him off. At least, I hope that's what happened and we don't have another zombie roaming around. When I stoop to take a sniff of the bag and try to pick up the guy's scent, I notice Mindy make an abrupt turn, as if she's avoiding an object that's not really there.

"Mindy?"

"Hmm?" She stops, smiling at me.

"Why did you zig-zag, kiddo?"

She points at open floor. "Umm. I didn't wanna mash my shin into the table."

"Table?"

"Stop messing with me." She folds her arms.

"I'm not messing with you." I forget about the bottle and walk straight up to her.

Mindy gasps and jumps back. "Ooh! How did you do that?"

"What did I do?"

"You walked right *through* that table like it's a hologram or something."

"I don't see a table, Mindy."

"It's *right there!*" she almost shouts. When I continue giving her a disbelieving look, she scoots around me, crouches, and starts patting thin air and feeling around the area. The effect is highly disconcerting, like she's a mime pretending to touch an invisible table. Come to think of it, she'd make a pretty good mime. "There's a table here with a bunch of magazines and shit on it."

I glance at the wood paneled walls covered in old Playboy centerfolds. "What do the walls look like to you?"

"Umm. Powder blue, like a dentist's office. There's some chairs around and a receptionist counter there." She points at blank wall, then walks over to the only chair still standing on its legs, and sits in it. "This is where I sat to fill out that questionnaire."

"Do you still have the flyer you found?" I ask.

"Yeah." She leans to the right and stuffs her hand into her left pocket. After a bit of a struggle, she extracts a crumpled up piece of paper and tosses it to me.

I unfurl the wad into an eight-by-ten sheet of paper with the same medical testing ad I saw at the campus. The one for $50 and the address in northeast Tucson… by the Chipotle. "Mindy, something's not right."

"Ya think?"

"No, I mean… I see this flyer as offering fifty

bucks, not five hundred. And it doesn't have this address on it."

She leaps to her feet and swoops in beside me, pointing at the $50. "Right there. Five-zero-zero."

I close my eyes and sigh. This is almost as frustrating as dealing with Tammy when she digs her heels in. "Mindy, I think you're hallucinating. I'd telepathically show you what I see, but your mind is closed off to me."

"That's not some kind of airhead remark is it?" She hooks her thumbs in her jean pockets and kicks at the floor.

"No. You're a… supernatural being. We can't read each other's minds." I'm not going to mention Tammy can. But then again, she's—at least I hope—still human and normal, so she doesn't count as a supernatural being.

"So you don't see this table?"

"Nope." I describe the room as I see it: fading pictures of boobs, a beat up desk, wood paneling on the walls, and three folding chairs.

"Whoa."

"Let me try something," I say.

"Okay."

I stare into her eyes and try to read her thoughts or project mine into her head, but I have about as much success at it as a millennial trying to afford a house. While I'm examining her, I catch a psychic whiff of an odd energy. It triggers a weak itch to reach for my sword, but not as strong as even what I felt on Doctor Roberts. All this time in her presence and it didn't hit me until I really focused hard on trying to 'read' her. Like trying to grab a thread floating in water, I hone in on the essence of it. She can't be possessed, which is my first thought, because she has a dark master. Or probably does. They don't really like roommates—well at least roommates inside her body. The two she's sharing a house with probably won't piss the dark master off.

My gaze eventually falls on her left wrist, drawn to her charm bracelet.

"What's that?" I point at it.

"A bracelet."

I smirk. "Obviously. Where did it come from?"

"Oh. It's my good luck charm. I was having a crappy day a couple weeks ago, and I found it in the grass near the health sciences building."

"May I?"

She nods.

I grasp her arm and lift it up to take a closer look. Seems like an ordinary charm bracelet. Steel chain with a bunch of random little things hanging off it, mostly tiny animals and some pink beads. While I doubt the thing's worth much more than thirty bucks, it has some definite energy surrounding it.

"Have you taken that thing off since you found it?"

Yeah, a couple times, mostly to shower, but I usually put it back on.

"I need to try something."

She stands still when I reach for the clasp,

offering no protest. The instant I pull it away from her skin, she lets out a startled shriek and jumps back with both hands clamped over her mouth.

"Holy shit! The whole place just changed!" She spins around, mouth hanging open. "Ugh. Eww. Creepy porn magazines. You're right. Wood paneling."

I hold up the flyer. "Does this still say $500?"

She reads it over and starts to tremble. Imagine being seven or eight years old and your parents driving you into the middle of nowhere to abandon you. The way you'd look at the car driving away when you realize they're not coming back? Yeah. That's the look Mindy's giving me now. Total destruction of her world.

I can't take it for much more than a few seconds without my mom instincts kicking in. When I hug her, she bursts into tears.

"What's going on, Sam?" She sniffles. "This is so trippy. Everything just changed."

A few minutes of squeezing and back-patting calms her. She stops clinging to me and looks around in awe. I glance down at the bracelet in my hand, getting a definite sense of demonic energy from it.

"I have good news and not so good news."

"What's the good news?" She bites her lip. "I could use it."

"You weren't targeted specifically. At least, I don't think so. Something left that bracelet on the ground for anyone to find."

She scratches at her head. "Oh, yay. I'm still a zombie. Does it matter if someone did it to *me* on purpose? What's the bad news?"

"The 'something' that planted the trap is probably a demon."

"Umm. Demon?" She looks about to go off on a rant, but stops and stares at me for a few seconds. "Okay. I'm a zombie talking to a vampire. I guess demons don't sound that farfetched."

I grab the charm bracelet in both hands and pull, grunting from the effort.

"What are you doing?"

"This thing is a demonic trap. I'm trying to break it so it doesn't get anyone else."

"Oh." She makes a sad little pouty face.

"I'll get you a new one—without the dark energy." I grunt and struggle to snap the chain, but it still doesn't give.

"Wow. That thing's tough."

"Yeah," I say between clenched teeth, still straining.

A sudden blast of energy emanates from the charm bracelet, knocking me on my ass. The still-intact jewelry falls to the floor where I'd been standing, then exudes a dense cloud of black vapor. By the time I scramble back to my feet, the cloud has grown seven feet tall. Mindy stares in shock, taking a step back as the vapor whorl widens and solidifies into a mostly-humanoid shaped creature. Its head is almost as wide as its shoulders, without much of a neck. Both eyes glow with yellow light, though the left one's about six inches across and the other is human-sized. Thorny barbs stick out of its coal-black skin here and there, bigger ones at the elbows and knees. It stands upon bird-like feet with two forward toes and one rear toe, and a cloud of stench wafts off it somewhere between fermented diaper pail and spoiled eggs. No, make that a fermented diaper pail lit on fire.

Mindy regards the demon for a few seconds before glancing at me. "Umm. Sam?"

"Yeah?" I ask, easing my hand toward my invisible pouch.

"Is fighting a demon gonna cost extra?"

Chapter Twenty
Some Light Remodeling

On second thought, I decide not to whip out the Devil Killer right away.

This thing would probably do whatever it is that demons do equivocal to shitting its pants at the sight of it. I don't want it running away... or shitting its demon pants. I want it dead.

"I'm technically doing this one pro bono. Greater good and all." I go to extend my claws… forgetting myself. "Aww, crap."

"Oh. Cool," says Mindy. Remarkably there's no fear in her voice. "And wow, this guy smells. Holy crap! I thought I smelled bad eggs when the doctor was testing me."

The demon snarls at her and whips its arm around with a backhanded slap to the face that knocks Mindy through the wall into the next room.

DEAD MOON

It emits a low, grating chuckle and swivels to face me—since it can't really turn its head.

"So, Mr. Tall, Dark and Neckless... you come here often?"

"Hey, cheap shot," yells Mindy from the hole in the wall, before stepping through, not a mark on her at all. "I wasn't ready."

The demon lunges at me. I duck its swiping arm and slide around to the left. It's too early to show the Devil Killer, and I've been declawed... an idea hits me. I hold out my arm the way Annie did when I first tangled with the Red Rider, picturing the amber blobs of energy she threw at it. Right as the demon recovers from its first swing to face me again, a little scrap of light flies away from my hand and burns a hole into its torso about the size of a golf ball. It howls in pain and staggers a few steps away, dribbling steaming black ichor on the floor. Yowch. Its blood looks boiling hot. I'm *glad* I don't have claws anymore. Sticking my fingers into that body would've hurt.

Unfortunately, that feeble little attempt at casting an attack spell didn't do much more than cause pain. It's doubtful I'll be able to kill a demon with my magic—at least not without a lot more practice.

However, whatever I did to it seemed to pack a punch at least in terms of ouchiness. And no, I don't care if that's a word or not. The demon objects wholeheartedly to it, and whirls on me. I dive into a somersault to avoid two fists mashing down on my head. He swings so hard he almost falls over from missing me. Enraged, he lurches up to a charge like a cartoon bull. For a big thing, he can move pretty fast. But turning, not so much. The demon tries to stop when I dive out of the way, but huge taloned feet don't do too well on bare concrete. He slide-stumbles headfirst into the wall, getting a face-full of Miss September 2001.

Danny's parents always did say porn leads straight to hell. I didn't realize how literal that could be. It would probably kill them to learn that their son wound up owning/managing a tittie bar for a few years. Something tells me he didn't share that factoid with them. While it's somewhat tempting, I haven't either. After all the things he no doubt said about me following the divorce, they wouldn't believe me anyway.

"Ugh," says Mindy, slapping drywall dust from her shoulders. "How can you stand being so close to that thing without throwing up?"

"Oh, it's not the worst thing I've ever smelled," I say, ducking another series of claw rakes.

The demon spits a piece of Miss September to the side, then tries to bite me. I pound my fist square into its forehead, knocking it into a backward stagger—and breaking pretty much every bone in my hand.

Ow. Shit.

"Seriously?" Mindy walks over to me. "What's worse than this? Gah. It's awful!"

"Have you ever changed a diaper of a one-year-old who got into the refried beans?"

Mindy shakes her head.

Oh wow. Healing is faster. Stunned, I watch as the bones in my hand knit before my eyes. Okay, ouch. The knitting hurts almost as much as the breaking. Back in the day, back when I hosted Elizabeth, my bones took hours to knit. Okay, this is cool.

Once the bones in my hand knit, I make a fist. "This guy's got a hard head."

The demon recovers his balance and roars. A tiny ember lights up at the back of its throat. Time seems to slow down to me as my vampiric reflexes kick in, speeding me way beyond human agility. There's two things that will really mess up a vampire's world: sunlight and fire. For me, sunlight isn't so much of an issue now but there's no reason to roll the dice with fire. I tackle Mindy out of the way barely a second in real time away from a flamethrower-spew of dark, crackling crimson.

Mindy hits the ground on her back and I wind up riding her like a sled straight into the wall from the force of my jump.

"That's not normal fire," rasps Mindy.

"What was your first clue? The dark red or that it came out of a demon?"

"No." She points. "Cinder blocks aren't supposed to melt."

I twist around and gawk at a magmatic hole in the wall. "I don't suppose you have a Tums the size of a car tire?"

"Huh?"

"Forget it." I stand and pull her upright.

"What are we gonna do?" yells Mindy.

"Kill it," I say.

The demon appears to find this amusing and delays his next attack to laugh at us. Ashes of burned Playboy centerfolds float around him like grey snow flurries. He snarls, rakes his foot at the floor, then charges at us again.

This time, Mindy steps forward into a straight jab, emitting this cute little grunt. Her knuckles slam into the demon's cheek, launching him off his feet. He flies, arms flailing, into the wall and blasts through it into one of the small conference rooms. The demon jams into the floor like a lawn dart on his head, slides a few feet with sparks spraying from his horns, then tilts over and lands flat on his chest.

I gawk at Mindy. "Whoa."

She examines her fingernails. "Took karate as a kid."

Her hand didn't even break. Okay, my girl here isn't anywhere near as brittle as she looks. I glance at the hole in the wall, the demon moaning on the floor, and back to her. Wow. Momvan got off light.

"Good grief, I think you knocked it senseless. I didn't think it was *possible* to knock a demon loopy." I chuckle. "He looks drunk."

"*Can* we kill a demon?" She gives me the side eye.

I wink and mouth 'play along' without adding voice. "I'm not sure. Maybe if we keep hitting it, it'll eventually die."

Mindy scrunches her nose. "Huh?"

"Trust me," I whisper. "Beat it senseless."

"Oh, okay."

The demon drags himself upright and climbs back into the room. A ripped section of a Playboy page flutters down and adheres to his chest, making it look like he's got a tiny pair of D cups.

Mindy points at him and giggles.

He raises his clawed hands as if to attack, but pauses, staring at her. She keeps laughing. He glances down at his chest, notices the page, and grumbles, flicking it away. Not sure if he thinks I'm an easier kill or he's still pissed about the painful smoking hole I gave him, but, he rushes at me. I see the claws coming, but, too late, realize he's faking me out and I leap straight into his other hand, which closes around my throat.

The demon twists at the waist, throwing me across the room. I fly into the door that leads deeper into the place, shattering it, and bouncing head over ass a few times before sliding to a stop on my back.

Deep roaring from the demon and higher-pitched female growling accompany a series of fleshy thuds and smacks. He emits a wail of pain, and a tremendously loud *whap* follows. Mindy's scream zooms by on the other side of the wall, along with a *wham* every few seconds as she blasts holes in several successive walls.

"Sam?" yells Mindy from *way* behind me. "I think my neck broke. My head's all wobbly."

"Give it a minute," I shout back.

The demon grabs the doorjamb at the end of the corridor and rips it wide enough for his shoulders to fit. Damn. I have nowhere to go in this hallway to dodge him. Things are going to get tight... unless...

I concentrate on the little flame as he comes storming toward me. Mere seconds before claws tear me in half, I teleport into the 'waiting room' and cringe at the heavy *whud* of the demon running into another wall.

"Missed me," I yell, then lean to my right and gawk at six Mindy-shaped holes creating a tunnel spanning multiple rooms. In one or two spots, I can make out where her legs were. This is seriously like something out of a Bugs Bunny cartoon.

"Grr," says Mindy, standing into view at the last hole. Aside from covered in white plaster dust, she doesn't look *too* hurt. Though, blood does leak from her nostrils and she's sporting a giant bruise on her face.

The demon pulls his head out of the wall in the corridor and wheels around, snarling at me. Oh, he's pissed. Good. I want him irrational. He might actually be angry enough not to flee the instant I pull out the sword. Single demons are chickenshits when it comes to final death. A whole mob of them whip each other into a frenzy and would probably still come at me even if I had the sword out, but one? Yeah, he's gonna haul ass.

His running back charge comes to a sideways halt as Mindy dives through the wall and tackles him. He lands on his chest, sliding with a painful skin-on-smooth tile squeaking noise that reminds me of the first (and only) time Anthony went face-first down a metal slide shirtless. I cringe at the sound now just as I had all those years ago.

Meanwhile, Mindy pounces on his back, grabs his two main horns like handlebars, and proceeds to repeatedly hammer his face into the floor. Gone—long gone—was the tormented, down-on-her-luck college girl, to be replaced by something rarely seen outside of a superhero movie.

Sweet mama.

The demon flails for a few seconds then gets the bright idea to put one of his arms between his face and concrete. Before Mindy realizes she's not doing much damage anymore, he rams his right elbow into her, launching her backward into the wall. But she only hits it hard enough for her butt to punch through the wall. She hangs there briefly, her rear end probably sticking out into the room behind her.

I hurry into the corridor while the demon's struggling to stand back up. He looks severely disoriented. Black blood gushes from his mouth and nose, forming a steaming puddle. Whoa. She even knocked a few teeth out and his eyes have crossed. Now's a good a time as any. After boosting my speed to make absolutely sure I don't screw this up, I zoom toward him like some kind of Valkyrie avenger.

The sword appears out of thin air as I close my hand around apparently empty space at my side.

Azrael's wings unfurl behind me like a giant black shadow. The demon's smaller eye opens as wide as it can, the merest beginnings of an 'oh shit' expression forming as I slash my blade into the top of his head.

My downward attack cleaves roughly to the demon's mouth, with an open split going upward from there to the top of its head. A low moan begins to come out of him, but cuts off when I yank the blade loose and spin around into a beheading stroke.

And dammit, cutting this thing's head off is *not* easy. This sucker's got no neck.

My 'heroic moment of victory' isn't quite the glorious, graceful movie-beheading I'd like to picture.

There's some sawing involved.

Okay, more than 'some.' There's a *lot* of sawing involved.

And a good deal of painfully hot blood spraying everywhere.

When I manage to force the blade a couple inches past where its spine would be, the whole demon explodes into a greasy cloud of black smoke.

Mindy walks over, wide-eyed, staring at me.

I glance around at the ruined cinder blocks, holes, small fires, and mashed up floor. "Someone's going to lose their security deposit."

"Wow, Sam. You're just full of surprises." She runs her fingers down the leading edge of my right wing.

"You don't know the half of it." I wink.

Chapter Twenty-One
Cats and Dogs

"This is freaky," says Mindy.

"Welcome to your new reality." I stash the sword back in its pocket dimension and put the wings away. "Though, I doubt you're going to have quite as weird a trajectory as my life has taken. I used to think being a vampire was weird, but the first few years were pretty normal by comparison to now."

"I'm not sure I trust the opinion of a vampire with wings as to what constitutes normal."

I laugh.

"Oh, hey, the bracelet's still there." Mindy hurries over and picks up the charmed accessory, dusting it off. "Is it still... bad?"

"Let me see it?"

She hands it over.

"It's not giving off any weird feelings anymore." I toss it to her. "Keep it if you like."

"Holy crap. Was I carrying that giant thing around with me the whole time?"

I shrug. "Maybe. Or maybe it was only using the bracelet as a focus for energy it sent across from its home."

"So a demon made me a zombie?" She scratches her head.

"I think the collective consciousness of humanity decided to make zombies into a 'thing that exists,' and well, the demons helped. Maybe they sensed it coming and tried to hurry it along."

"What about all that dark master stuff?"

I think about that. I had thought this had been a dark master plan to deflect attention away from them... but, perhaps, this had been a demonic plan all along, meant to deflect attention away from... me. After all, I had been deputized to kill these suckers. Keeping me busy fighting a zombie attack would surely buy them a lot of time. Then again, not everything was about me.

"It's looking more and more like a demonic attack—"

"But what about the flame in my eye?"

"Good question. C'mere."

She does and I take a good long look into eyes that are just beginning to cloud over. The girl was gonna need some brains, stat. She also had a possession problem. "It's still there."

"What is it? A demon?"

"That, I don't know. I say we worry about it later."

"Is there any way you can like, 'fix' me? Maybe kill the head demon and I go back to normal?"

"That doesn't even work for vampires, hon." I pat her on the shoulder. "The one who made me is long dead and I didn't wake up normal." Of course, the one who had made me had been my one-time father, Jeffcock Something-or-Other. Long story.

"Well, crap." She grumbles.

"Don't feel *too* bad. I'm almost jealous of how strong and tough you are."

She shudders. "Yeah, but… I'm dead."

"There are worse things to be than dead." I shrug. "You could be a Kardashian."

"Hey, I like them."

"Really?"

"What do they call it? They're my guilty pleasure."

"Fair enough."

I head into the building again, exploring. She trails me like a lost kitten following the first human to be nice to it. Fortunately, I'm not getting any feeling of oddity from this place anymore. Maybe that demon was here all along and not in the bracelet. It just sensed me tampering with its toy and came out thinking it could squish us. Maybe it was merely a sentry of sorts. Not the brains behind this. Truth was, it looked about as far from the brains as possible.

"Let's get out of here before someone shows

up."

Mindy steps over some broken drywall. "Or something."

"Exactly."

We hurry outside and hop in the Momvan. I drive a couple blocks away, then pull over and take out my phone. Mindy gives me a 'what'cha doing?' look.

"Pinging one of those friends I mentioned."

I call Fang… and feel like an idiot. He's not going to be awake. Still, I get his voicemail… and I probably shouldn't leave a recording of the stuff I want to say. So, I just say, "Hey, Fang. Got a weird case. Need to pick your *brain*. Call you later." I wonder if he would catch my coded message.

"What now?" asks Mindy.

"Well. I think we might've destroyed the demon responsible for what happened to you."

"But do you really think that slobbering, evil thing planned all this?"

I put hands on hips and take in some worthless air. "If I had to guess, I would say that demons and dark masters are working together."

"That can't be good."

"No," I say. "Not at all."

"Kinda sounds like cats and dogs working together." She giggles.

I laugh. "Nah. I think demons and dark masters are a bit more aligned than that."

"Maybe I can help you?"

"Possibly," I say. "Now, our focus should probably be on helping you adjust to your new normal."

"Good luck." She rolls her eyes. "I never really adjusted to my old normal."

"Problems at home or with school?"

She shrugs as I start driving again. "Not really. I mean... I never thought of myself as much of a homebody, but the town I grew up in is really small. Tucson is huge. Makes me miss home, yanno? Still can't get used to having so many people around, and I miss my friends. But it's okay. I can deal. At least I don't have to be so nervous around strange guys anymore. I mean, it's not like roofies work on me now, right?"

"I doubt they would. More brains?"

"I thought you'd never ask!"

Chapter Twenty-Two
Roommates from Hell

We swing by a Mexican grocery and get some more *cerebros de vaca*.

While we're wandering the aisles, I notice Mindy fixate and stare at the meat cooler. Her expression has got to be pretty much exactly what I looked like while wandering around a blood-soaked Civil War battlefield—assuming that really happened. Hmm. Some zombie movies have them eating any sort of raw flesh, not only brains. Can't hurt to test that out, so I grab a couple packs of fajita beef as well.

Soon, we're back at her place. One of the roommates, Natalie Hernandez, is sprawled on the couch glowering at a tablet. She looks up at us.

"Oh, hey. Wow, did you blow up a coke factory?"

"Huh?" asks Mindy.

"You're like covered in white dust."

"Oh, umm…"

"White dust?" I ask. "Where?"

Natalie blinks as I encourage her not to notice the mess we are. She looks around again, and shrugs. "Never mind. Oh, who's this?"

"Nat, this is my cousin, Sam," says Mindy. "She's going to California and stopped by to visit for a day or two."

"Oh, cool." Natalie waves.

"Hey." I return the wave.

The girls spend a few minutes talking, mostly Natalie complaining about what she's been reading on the tablet. Evidently, the textbook is 'complicated, dense, and boring.' Dense as in a lot of information crammed into few words. So, she's struggling to absorb it. And yeah, apparently text books are on tablet computers these days.

I head to the kitchen and put the meat in the fridge, although I suspect rotten wouldn't phase her, and return to the front room and siphon some energy from Natalie. I don't take too much, but she yawns. Since they're still chatting away, I decide to 'go to the bathroom.'

After locking the door, I close my eyes and call the little dancing flame, drawing it closer and closer until it engulfs me. My surroundings shift, and I'm standing in the shadow of the dumpsters at my local Starbucks back in Fullerton.

Ahh. Come to mama.

I head inside, feeding from everyone in line. On a whim, I get a pair of pumpkin spice lattes, then teleport home to check up on the kids. Tammy's not there, but Anthony's in his room on the computer again. It's unreal how much time that game can absorb. He's not apparently doing anything involving other people at the moment, so he has no trouble logging out for a little while for my benefit.

His homework's all taken care of, Tammy's over at her friend Veronica's place, and things here have been quiet.

"How much longer are you gonna be away?" he asks.

"Not too much longer, I think. Case is pretty much over. I just need to help someone adjust to her new reality."

"Ugh." He sighs. "Another vampire?"

"Not exactly." I sit on the edge of his bed. No sense BS-ing the kid, especially since supernatural stuff seems to have a distinct habit of interfering with my entire family. So, I explain about Mindy and how I think she's pretty much a zombie of sorts.

"Huh." He rubs his chin. "Maybe she's like a 'revenant' or something."

"What the hell is that?"

He points at the computer. "There's a monster in the game called that. Basically, they're like zombies in that they're undead former humans, but they still have their minds and they don't look all gnarly and decaying, just creepy pale with blue glowing eyes."

"Hmm. That does sound a lot like Mindy except for the glowing eyes. What about eating brains or flesh?"

He shrugs. "It's only a video game. They don't go into that much detail. It's a bad guy monster."

"Right."

"Okay, well... I should probably get back before they break down the bathroom door." I chuckle.

He stands and hugs me, then flops in his chair and puts his headphones back on. "Love you, Mom."

"Love you too, Anthony." I can't help myself and sorta-hug him by pulling his head against my side.

Leaving him to his game, I send myself back to Mindy's bathroom. She's in the kitchen waiting for me and killing time by stuffing her face with Doritos. There's an obvious milky haze over her eyes, more noticeable than earlier.

"Looks like you're hungry." I hand her the second pumpkin spice latte.

"Ooh. Thanks!" Mindy jams a handful of chips in her mouth. "Yeah. But these aren't even taking the edge off."

"I mean..." I lean close and whisper, "Your eyes look a little hazy. Dealing with that demon made me hungry, so I think it's probably the same for you. I want to try something."

"Okay. What?"

I grab one of the packs of beef from the fridge and hand it to her. "Eat that."

As casual as can be, she peels the plastic film off and stuffs a strip of steak into her mouth raw. If her expression is any indication, my hunch is right. She lights up the way I used to while splurging on chocolate after a bad day at the office. One by one, she devours the four strip steaks, then stares imploringly at me with cow blood dribbling off her chin and fingers.

"Need. More." The manic look in her gaze tells me the beef's a winner.

Good thing we bought four packs. I hand her another, and she makes short work of it, too. By the time that package is gone, her eyes have gone back to normal. Or at least minimum haze.

Mindy licks her fingers clean, then wipes her chin and licks her hand again. "Mmm. Okay. That kinda worked. It's weird though."

"How so?"

"Well, like, I kinda prefer the texture of the beef to the brain. But I also kinda felt like I needed more of it than I needed of the brains." She sighs. "I'm still hungry, but only 'snack hungry' now."

I smile, take her hand, and guide her down the hall to her bedroom. "Don't need your friends overhearing stuff."

"Oh. Yeah." She sits on the edge of the bed.

"Well, this is good news." I flop on the folding chair by the computer. "It's a lot easier to find beef than brain. I imagine you'll probably be able to survive on pretty much any kind of raw meat. Taking a guess here, but there's probably something of a zombie food pyramid. Brains are at the top, then most likely organs like kidneys or the liver, and then red meat. Not sure if poultry is better or worse than red meat. No idea about fish."

"Ick. Raw fish?"

"Never had sushi?" I raise an eyebrow. "It's really good."

She shivers.

"Hang on, girl. You ate raw cow brains, but you're squirming about sushi?"

Mindy stares at me blankly for a moment before bursting into giggles. "Yeah, okay. That's a valid point. Maybe I'll try it. The idea used to make me sick, but… things change."

We spend a while chatting about potential nutrition. She's much happier thinking that beef is a viable option since it's pretty much universal. Until she arrived in Tucson, she didn't even know that 'cow brains' were a thing people could buy, much less *want* to eat… though the tacos are cooked.

I spend some time going back over my feelings on dark masters and how they want to become stronger and could eventually overwhelm her entirely. That is, of course, assuming she has one. She so far hasn't reported hearing any whispery voices, but it's only been a few days. "And, it's in your best interest to do as much as you possibly can to avoid consuming *human* brains or flesh."

"Eww." She shivers.

"Good." I hold her hands. "That your reaction is 'eww' is a great sign. However, you need to be prepared for the probable reality that if you are confronted with the sight or smell of human brains, you may think of it in a completely different way, especially if you've ended up in a state of near-starvation when your mental faculties start shutting down."

A distant stare comes over her.

"Mindy?"

She blinks, shakes her head, and forces a smile. "Oh, yeah. I was just remembering that image on the TV. The guy who like popped open all over the sidewalk."

"I know it's going to smell wonderful and be more tempting than anything you've ever seen… but you need to be strong. The thing inside you is going to want to take you over, and if you keep giving in to it, everything that is Mindy Hogan could disappear."

She shivers.

"If you have a dark master, it might try to offer a compromise."

I know Dracula had some sort of working agreement, but I also suspect the one-time prince had given in a little too much. My guess... Cornelius had been calling the shots for a long time, and Dracula was only occasionally permitted out. Then again, that was all a moot point if Dracula the man had been destroyed after the fall of the Void.

"So, a dark master is like having a roommate

from hell… only in a more literal sense," says Mindy.

"Right."

"Are they demons?" Mindy gasps.

"No. Not exactly. They were once people, evil people, who used dark magic to cheat death and avoid the punishment the afterlife had in store for them."

"But now they've all escaped from their prison."

"Most, not all. Some are still bound to their human hosts."

"So, most likely, I am not hosting an actual dark master. Just some of that latent dark energy."

"That sounds about right. But it's not random. This was pre-meditated."

"With the help of demons."

"Dark masters and demons working together to bring forth something potentially catastrophic to humans. Seems about right."

"And all of it was set in motion because of the collective consciousness of mankind's belief in zombies?"

"Belief might be too strong. Not sure many people actually believe in zombies. But being front and center in so many minds was enough to set it in motion."

I spend a while talking about how the creative force or The Universe or whatever it is tends to respond to people's beliefs. If enough of a collective consciousness develops around an idea, it manifests in reality. Zombies have been present in fiction for a long time, but these days, there seems to be a growing number of people who've started taking the idea of a zombie apocalypse as something they think might actually happen.

"And the dark masters were aware of this?"

"Hard to guess what they knew in the Void. The demons might have sensed a coalescing of something that might be called 'zombie energy.' At some point, a plan was hatched."

"And I'm a result of that plan."

"I think so, yes."

"So the thing inside me..."

"Might be less a thing... and closer to intelligent energy. Maybe even black magic."

"Gee, way to pick a girl up, Sam."

I shrug. "We're asking questions pretty much never asked before. We're doing our best to answer them."

"I know. I can sort of... feel it inside of me. It almost feels like it swirling through me, around organs and bones, through skin tissue. Moving, moving, anxious, alert, poisonous. But no real thought. None that I can detect. But something is there... and it seems to have purpose."

"What purpose?"

Mindy closes her eyes, and sits quietly, with no attempt to breathe. I might need to work on her about that. In some situations, she might need to consciously think about simulating taking breaths, if only to appear normal and not draw attention.

"To make more," she says. "Lots and lots

more."

"How?" I ask.

"Biting. The bigger and deeper the better... faster that way. A bite, exposure to the blood stream... causes the thing inside me to flow free... to expand, to grow."

Despite my sudden alarm at her words, I nod. "It's one entity, perhaps. Magic or otherwise. It's like one of those root systems... one entity, connected to many, many others."

"Pando," says Mindy. "I just learned about it in my biology class. Aspen trees connected by identical genetic markers, but comprised of like a single, huge root system."

I nod. "Took the words right of my mouth. And, yeah, that. Zombies... one mind, one entity, growing and learning and spreading."

"It wants out," says Mindy. "It wants out so bad."

I nod, taking her hand. "Take your attention off it. Learn to lock it away, learn to seal it away and shove it deep down inside you."

"Will you teach me how?"

"Of course, sweetie."

"I... I don't know if I can control it."

"You can. I know you can."

She nods, takes a breath, then forgets to let it out. I can almost see her mind looking for anything else to focus on, anything but the darkness within. Then she nods, gives me a small smile, and rummages the milk crate nightstand and pulls out a pack of Hostess cupcakes. "Used to keep these around for when I needed an energy boost."

"Not a bad idea. They'll basically last forever."

She laughs. "Looks like I can still eat whatever I want."

"I don't think you're getting much nutrition from it, but I could be wrong. You might actually be able to process it… since you can eat solids, so to speak. Normal vampires can't eat anything other than blood. So, that you *can* eat things could mean it does something for you, though you might need a huge amount of 'not meat' to derive any benefit. Then again, werewolves eat normal food, too. But they're kinda weird. Their obligatory meals are only once a month."

"Obligatory meals?" She tilts her head.

"What our supernatural nature demands. I used to need blood around twice a week. Now, I have to feed daily—on energy, mind you—but feeding has gotten *so* much easier. Werewolves need a large amount of raw meat once a month. Some of them prefer rotting meat." I shudder, as does Mindy. "Though, a friend of mine mentioned mermaids. He said they tend to eat with a frequency close to humans, though either dead flesh or living seafood."

"Stop talking about mermaids," says Mindy. "You're making me jealous."

I laugh.

"So what else is real?" she asks.

"Well. Vamps, werewolves, apparently those things you don't want me mentioning, there's a critter that's kind of like Frankenstein's monster. You've seen a demon. And, apparently, there are zombies. But you may be something else. Someone I know suggested you're a revenant."

"A rev-a-what?"

"It's a supposedly fictional monster that sounds a lot like you. An undead human who doesn't rot and still has all their mental faculties. This is all still new to me."

"Me too."

We stare at each other for a few minutes.

"Oh, and there are witches."

"Well, duh."

Mindy hits the shower to get plaster dust out of her hair, then hurries out the door to catch a 3 p.m. class. I avail myself of the shower as well for the same reason. To escape boredom, I decide to take a nap and pass out.

Hard.

Chapter Twenty-Three
The Bright Side of Pale

I wake upon Mindy walking back into the room. One strange side effect of how I sleep—which hasn't changed—is the ability to sense when someone approaches. She appears to be in reasonably good spirits until she sits in front of her computer. Out of nowhere, she bursts into tears.

"Undead mood swing?" I ask.

She sniffle-laughs. "No. I got fired from both of my jobs."

"Ugh."

"I understand why they did it. I mean I disappeared for three days. Still sucks. Hopefully, I can beg my parents to cover my share of the rent this month."

"Well you did get the $500, right?" I ask.

"Oh, that…" She shakes her head. "No. It was

fake, too. I checked the jeans I had on that day. I had a wad of Playboy pages stuck in my pocket. I saw it as money."

"Damn. Well, if you need help finding a job or want your old one back, I can"—I wag my eyebrows—"*talk* to the manager for you."

She grins. "Being way strong is cool and all, but I wish I had mind powers. That must come in *so* handy."

"Yeah. It does. Why do you think the vast majority of the world still thinks vampires are fictional?"

"Oh. Good point."

The other roommate, a blonde named Alisha, pokes her head in a little after five to invite Mindy to a party. She politely declines, claiming her 'cousin' is here visiting and it would be rude. Alisha suggests I go along.

And that's how I wind up attending a frat party as a forty-four-year-old mother of two.

But I'm in disguise as a twenty-seven-year-old who could pass for a little younger in the right lighting. I go mostly because Mindy needs the morale boost, and I want to keep an eye on her. About half of that 'eye keeping' is me trying to make sure she doesn't eat anyone and the other half is being wary for outside threats. I'm doubtful that this is the work of a single demon or a handful of dark masters. First of all, demons never operate alone. And second, I was suppressing their prized pupil.

Meaning, after all the work they'd done to begin

the zombie invasion... here comes Sam Moon to once again thwart their nefarious schemes.

Thank the good Lord no one could hear my thoughts. Thwart? Nefarious? Oh, yeah, Tammy would have had a field day with those words.

Then again, that last demon was on the strong side, so who knows? That said, why did the dark masters need to bring in demons? Well, demons are free radicals, let loose once I killed their creator, the Devil 1.0. How much they could think, I hadn't a clue. I certainly hadn't sat across from a demon and had a smoothie, like I'd done with the Devil. Still, they must have some semblance of synapses. Clearly, they had worked with and took commands from the Devil.

Oh, hell no...

With the Devil gone, and the demons—who may or may not be mindless—free to roam the Earth had the newly emerged dark masters somehow taken control of them? Had the dark masters, in fact, become the demons' new masters? But how? I didn't know, but these creatures—which had sprung straight from the mind of the Devil himself—were the ultimate henchmen, so to speak. Heavies who could guard, defend... and possess.

And one of my jobs as the Angel of Death's assassin was to do away with these things. Great. I'm going to be busy. Hoping this wasn't somehow true, I did my best to enjoy this party.

About forty minutes into it—and damn, what the hell is it these kids listen to these days?—some boy gives Mindy a drink. Five minutes later, he looks perplexed and walks away. I sidle up beside her.

"Looks like we were right about roofies," I mutter.

"Huh?" she shouts over the music.

I lean close and talk right into her ear. "That guy slipped you something. See how confused he is over there? He can't figure out why you're not delirious."

She blinks at the cup, at him, back at the cup. "I thought it tasted a bit weird." She glares at him. "You roofied me!"

The guy tries to run, but she grabs his jacket, swings him around, and drives him face first into the floor. His head bounces up with a dense *thud* that most people seem to think belonged to the sad excuse for music blaring in here. Fortunately, she didn't kill the guy, but he is *out.*

When Mindy draws her foot back to kick him, I grab her arms and pull her away. "Easy, tiger. You got him."

"Ooh!" She fumes. After a moment, she stares at me, blinks, and starts sobbing.

Crap. I don't even have to see into her head to know I'm about to have the 'I can never have kids' talk. We wind up in an upstairs bedroom, the music shaking the floor beneath our feet. The whole 'I didn't really want kids but now I can't have them and it's depressing as hell' conversation goes in circles for the better part of the next half hour.

I share the same feelings I had when that realization hit me. Of course, by then I already had my two. So I was irrationally depressed over not being able to have any *more* kids. To be honest, I'd never even thought of trying for more until I suddenly had no choice in the matter. We commiserate over our uterine dysfunction for a while before she jokingly suggests she probably shouldn't be around kids at least until she knows for a fact she won't freak out and lose control of herself.

My phone rings.

It's Fang.

"Oh, cool. Hang on. Need to get this."

She nods.

"What's up, Moon Dance?"

I sigh. "I've got a rather interesting case…" I proceed to tell him about Mindy and everything I've observed before, including Anthony suggesting the term 'revenant.'

"Oh, yeah. That's a thing. Could be. Heard some old folklore awhile back. They're kind of like a 'master zombie' yanno? They supposedly have powers to influence or control lesser undead."

"What the heck is a lesser undead?"

"Anyone who works in telemarketing," mutters Fang.

"Oh, very funny."

"Seriously… some of the simpler Lichtenstein monsters may count as that… the ones with piss-weak parasites in them. And some things I've read about those alchemists lead me to believe one or two of them may have reanimated dead things in the past. But those stories make them sound like ye-olde traditional moaning, shambling sort of zombie. So this girl looks normal?"

I give Mindy a once-over. "Yeah. Other than being *really* pale, she's fairly hard to tell apart from a normal person."

"Fairly hard means possible."

"Yeah. Her eyes have a faint haze in them. Most people probably wouldn't notice or mistake it for a medical issue." I cover the phone and ask her, "Do you have problems seeing?"

"What? No. Well, only when you first found me, back when it was really bad. I don't notice anything now. Though, it's not as dark as it should be in here. Oh, and I can still hear people talking downstairs."

"Well, they say zombies have excellent hearing." And by 'they,' I'm referring to Anthony. "You can also see in the dark I bet."

"How's that work?" asks Mindy.

"Long story. I'll give you the details later, but for now, know there's this energy flowing around in everything and you've been awakened to it." I turn back to the phone. "Anything else you can think of, Fang-a-licious?"

He chuckles. "Nothing comes to mind but I can look into it for you."

"Thanks. I owe you one."

"Any time. And you need to stop by in person sometime. Hang out for a night. Bring the hairy bastard if you want. Hey, as soon as the paperwork for the house is all signed, I'm going to have a party there. You absolutely must attend."

"Sure. Count me in. You're right. It has been too long. Talk to you soon," I say.

"Take care of yourself, Moon Dance."

I grin at the smile I can hear in his voice, and hang up.

"Okay," says Mindy. "So I'm not a"—she pantomimes a moaning zombie—"shambler. But I'm still weird as fuck. Sorry."

"That's fine, Look on the bright side. As long as you stay fed, you look reasonably normal… just a bit pale."

Mindy pulls her hands down her long, brown hair. "Think I should go goth and dye it black?"

"Up to you."

"Nah." She tosses her hair behind her back with a twist of her head. "My parents would kill me."

Chapter Twenty-Four
Inevitable

Mindy spends the next maybe hour or so going around in mental circles.

She can't make up her mind if she should tell her parents the truth or try to carry on like nothing unusual happened. On one hand, she can't bear the thought of them finding out she technically died, especially if she starts falling apart. However, her parents have always been somewhat on the coddling side, so she thinks having their support coping could be a big help.

There's also the matter of school, though on that note, I do encourage her to keep going. Considering she doesn't have an awkward relationship with sunlight, there's no reason she can't at least make a passing attempt at the whole normal life thing… at least until people start noticing she still looks twenty years old thirty years from now.

"Did you tell your parents?" asks Mindy.

"No… they still don't know. But then again, I was thirty-one when it happened and I didn't have the closest relationship with them."

"Oh wow, really?"

"Yeah, things were kinda strained between us."

Mindy grins. "No, I mean that you were thirty-one. Damn, girl, you don't look much older than me."

"Good genes." I laugh. "Honestly, it's the vampiric thing. Over the first few days after my change, the clock turned back a bit. I used to have some wrinkles around my eyes and I lost the weight I put on having kids."

"That's cool." She fidgets. "Ugh. I wish I knew if I was going to fall apart. Okay, so it's a little vain of me, but I don't wanna rot."

I give her a sympathetic look. "Totally there with you on that. However, you still don't smell like a walking corpse, so I'm guessing your appearance is pretty much static."

"Static? Like electricity?"

"It means no change."

"Whew." She flops back on her bed. "So do you think I should tell them?"

My pocket picks that moment to beep.

A text from Tammy flashes on the screen when I pull the phone out: 'Everything's okay. We're alive and the house hasn't burned down.'

I start typing back a 'that's good to hear,' but

before I can send, she adds 'yet.'

Chuckling, I respond with 'Good. Keep it that way. No burning. Fire bad.'

'When R U coming home?'

I glance at Mindy, ponder a moment, then send, 'Probably soon. Almost have things sorted here. Helping someone settle in.'

'Can I inv ppl 4 a party tomorrow?'

My eyebrows go up. Well… she *is* seventeen. I'd rather have her in a safe environment. 'No alcohol and you will clean up after.'

'Holy shit really?' A pause. 'Umm. I mean cool! Will clean up and no drinx. UR awesome.'

'Everything else ok?'

'Yeah. Ant is on computer, lol.'

'Okay. CU soon.'

I stick the phone back in my pocket and sigh. Perhaps giving Tammy the okay to have a party in the house is going to bite me in the ass, but I need to let her know I trust her—at least unless she gives me a reason not to, satanic mental influence notwithstanding. Much better she has a party at home and things get slightly out of hand than she's at a stranger's place and… yeah.

"Who was that?" asks Mindy.

"My daughter."

She blinks. "Wow. Oh, that's right. You already said you had a kid."

"Two. And before you ask, I had them before my change."

"Oh." She sighs and starts to slouch, but snaps

upright again, staring. "Wait, you're still in contact with them?"

"Yeah."

"Didn't do the fake death thing? Like do they know you're a vampire?"

I nod. "I tried to keep it hidden as long as I could but they're both pretty sharp and figured it out eventually."

"So your family knows." She folds her arms.

"Just the kids and my sister… and a friend of mine on the police force. But, yeah, since you can't wipe out people's memories, you should probably try to be as subtle as possible. Though, anyone you spend a significant amount of time with is going to eventually notice things aren't quite normal."

Mindy giggles. "Yeah, I think they might start asking questions when I eat four pounds of raw beef." Her smile dies a slow death, and she winds up giving me the forlorn kitten face after a few minutes. "You're not going to stay around here, are you?"

"I'm afraid I can't. I need to get back to my family. I'm from California."

"Yeah. Figured that since your van has Cali plates." She swipes at her hair, moving it off her face. "I think I want to tell my parents about what happened."

"Okay," I say in as comforting a tone as I can manage.

She stares down. "I don't think I can do this totally alone, yanno?"

"Well, you wouldn't be *totally* alone. You can always call me."

"Thanks. I probably will. But I need to at least try. Hey, if they don't take it well, can you make them forget about it?"

"If I do it fast enough, I should be able to erase it without a problem. If they've been stewing on it for a while, it becomes harder to completely eliminate."

Mindy scuffs her feet side to side on the rug. "Is there any way I could maybe ask you to give me a lift home? I don't have a car. It's like an hour or so away."

Part of me wants to grumble in frustration at another delay, but this poor girl looks so sad I don't have the heart to refuse. "Okay. When do you want to go? You're not skipping classes are you?"

She grins. "No, *Mom*. My next class isn't until Thursday, and it's Tuesday night."

I check the time on my cell phone. "Actually, it's Wednesday morning." I chuckle.

"Still. I have all day tomorrow. And I'm not planning to bail on college. Mom and Dad are spending a lot of money for this. Though… if I had a car, I might move back home. I'm only living in Tucson because I don't have wheels."

After being a bloodsucking vampire for thirteen years it's strange to look at a clock, notice it past one in the morning... and yawn. "Your parents are probably asleep now, right?"

Mindy nods.

"Why don't we go in the morning then?"

"Okay. Umm. I feel kinda bad asking you to sleep on my floor again."

"It doesn't bother me really. When I'm out, I'm *out*. I could sleep on a morgue slab and not be uncomfortable."

"Little too on point." She shivers.

"True…"

Considering it's 1:33 in the morning, we don't do much 'hanging out.' Mindy goes to sleep as soon as we plan to head to her hometown, a little place called Canelo about an hour south of here. I check it on the GPS app with my phone. That thing says closer to an hour and twenty, but it's not factoring for the driving habits of a twenty-something. It then occurs to me that Tammy sent me a text message at around 12:38 a.m. And that Anthony was still awake at that hour too since she mentioned he was on the computer. In my head, I picture Tammy getting home from her friend's house, finding a note or something from Anthony that I popped in before, and sending me an 'all clear' text before going straight to bed.

I hope she went straight to bed.

Am I being overly strict by requiring a seventeen-year-old be asleep by midnight? I don't exactly have the best frame of reference. My parents never cared what time we passed out at night. I remember staying up 'til midnight when I was nine. Of course, that made waking up for school such hell I usually crashed around ten. But they never set a bedtime.

Meh. She's less than a year away from eighteen, and I can't see myself enforcing any kind of 'bedtime' rules once she's a legal adult. I need her to listen to me on the important things like 'don't try taking on any greater extraplanar evils alone,' so I don't make a big deal about the trivial stuff like bedtime.

So, yeah. I flop in my temporary 'bed' and lay there feeling maudlin about my children no longer being little. I make the mistake of wondering where we'd be if I'd never become a vampire. Tammy wouldn't be the mother of all telepaths, Anthony would be dead. Danny would probably still be alive, still a lawyer, and never would've gotten involved in that strip club. The 'Anthony being dead' part trumps all.

No regrets.

For the tiniest moment, I find myself almost grateful to Elizabeth for picking me. In a roundabout sort of way, if not for her, my son would be gone.

I wonder how she'd have reacted to me feeling grateful for something she did. A part of me thinks she might've done the human thing and tried not to exploit the moment of a mother's greatest dread. Could it be that Elizabeth is *not* a complete monster? Her feelings of loathing and disgust at the Red Rider for what he did to those innocent girls had felt genuine. But then again, so had her 'anger' at me for trying to contain her… when containing her had been a lie all along Ugh. I shouldn't go down that mental road. The things she's done? How could someone like that have the least bit of empathy for me mourning the theoretical death of my then six-year-old son?

Anyway. Can't quite sleep yet.

I borrow Mindy's laptop and do some research. Trying to look up the word 'revenant' leads me to a movie with that title, and even a wiki article. Though that describes them as appearing to be rotting and makes reference to a supposed real-life revenant as described by a man named William of Newburgh.

Impossible to tell if the guy encountered anything real or spun a yarn. I find a bunch more links to movies, none of which bear any resemblance to Mindy's condition. One article says they are returned dead who were evil in life. Another describes a guy mauled by a bear. My son's use of the word came from his video game, and 'basically a zombie that's still intelligent and doesn't rot' so far is the closest thing I can find to Mindy. So I'm pretty much left to guess for myself.

She'd been dead for three days before I found her and, while she had almost no coordination, couldn't see well, and couldn't talk much beyond moaning, she didn't stink or appear rotted. After three days in the Arizona sun, a corpse with plans to rot would've been well underway. I feel safe in ruling decay out. Though, severe starvation may or may not affect that.

Mindy's ridiculously strong, and evidently

tough. No idea if she has any kind of Talos-like transformation in there, but then again, she's not even a week into her new existence yet. It took me quite a while to find that… which scares me how fast Anthony found his. Then again, he's an entirely different situation, having become what he is *before* a dark master (even a dinky one like my ex-husband) decided to possess him.

The word 'zombie' makes me think of those things from the TV show my kids like. Rotting corpses barely able to walk, unable to speak, and driven entirely by hunger. Mindy's some kind of 'zombie 2.0' type critter. And while it may not be accurate to folklore, I'm going to think of her as a revenant anyway. Mostly because I'm biased to my son suggesting it. Not that I really expected to find too much useful information about paranormal things on Google, but I keep on reading for another twenty minutes and get no closer to understanding what I'm dealing with.

Right.

This is uncharted ground.

Wonderful. Since I'm not getting anywhere, and it's getting close to two in the morning, I yawn and sack out. This whole 'going to sleep at night' thing is nice.

J.R. RAIN & MATTHEW S. COX

Chapter Twenty-Five
Living Impaired

Around four in the morning, I wake when Mindy gets up and walks out of her bedroom.

A moment later, the *clunk* of a door elsewhere in the house closing breaks the silence, then the *clonk* of a toilet lid. I feel a bit like the naturalist David Attenborough and am half tempted to go check out what's happening purely for scientific purposes. Or maybe Jane Goodall since I'm sharing living space with the subject at the moment. Then again, Mindy is a lot less hairy than a community of chimpanzees... and a lot more dead. I don't bother getting up to watch her in the bathroom. Bit awkward. After a few minutes, a flush, then the creak of a door.

Mindy autopilots back into the room. I've felt like a zombie in the middle of the night (or day) while staggering to the bathroom, but the girl's taking it a bit literally. She walks straight into the footboard of her bed, trips over it on her face, and lays there with her butt sticking up in the air, not even bothering to crawl the rest of the way onto the mattress.

Soft *thumps* go by in the hallway, one of the roommates walking. I don't pay her much attention until the gagging and choking starts.

"What the fuck," rasps a young woman. "Oh, god, that's foul…"

A louder *thud* makes me picture someone falling to their knees. Brief vomiting/splashing noises follow, then the unmistakable *thump* of a body hitting the floor.

I throw the covers off me, squeeze past Mindy's butt, and dash out the bedroom door.

The blonde roommate, Alisha, is laying on the floor of the bathroom near the toilet in a yellowish gossamer nightie that doesn't leave a whole lot to the imagination. Puke's spattered on the toilet, as well as the floor near her face.

An urge to retch hits me, but not from the sight of her vomit.

Imagine a stink so horrible that a normal person would be on the floor throwing up before they consciously realized they smelled something. An aerosol horror lurks in the bathroom, strongest near the toilet. Despite my being a vampire, I nearly throw up as well. I've only encountered a smell like this once in my life back when I worked for HUD. I think I'd been on the job four months or so when we went to do a property inspection and found an elderly resident dead in his bed. The man had been deceased for around ten days in August with no AC. What I initially assumed to be patterned wallpaper turned out to be flies.

And yes. I threw up. So did Ernie Montoya. That had been pretty early in my career, before I partnered with Chad. Ernie had 'seen some shit' as they say, and the stink even got him. This poor girl started to throw up and put her face over the bowl—only she got closer to the source of the stink… and passed clean out from it.

Note to self. Do not follow Mindy into the bathroom. I should probably suggest she get a spray or something, but then again, garden variety Glade isn't going to scratch this. Well, I can't leave the girl on her face. Being a mother is about 50% cleaning up puke (or other bodily fluids) 30% worrying about your kids, 10% feeling proud of them, 5% wondering why the hell I ever decided to get pregnant in the first place, and 5% wanting to keep them small and protected for their entire life.

Puke I can handle.

While she's out cold, I take the liberty of making her forget the stink. Mercifully, she only got a little of the puke on her nightie. I wipe it off with a wet rag, and carry her back to bed.

That done, I go open the damn bathroom window.

***

I wake up around eleven the next morning, Wednesday, to find Mindy on the chair by her computer desk.

"Morning," I say.

"Hey." She spins around to smile at me. The smell of strawberry shampoo hangs in the air. "Are you still up for giving me a ride home?"

"Yeah. Though, we need to talk about a small detail."

She tilts her head. "Gas money?"

"No. I'll tell you on the ride."

"Cool."

Both roommates are away at class, so it's no trouble getting the Momvan out of the driveway. Mindy gives me her parents' address, and once I've loaded it up in the Garmin, we're on the way.

"So, what did you want to talk about?" She leans against her door, almost sideways in the seat.

"Forgive the indelicate question, but you went to the bathroom last night. Was it the first time since you changed?"

"Became an awesome zombie? Yeah. Why?"

"Let's just say you're evidently carrying a weapons-grade payload."

"Huh?"

"*Bad* things happened to whatever you ate before it came out." I describe Alisha fainting after throwing up all over the bathroom.

Mindy's face briefly looks human again, color

wise. I think she's blushing. "Does that mean I'm rotting inside?"

"If you were rotting inside, you'd be all swollen up and purple."

She lifts her T-shirt up to examine her pasty-white stomach. "Holy crap. I have abs. I haven't had abs since I was eighteen."

"So like an eon ago."

She laughs.

"Vampires lose a little weight too. I think it's related to the 'being dead' thing."

"Ahh." She drops the shirt. "So, I guess I should get some air fresheners. How bad was it?"

"Corpse left in the sun for a week bad."

She cringes. "Are we really talking about my... poo?"

"I'm not sure whatever came out of you still qualifies as poo." I chuckle. "But, you should be aware that it can make you stand out as not normal."

"Right." She twirls her hair around her finger while staring into nowhere for a bit. "Umm. I just realized that if I spend time around my parents they're going to know something's wrong. Remember how I said I was always so fidgety?"

"Yeah."

"I'm not bouncing around and acting like a chihuahua on crack anymore. They're going to think I'm doing pot. Or depressed. Or something. So, I hope they don't freak out."

"Fingers crossed."

She shifts to face forward in the seat. "Promise you'll make them forget I told them anything if they flip out?"

"No worries. I got your back. I'll just follow your lead."

***

The ride to Canelo is pretty boring.

Desert on all sides, scrub brush, hills. It takes us about an hour and nine minutes, after which we roll into this area that's more a loose affiliation of buildings than a 'town' per se. If ever a place existed that a potentially contagious zombie should call home, this would be it. We still haven't figured out if her bite can transmit anything… and I'm not too keen on testing that. But if I was a betting woman, I would bet 'hell, yeah.'

Mindy directs me around a few small roads, one of them paved only with dirt, to a large-ish one-story home with a covered porch spanning the entire width of the front. While big, the place doesn't appear in the best repair, though they have solar panels and a satellite dish. An old pink bicycle leans against the steps, probably lying where Mindy left it years ago.

"Do you have any siblings?"

"Yeah, a younger brother, but he doesn't live at home now. Just me and the parents," she says, a strange placidity in her voice.

I'm guessing familiar surroundings help her

somewhat. We hop out and I follow her up to the front door. It's unlocked, and she goes right in without knocking or ringing the bell.

"Mom? Dad?" calls Mindy.

A brown-haired man in a blue button-down shirt enters from an archway on the right with a pleasantly surprised expression. The guy looks like the generic 'dad' from a TV sitcom, closing in on fifty, squarish jaw, on the tall, thin side.

"Hey, sweetie." He hugs Mindy, then gives me a curious glance. "Who's this?"

I about cough when I sense the guy dreading the next words out of his daughter's mouth are going to be something like she's in love with me. That leaves me blank and unable to come up with anything to say for a few seconds.

"Oh, that's Samantha," says Mindy, jumping in. "She's umm, helping me with something."

A woman walks in from a small corridor leading straight back from the living room. She's sandy blonde, rocking the flannel and jeans look, and probably a few years younger than Mr. Hogan. "Mindy! What are you doing here?" Her mother hurries into a hug. "What a surprise. Is everything okay?"

"Sorta." Mindy bites her lip. "Some weird stuff's been going on. I just needed to see you guys."

The man approaches me with an offered hand. "Arthur Hogan."

"Samantha Moon," I say, shaking hands.

"That's my wife, Louise. What exactly are you helping our daughter with?"

Mindy forces a smile. "She's an occult specialist."

"Occult?" Louise blinks. "Since when do you believe in that stuff?"

"Uhh, since odd things started happening." Mindy bites her lip. "I found this bracelet on the ground and I think it had a curse on it or something."

"Oh. We don't put much stock in that sort of thing," says Art. Frowning, he looks at me. "What exactly is it you do?"

"Mostly, I'm a private investigator… but I have some experience dealing with matters of an occult nature."

Louise raises both eyebrows. "You sound rather serious."

"It can be. There was something affecting Mindy, but it's dealt with." I glance sideways at her. "She's had a bit of a scare and needed a dose of familiar surroundings."

"And how did you two meet?" asks Art.

"We just sort of ran into each other, Dad."

He squints at her. "You're not experimenting with things, are you?"

"No." Mindy looks down.

"Drugs?"

"No, Dad. Sheesh."

"Are you sick, dear?" asks Louise. "You seem a bit, I dunno, listless."

"Maybe." Mindy picks at her shirt. "I haven't been sleeping well since this thing started."

"The thing with the bracelet?" asks Louise.

"Yeah."

"Is that it?" asks Art, pointing at her arm.

Mindy twirls the charm bracelet around her wrist. "Yeah, but it's cleansed now."

The parents exchange a glance.

"Well, thank God for that," says Louise, winking.

"Come on in, have a seat," says Art, gesturing at the sofa.

Louise runs off to the kitchen to get iced tea… and we proceed to pass an incredibly awkward hour or so sipping it as Mindy talks about school. So far, she's chickened out telling her parents about anything more. Which is fine. Let her work up the nerve. I wasn't in a terrible rush to leave, anyway. Mindy next expresses her frustrations at barely making ends meet, and tells them that she lost both her jobs because she called out sick last weekend.

"Well, you're clearly sick," says Louise. "I can tell by looking at you."

Art leans over and puts a hand on her forehead. "You're pale as a ghost, and clammy. And cold."

"Yeah." Mindy breaks eye contact. "Been feeling weird, too. But I'm getting better. And it's not like it's *that* hard to find a crappy job, although I did kind of like the waitressing one."

"I could talk to her boss," I say, smiling. "I've been known to be persuasive."

"Can you guys help me with my rent this month? I'm short like two-hundred."

Her father nods. "Shame landlords don't take students into account."

"Well, I'd stay here and commute if I had a car."

"We talked about this, hon." Louise pats her hand. "We don't want you driving an hour each way, especially at night. It's too dangerous."

"Yeah, I could drive tired and go off the road and hit, I dunno... some *sand*." She sighs.

Her father chuckles. "It's not you we're worried about. It's all the other idiots."

While the Hogan family debates driving and their twenty-year-old daughter, I lean back in the sofa and confront the truth of me having to deal with a seventeen-year-old on a learner's permit. It won't be long before she has a full-on license and I get to experience the pure joy of worrying myself sick whenever she's going somewhere. And of course, she's going to want a car of her own as soon as she has a license... and especially after I come into some serious money soon. And, naturally, she's going to know exactly how much money I have.

For now, I'm driving a fourteen-year-old van for more reasons than pure sentimentality. I'd learned long ago how to forfeit my needs for others. In this, to put food on the table for my kids. I didn't need a big monthly car expense, especially during the lean months of work. So, yeah, if Tammy wants her own car, she's going to need her own job. Or she can have the minivan once I treat myself to a new car. Either way, she's going to need to earn her own money for gas and insurance—oh, crap.

I stare into space as a heavy realization slaps me across the face like a clown with a forty-pound raw salmon. Why else would an incredibly telepathic girl about to hit driving age want to go to Las Vegas… so she can lie about her age, go into a casino, and cheat like crazy. Like poker or something where she can see what cards her opponents are holding.

I grapple with the question of should I be angry with her for that, or if I'm now the one going over the deep end. She might not have even considered that. But, knowing Tammy—she's industrious, crafty, and far from stupid—I bet it's crossed her mind. She's also inherited Danny's unfortunate tendency to get something in her head she wants and have this near manic drive to accomplish it. I just hope she didn't inherit all his scheming. Then again, she could just be making a joke.

Time for a five-percent moment. I want to compress her back into a sweet, innocent six-year-old and hold her like a doll. Ugh at the teen years. On second thought, once the deal goes through with my sire's mansion, maybe I will get her a car... a reasonable and safe car. It's the least I could do for my baby girl, whom I put through so much.

And knowing me, I'll probably just keep using the Momvan until it breaks down beyond repair.

"That's great mom. Sam?" asks Mindy, snapping me out of my spinning thoughts.

I glance over at her, feeling a bit like I'd fallen asleep in class and the teacher just called on me. "Sorry. Was lost to my thoughts."

"Oh. It's okay. My parents want us to stay for dinner, but it's okay if you need to go. I'm sure they can give me a ride back to Tucson."

If not for my recent dream of being hip-deep in a zombie invasion, I would have. I can't shake the unsettling feeling that I need to stay right where I am. "Oh, that's okay. I don't mind. Still working out some of the particulars of the... haunting."

She nods, knowing that I am, in fact, referring to her newfound condition.

Still clueless, the parents exchange concerned glances.

"C'mon. I'll show you my room." Mindy stands.

A bit of her old self comes out as she heads across the house and down a hallway like a sugared-up tween excited to have a friend over. The display of energy appears to placate her parents in an 'oh, that's more like her' sort of way. I offer them a polite smile and follow.

Her room is pretty typical, I suppose, for a girl who grew up in the middle of effing nowhere. She likes horses apparently, to the tune of three pictures and numerous figurines. The furniture has a rustic, older look. Yeah, it's clear her parents aren't loaded, though they aren't *poor* either. A particleboard computer desk stands against the left wall, full of books and cheap jewelry boxes. The spot where the laptop had been is obvious by its emptiness.

"So, yeah. I choked," says Mindy. "I couldn't do it to them. As soon as I looked into their eyes, I couldn't tell them what happened to me."

"I can do it for you if you like… and wipe it out if they can't handle it."

She kicks her sneaker at the not-quite-pink-anymore rug. "I dunno. Can I have a little more time? I'd prefer to tell them myself."

"Well…" I almost say I'm going to drive home after dinner, but that damn dream keeps my butt planted here. "Okay. I suppose I can wait."

"Sorry. I just…" She paces around. "I'm freakin' dead. How do you tell your parents that?"

"Might be no easy way, other than jumping in. But yeah, I get it. I'll wait."

I catch her in a hug right as she bursts into tears. Mindy presses her face into my shoulder, trying to muffle herself. She clings, sobbing desperately for a few seconds.

Crack. A spear of pain jolts my side.

Mindy looks up; tears shut off like a light switch. "What was that?"

"A rib I think," I wheeze. "You're damn strong."

She gasps. "I'm so sorry…"

I hold up a 'hang on a sec' finger, searching for meditative calm amid the pain. As soon as the click of knitting bones begins, the agony stops. "Okay. Back almost to normal. Give it about twenty minutes." Whatever sort of immortal I've become is a definite upgrade over my old vampire self. Used to take hours for bones to knit.

"God, that's weird."

"Hey, we're both pretty damn hard to kill." I wink. "I bet you could bounce off the grille of a tractor-trailer sailing down the highway and sit up with only a mild nosebleed."

She cry-laughs. "Oh, come on. I'm not *that* tough. Still. I'm"—she drops her voice to a whisper—"dead."

"Eh…" I shrug. "You get used to it."

We sit around for some time talking about random stuff. I try to coax her into searching for the flame in her thoughts similar to how I call Talos or teleport. While making a series of weird faces, she stops abruptly, staring at me.

"Okay, that's weird."

"What's weird?" I scratch at my head. "I can't see into your head. You need to give me a little more than 'that's weird.'"

She puffs air, rolling her eyes like an annoyed teenager. "I was getting there. Didn't see any flame, but when I closed my eyes, I saw this strange lump far off in the blackness. It took me a moment to figure out what I was seeing, but I'm sure it's Tulip, my dog."

I tilt my head.

"She died like a year ago, and we buried her out back." Mindy points her arm to the right and somewhat behind. "Over there. It's like I can see her bones."

"Hmm. Maybe you have some kind of 'corpse radar' for hunting brains to eat?"

"Eww. Like dig people up and eat their brains?"

I shrug. "Who knows? Some supernaturals prefer decaying food. A werewolf I'm acquainted with only eats deer that are well into decomposing. It's kinda nasty… but to him, it's filet mignon."

"What's that?"

"Filet mignon?"

She nods.

"Expensive steak."

"Oh. Never heard of it."

A knock at the door precedes Art poking his head in. "Hey, hon. Dinner's ready." He nods invitingly at me.

We head out to the dining room and have a nice meal of pot roast, mashed potatoes, and string beans. Painfully normal. Dinner conversation is a little strained as Mindy keeps dodging her parents' attempts to ask about the 'occult thing.' It further strains when they take note of her voracious appetite. I have half a mind to think she could kill that entire pot roast by herself, but she restrains herself to enough meat to feed two large men.

"All right. Something's up," says Art. "You're never this quiet… or still... or hungry."

Mindy looks at me with a 'get ready to hit the history eraser button' face.

"Sweetie?" asks Louise. "What's wrong?"

"I have to tell you guys something, but I don't

want to alarm you." Mindy grabs the napkin and cries into it.

Art gives me the side eye. "It's all right, dear. Even if you're, umm… seeing a wom—"

"Dad. No. It's not that. I was really stupid. I did something super dumb and got hurt."

The parents stare at her.

Mindy explains about the medical testing thing, the $500, and how despite being scared she went there anyway.

"They got you hooked on the acid?" asks Louise.

"No, mom. I'm pretty sure they killed me. I'm like a zombie now or something."

"Um, what?" asks her dad. I note the sweat beginning on his brow.

"You know, like 'living impaired?'" Mindy fidgets her hands in her lap. "Sam's been helping me try and figure out what's happened to me, and it's not as bad as it sounds."

"Zombie? What's going on?" asks Louise. With each word, her voice rises an octave.

"You tried some drugs and you're having a flashback or bad trip, right?" says Art. His sweat is beading.

"No, Dad. I wish. They gave me something and it turned me into whatever I am now." Mindy gets up, walks around the table, and picks up her father and his chair with minimal effort.

"Whoa," he yells, flailing his arms.

Louise faints.

"Mom!" Mindy puts her father back down and runs over to scoop her mother off the floor. She sets her back in her chair. "Mom…. wake up!"

Louise's eyes flutter open. I dip into her head and watch her thoughts swirl around as her brain tries to reject the sight of her daughter holding Art–plus his chair–off the ground like he weighed nothing.

"It's real, Mom. Feel how cold I am. I don't have a heartbeat."

Her mother listens at her chest for a moment before bursting into tears.

"I'm still me inside, Mom. Please don't freak out on me. I didn't want to tell you because I love you guys too much to make you go through having to deal with me dying."

Art rubs his chin. He eventually reaches over, takes Mindy's hand, and feels at her wrist for a pulse. The color gradually drains out of his face. Much to my surprise, he seems to take it in stride. "All right. So, assuming this occult shit is real, what does that mean for my daughter?"

Louise blinks at him. "Art, you seriously believe what she's saying?"

"Did you hear a heartbeat?" he asks.

"I... maybe I missed it."

"You can't miss a heartbeat. It's there or it's not."

"Guys, I'm in a really vulnerable place right now. I really need you two or I'm not sure I can cope."

Art turns his head toward me, eyes narrowing. It's obvious he needs to direct his anger at someone, and I'm an easy target. "So, what are you really doing here?"

"Like Mindy said, I randomly ran into her. She was wandering around out of it and disoriented by the change. Having had some experience with supernatural entities before, I tried as best I could to help her cope with what happened. We also managed to destroy the thing that did it to her."

"Oh, this I gotta hear," says Art.

Louise stares into space the whole time Mindy and I give them a mostly true version of events. We leave out that I'm a psychic vampire, and I don't bother going into the whole dark master thing. That's a level of detail that they don't really need to be privy to. Plus, I'm still not one hundred percent sure what happened to her. Even if Mindy turns out to be weak-willed enough for her dark master to eventually take over, her merely attempting to hold it off will delay the process well past when they'd pass from old age.

Then again, I suspected the thing within her—be it dark master, demon, or something else—might be particularly powerful... judging by her great strength. Worse, I suspected it was commanded or created to multiply at all costs. Such a compulsion might be particularly hard for her to resist.

"So, basically," I say, "your daughter is close to indestructible and amazingly strong. However, she's going to need a particular diet. Animal brain is probably the most preferable, followed closely by organ meat, then raw red meat. She can probably gain nutrition from any meat-based item, but the farther from brain it gets, the more she'll need to consume. Based on my observations over the past few days, if she doesn't overexert herself, she can probably last between three and six days between meals." I explain how the faint haze in her eyes worsens when her true hunger deepens.

Art nods. "Okay. So if her eyes look milky, she needs to eat soon."

"Yeah." Mindy nods. "If I go too long without eating, I get clumsy and might forget how to talk. If I start doing like word-association stuff, that means I'm starving."

"Well, this is certainly a pickle," says Louise, still with a shell-shocked expression. That might have been the understatement of the year.

Mindy glances over at me with a questioning look, so I dive into her mother's thoughts. The woman is borderline between filing this away as a weird hallucination, ignoring it completely, or being fitted for a straitjacket. Since this girl really needs her parents' support, I give the woman a strong push toward regarding Mindy's condition as a totally normal thing that sometimes happens to people—but still one she shouldn't talk about to anyone.

Louise blinks away her mental fog and smiles. "So nice to have you home again, dear."

"Thanks, Mom." Mindy shoots me the side eye.

I flash a broad smile. "Your parents are going to help you adjust."

"Awesome," says Mindy.

J.R. RAIN & MATTHEW S. COX

Chapter Twenty-Six
A Matter of Grave Importance

Drifting in a fog, Mindy lay in bed, neither asleep nor awake.

The familiarity of her old bedroom had soothed her. A flood of memories swirled around from her senior year of high school as well as the summer between her first year at U of A and the current one. All during her freshman year in college, she couldn't wait to get home but the summer turned out to be amazingly boring—and depressing. Not that she had a lot of friends in this little town, but the four she had were dear.

Unfortunately, Hattie and Christina went to school way out of state and didn't come back for summer break. Her best friend, Grace, didn't go to college and still worked at the Burger King in nearby Fort Huachuca. At least they managed to hang out a little last summer between shifts. Her last friend, Ellie, also didn't go to college but wound up in the Army. Mindy didn't even know where she'd been sent, not having talked to her before she left for basic training two weeks after high school.

Mindy had reluctantly decided to stay in Tucson this coming summer so she could work and save money and maybe build up a cushion. So far, sitting around home wasn't the best idea. It hadn't been as comforting as she'd hoped since none of her friends were around. She hated that her life had changed so much and she couldn't just go back to hanging out with her buds all day long.

But after waking up as a zombie, all the little memories of her past, all the fun she had here hanging out with her friends, wrapped her like a blanket. The more she thought about it, the more she didn't want to spend all summer working. No, Mindy needed to hide in her bedroom and be a teenager again, without worry or responsibility.

They're so close, whispered a voice in the back of Mindy's head.

"Mmm," mumbled Mindy, half awake.

Close. So very close. Go to them.

"Huh, what?" asked Mindy. Her bleary eyes peeled open to stare at a white ceiling blued from moonlight. "Sam?"

Her bedroom remained utterly silent. It occurred to her that she couldn't hear the sound of her breathing or heartbeat. All her horse statuettes remained as she remembered. She smiled at them, remembering each one's name and the day she got them. "Okay. I'm a dork. A very bored dork."

Close, said a whispery voice at the back of her mind.

Mindy sat up and wrapped her arms around her legs. Her best friend, Grace, would probably be at home in bed now. That girl didn't have 'college drive' as Dad put it. She'd probably wind up marrying Tyler at some point once he got around to it.

She couldn't stop thinking about her friends and how lonely she'd become. Fond memories of pajama parties with Grace, Ellie, Hattie, and Christina swarmed around her head like a buzz of angry wasps. A town this small had little to do, but they'd always managed to entertain each other, even before Hattie got a PlayStation for her thirteenth birthday. Mindy's parents never got her anything like that, but she didn't mind. Some things cost too much.

But Mindy needed friends now. She'd never felt so alone in her life. Somehow, she'd made it to twenty without having a boyfriend who lasted more than six months. Of course, every boy she dated had lived in Tucson or Fort H. She'd always figured, like Dad said, a boyfriend could wait for college. Only, once college happened, she barely had time to think between classwork and jobs.

Mindy curled up in a ball, shaking from how bad she wanted to not be alone, which was weird. Why the sudden need for friends? Hadn't Sam, who was asleep in the guest bedroom been with her 24/7 for the past few days? She had... but Sam would be leaving soon.

They are so close, rasped the voice in her head. *Friends...*

An urge not of her doing moved her leg. Too lost to loneliness to care, she stared glumly at the floor as she climbed out of bed. Snow-pale legs flashed back and forth in her vision, but she didn't register them as hers. Her body moved, driven by her subconscious. If she only took a few more steps, she could find her friends... her new friends.

Mindy had an overwhelming sense that new friends awaited her. True friends. Friends who would never, ever leave her side. She liked that. Suddenly, in this moment, she liked that idea very much indeed.

She meandered down the hall to the living room, went to the door, and stepped outside into a mild breeze. The wind brushed across her bare legs, neither cold nor warm. Friends waited for her nearby. She didn't have to be alone anymore. Mindy smiled at the idea, reaching her arms out at the night while padding down the long dirt driveway away from her home. After a little while, she veered off over the untamed scrubland. An occasional rock or bit of bush met her bare soles, though nothing hurt.

A confused *mrff* noise to the left drew her attention to a medium sized black dog.

"Hi George," said Mindy, grinning at her three-house-over neighbor's pet.

The dog took a step back, emitting a nervous growl.

"Oh, he knows I want to eat him." Mindy chuckled. "Come here, George."

George backed up more, whining.

Mindy stopped. "Ugh. No. Not George. I don't wanna hurt him."

The dog licked his nose and started wagging his tail, though remained wary.

"I gotta go, George. Friends are calling me. Bye." She grinned and waved at the dog, then resumed plodding over the desert.

Moonlight sand stretched everywhere around her. She barely noticed the odd building or two, no trace of memory coming to mind about who lived there despite her having grown up here. She didn't find that odd, her thoughts too occupied with the need to go to her new friends.

One step became ten, then fifty, then a hundred. Mindy closed her eyes but kept walking. Soon, the prone shapes of bodies glided into view in neat rows amid the darkness. She smiled.

Friends, rasped the voice in the back of her mind.

Mindy walked toward the bodies, all floating six or so feet below the ground in the pure black world of her closed eyelids. She stopped near the middle of the formation, and grinned from ear to ear.

"Hi, everyone," said Mindy.

A few distant rasps and moans emanated from the figures. She opened her eyes and found herself amid a field of gravestones, no longer able to 'see' the people under them. Again, she closed her eyes and her friends reappeared. Some indefinable sense told her she could talk to them. They all felt awake and aware of her being here, but none moved or spoke back in anything but ghostly moans or wheezes.

"Come on! I'm really lonely," said Mindy. "I don't want to be alone anymore. I want friends."

She opened her eyes and blinked.

"Did I say that? What's going on?"

Myriad groans and whispers rose up in her mind from all directions.

"Whoa…" She turned, looking around at the gravestones. "How did I get here?" Something inside her stomach moved. Mindy grabbed her gut, swooning to her knees from a sudden crippling nausea.

You are lonely, Mindy Hogan. So, so lonely.

"I'm…" She lurched over forward onto all fours, her fingers stabbed into the dirt. "I'm…"

Mindy heaved, gagged, and heaved again. She threw back her head as an eruption of black slime flew out of her mouth, a five-second stream that arced ten or twelve feet before striking the ground. When the horrible flow stopped, she collapsed flat on her chest, staring over the dirt at a mass of tar-like ooze seeping into the earth.

The sight of it made her stomach churn again. She heaved in disgust, though nothing came up.

Exhausted and overwhelmed, Mindy passed out.

Chapter Twenty-Seven
The Occult Specialist

So this is what I get for trying to do the right thing.

I'm stuck in this nice couple's house, taking up their guest bedroom reading a bodice-ripper on my phone when I really want to go home. I'm not *too* worried about my kids. This time, I want to get back to my routine already. Property taxes won't pay for themselves, and even my kindness has its limits. Pro bono work doesn't put food on the table for my children.

Then again, I had that damn dream. It alone is cause enough for me to pay attention. Back in my blood-sucking days, my dreams were largely prophetic in nature. I had no reason to think different now. Other than Elizabeth's negative effects having been removed, I still retained all the good. That is, those positive gifts contributed by the containment of my powerful soul in this tiny little body. Being warned of future calamity struck me as a good gift.

"I guess we'll see," I whisper.

A soft rap at the door gets me to peer over my phone. "Come in."

Mr. Hogan leans in, seemingly surprised to find me still dressed and sitting *on* the bed as opposed to under the covers. Truth is, I'm not tired. Although my sleeping schedule is wide open now—meaning, I can sleep any time I wish—I still haven't totally adjusted to sleeping at night. Thirteen years as a night crawler will do that to you. I see dark skies, and I think... time to live it up, not sleep. That said, this body still needs rest, especially if it's been recently taxed. And that broken rib had only recently healed. Stuff like that needs an exchange of sleep. Back in the day, as a vamp, I suspected I needed sleep because Elizabeth and the gang wished to slip free of these corporeal bodies and convene in the Void with fellow dark masters. With nothing possessing me, and with my soul fully contained in this body of mine, I approached sleep differently. Truth be told, I'm still feeling my way through this. Which, kinda makes me feel like Mindy. We're both in uncharted waters.

Also, I haven't gotten rid of the pot roast yet. While I can once again eat normal food, it still tends to work its way through me quickly. After all, my body has no real use of it, being fully sustained now on psychic energy. Which means, yes. What comes in, must come out. Kinda gross, I know. However, that is a small price to pay for being able to enjoy food again. I really don't know how the ancient vampires can tolerate being stuck on only blood. And not even that it's blood—eating the same thing every meal over and over would drive anyone crazy. Heck, maybe that's why most of the super old ones *are* insane.

"Miss Moon?" asks Art.

The concern in his voice piques my attention. "I'm up. What's wrong?"

He steps in. "Mindy's gone and the front door's wide open."

"I'm guessing nocturnal somnambulation is out of character for her?"

Art goes glassy-eyed for a few seconds. "I figure that was English, but I ain't got no clue what the hell you just said."

"Does Mindy ever sleepwalk?"

"Oh. Nah. Girl always had ants in her pants, but she slept like a lump of cord wood. Swear a damn bomb could go off an' that girl wouldn't even bat an eyelash. Anyway. Seein' as your kind of our expert on the strange stuff, we were hoping you could either tell us somethin' ta make us stop worrying, or know what's going on... or where she is."

"I'm afraid I can't quite do either yet, but I'll go looking for her."

"I can help ya if need be. I ain't that old." He smiles.

"All right." I stuff the phone in my pocket and get up.

Art follows me to the wide open front door. I look around, but don't see anything that stands out.

"Why don't you go that way"—I point to the left of the house—"and I'll go this way. We'll find her faster if we cover more ground."

"All right. Give a holler if you find her," says Art.

"Sure thing."

I walk generally away from the house until he's out of sight. This little town is nothing if not desolate. Neighbors' houses are like a ten to fifteen minute walk in any direction if even that close. Confident that no one can see me, I sprout my angel wings and leap into the air. I love Talos to bits, but not having to strip is so damn convenient. Of course, he's bigger, tougher, has claws, and can spout fire… and I'm pretty sure he can fly faster, too, but I'm not in a specific hurry at the moment. Slower is even better for searching.

After flying up to about 150 feet, I start a spiral path outward from the house. High altitude plus night vision makes me a damn effective asset in search operations. If only the Park Ranger service had vampires, they'd find lost hikers with ease. Well, in the dark anyway. Not too long ago, I had helped in a search and rescue operation in the mountains of California. A little boy had decided to have the adventure of a lifetime. Except, of course, he had been ill-equipped to survive the rough terrain on his own. Little did he know that a werewolf and vampire had watched over him that night. But yeah,

I was particularly equipped to aid in search and rescues. Hmm. Maybe I should secretly volunteer my services if and when I hear of such cases.

Sam Moon... mom, private eye, demon slayer... search and rescue specialist.

We'll see how tonight goes.

On my ninth or tenth circular pass, I catch sight of something fluttering on the ground. Motion draws my curiosity, so I fly toward it. As I do, it's not very difficult to make out pale legs against the dark soil at night. Indeed, the shape of a young woman in a long black T-shirt fills in as I draw closer.

Mindy's flat out on her chest in the middle of a small cemetery. Ugh. Please tell me she's not having an emo attack and thinks she belongs here with the other dead people. I dive, swing my legs forward, and ride the wings like a parachute the last of the way to the ground. She doesn't react to my approach, so I take a knee and pat her on the shoulder.

"You know, that whole vampires and coffins thing is made up, right?" I ask. "Even if you are a zombie, you don't need to sleep in a graveyard."

She doesn't stir.

"Mindy?"

The girl still doesn't move.

I shake her a little harder. "Mindy."

Well, her father was true about one thing: she does sleep like the dead. It takes me almost a full minute of patting her face, but she eventually squirms, and makes a noise part zombie moan, part teenager late for school. Honestly, the two sounds are so damn close to each other it's hard to tell which one I heard.

"Huh? Sam? Bleh." She spits a few times to the side. "Blech. Eww."

"What are you doing out here?"

Mindy pushes herself up to kneel. Her shirt's long enough to cover her to mid-thigh like a dress. "Where am I?"

"About two miles from your house, in the middle of a graveyard."

She looks at me, eyes wide with worry. "I don't remember how I got here. I just…"

I wait for her to continue, but she lapses into a distant stare. "Mindy?"

"Sorry. I mean I just remember feeling super lonely. Like I was trying to go to sleep and my bedroom made me think about a couple years ago when I was in high school and had friends and didn't have to worry so much about working or… being dead."

"Are you sure you didn't have an emo attack?"

"Emo is totally not a thing any more. And no. I'm not depressed or anything."

I shrug. Learn something new every day. I totally thought emo was a thing. Would have bet money on it.

"One minute I'm in bed feeling super lonely and kinda nostalgic, then I'm here." She blinks. "Oh! And I had this weird whispery voice talking to me. Sam, am I going crazy?"

I hang my head. "No… that's probably your dark master talking to you. Or dark something talking to you."

"Eep."

"What did it say?" I ask.

"Umm. I don't really remember. Something about friends. It's almost like I dreamed it."

"That means it doesn't have a lot of influence over you yet. No offense, but I think whatever is in you is on the weak side, but not *too* weak. It slipped in during that point where you're between awake and asleep. Just remember, the more you resist it, the longer you'll still be Mindy Hogan and not someone else."

She nods. "I'm kinda freaked out, Sam. Can we go back to the house?"

"Yeah. Good idea." I help her up.

"Why am I in the graveyard?" she asks.

I think back to my dream, and I'm all of a sudden rather glad I decided to stick around. Nothing looks unusual, but I can't shake the feeling that this sleepy little town is about to wake up. Or maybe I got here in time to stop whatever this girl's dark side wanted to do.

"Did anything happen?" I ask, looking again at the dozens of graves and markers. Nothing seemed disturbed.

Mindy shrugs. "Not that I remember. Other than sleepwalking out here."

"Okay." I put an arm around her back. "Let's get you home."

Chapter Twenty-Eight
Friends

Mindy's mom is waiting for us in the living room when we walk in.

The expression on her face—panic and worry tinged with relieved anger—is one I've worn a few times when Tammy's been late. However, the woman's a master at it to the point where even *I* feel like I'm about to get in trouble.

"Sorry," says Mindy in a contrite tone, looking down.

"Why are you running around half naked in the middle of the night?" asks Louise.

"I'm wearing shorts." She holds up the long shirt to reveal them. "It's what I always sleep in. And I don't know. I just kinda sleepwalked to the old prospector cemetery." Mindy shivers. "I'm scared."

Her mother goes from accusatory to worried/comforting and steps closer. "Samantha, what do you think happened?"

Clattering from the corridor leading to the kitchen announces Art arriving via the back door. He runs in, still holding his cell phone. Guess Louise saw us coming and called him.

"What happened?" asks Art. "Where were you?"

"The Prospector's cemetery," answers Louise.

"What in God's name?"

"We're still trying to work out what happened." I set my hands on my hips. "Best I can figure out at this point, she might have some kind of instinctual urge to seek out graveyards. Or…"

Mindy coughs and a thin line of black liquid dribbles out of her mouth.

"Or what?" asks Art and Louise at the same time.

I shift my eyes to the left, staring at the line of ink rolling over her pallid chin. It evaporates in a wispy finger of black smoke. I'm pretty sure I'm the only one who noticed it. "Ah, hell."

"I don't like the sound of 'Ah, hell,'" says Louise.

Mindy cracks up giggling.

Her father and I both raise eyebrows.

"Oh, it's just that Mom never curses. It's so weird to hear her say that."

"Mindy? Did something happen when you were at the cemetery?"

She wipes her chin where the dark trail had been. "Umm. I might've thrown up."

I point at her chin. "Black stuff?"

"Yes, how did you know?"

"It's on your chin. Or was on your chin."

"Umm." Mindy's eyes widen with worry.

"What the devil are you two talking about?" asks Art.

"Let your daughter answer," I say.

"Umm." Mindy grinds her toe into the rug. "Well, I thought I was dreaming. But like, a whole bunch of black goo flew out of my mouth and crawled into the ground. All I really remember is wanting friends. I was so lonely."

"Lonely? You're surrounded by people all the time," says her father.

"Sweetie, is school too hard on—" begins her mother.

A male voice somewhere outside screams.

Mindy gives me an 'uh oh' look. "Maybe I should go put on real pants."

"Yes, that's probably a good idea." I glance at her thigh-length T-shirt with Kermit the Frog on it.

"I'm lost," says Art.

"Your daughter just summoned zombies." I rub the bridge of my nose, thinking about my dream. "And… they're probably about to invade the town."

Another scream, this time a woman, echoes far off in the night—along with a gunshot.

Mindy runs down the hall to her room.

"What do we do?" Louise eyes the windows.

"We don't have time to board up."

"Don't let one bite you. Don't touch blood. And, yeah, probably a good idea to stay inside."

"What about you, Sam?"

"Don't worry about me."

"But you can't go out there alone."

"I have a few tricks up my sleeve." I wink.

"What does that mean?" asks Louise.

"Don't you get it, Lou," says Art. "She one of them. She's like Mindy."

"Not quite," I say. "But close." And I promptly erase that exchange from their mind and encourage them to hide in the master bathroom with all doors locked.

The Hogans exchange a confused glance before hurrying off together down the hall to their bedroom and ultimately the bathroom.

Might as well get started. I don't have a terribly strong itch to touch rotting corpses, so I pull the Devil Killer out of thin air. These things won't have the mental faculties to be afraid of anything, even this blade.

Mindy sprints back into the living room having added jeans and sneakers to her outfit. "That's a cool sword. Ooh. I want one, too. Did it cost much?"

"Thanks. And nah, I got a devil of a bargain. Unfortunately, it's one-of-a-kind." I head outside, stop a few paces from the door, and look around like an Old West gunslinger.

A hollow metallic *scrape* comes from behind

me.

"Here." Mindy appears at my left and offers a big metal garbage can lid.

"A trash lid?"

She holds it against my left arm. "You need a shield."

"Seriously?"

Mindy nods enthusiastically. "Yeah. What if they like projectile vomit?"

I take the lid. "Okay." It's kinda tempting to bang the sword against it and yell 'Freeeeeedom,' but I resist.

I nod to myself. Time to fight some zombies.

Chapter Twenty-Nine
Knight of the Living Dead

A young couple appears in the distance, running like hell across the desert away from a slow-moving crowd of decaying bodies.

"Wow. There's a lot," says Mindy.

"How many 'friends' did you call?" I glance back at her.

"I dunno. It's all kinda blurry. Had this voice whispering in my head and the next thing I know, I'm vomiting black crap into the cemetery grass."

I nod. God only knows how many of the dead the black ooze had infected. Maybe all of them; that is, all of them with bodies intact enough to move.

"Where are they?" asks Art, emerging from the house behind us.

Ah, crap. I realize my mistake immediately. I encouraged them to go into the bathroom and lock the doors along the way, which they very well may have. But I didn't command them to stay. Rookie mistake.

I glance back at him, about to prompt him to go inside—and stay inside—but he's carrying a big pump-action shotgun. Louise hovers in the doorway behind him holding a handgun… probably a Beretta 92. I blink. Well, okay then. Guess I'm too used to California.

"Coming from the cemetery." Mindy points. "I see a group approaching."

"All right," says Louise. "We got your back."

I smile and adjust my grip on my 'shield.' "Actually, they're not much of a threat to me—or Mindy. But I'd feel better if you guys tried to keep as far away from these things as possible.

"Well, you've got a giant boot knife," says Art. "Best if you don't get close to them things, either. I seen the show."

"True, but they can't infect me. If you're going to do anything, check the town while I deal with the big group."

"You?"

"Well, me and Mindy. That is, if she doesn't mind fighting her new friends."

"They're not my friends. The thing in my head lied to me."

Art looks at both of us like we're speaking another language. Finally, he sighs. "All right. Please be safe, baby." He says this to Mindy, but I secretly accept it too.

He gestures for his wife to follow him. As she does, she looks back at us once, fear in her eyes. I send her a large heaping of courage. She nods, smiles, and climbs into the passenger seat. The truck roars off.

***

Okay, this is going to be a new experience.

Hopefully, these things are weaker than Mindy. A lot weaker. If not, I'm going to have to summon Talos... and he would be damn hard to explain to the town of Canelo.

I march toward the oncoming throng, counting maybe thirty or so. Some are exceedingly slow, lagging well behind the main group. A few speed-hobble, especially the strays heading for the town away from the pack. All of them look pretty much exactly as I expected zombies to look. So, yeah, I'm basically *living* Tammy's favorite show.

"Be right back," calls Mindy, before running to the house.

Maybe she's got a gun, too.

They are moving rather slow. Not like we don't have time.

If I stand here waiting, it'd be an easy ten minutes before any of them came close enough to engage... but I'm not exactly a patient person at the moment. Yeah. Tonight's going to contain a whole mess of suck—and probably a fair amount of fire.

I jog the hundred-plus yards to the nearest

zombie in the main group, some dude in a suit who looks like they stuck him in the ground during the fifties, which I find interesting. Don't corpses reduce to bones in a few years? Did whatever animated these bodies also give them temporary flesh? If so, why not give them full-on flesh? Why just bits and pieces? After all, gaping holes in his cheeks expose his yellow teeth. His eyes have gone completely white, so opaque I can't even see an iris.

I know the answer as soon as I ask the question... because this is what the world expects to see. No matter how much dark masters and demons scheme, they still must work within the confines of creation. Mankind collectively summoned these things, and the dark masters and demons were only too happy to help it along. Undoubtedly, these zombies fit beautifully into their plans. If anything, that scared the hell out of me.

At this distance, my count revises to fifty or so, and the stink of formaldehyde is eye-watering. There's no way they all have dark masters. One woman in the distance keeps falling over every few steps when her left leg keeps detaching at the hip. The endless cycle of fall over, put leg back on, stand up, take two steps, fall over again doesn't seem to bother her.

Call me an elitist, but I can't imagine an individual dark master wanting to put up with that bullshit. The theory of one powerful dark master spreading to many vessels is looking more and more likely.

When I get close, I round the Devil Killer in a fairly telegraphed sideways slash and neatly take the head off Mr. 1950. He doesn't even attempt to duck. Skin smolders and chars at the magic in the blade. A spray of brackish brown liquid gushes upward from the neck. His body keeps walking, and the jaw continues opening and closing after the head rolls to a stop a few feet away.

A woman in a once-nice dress hurls herself at me. I leap backward, causing her to face-plant the ground. Before I can take a swing at her, another man in a horrid suit he probably bought at Walmart moans and barfs green goop at me.

Trashcan lid for the win.

Still, I get some on my legs. Damn. Now I'm gonna have to burn these jeans.

I duck another grabbing hand and chop at Mr. Puker, hitting him straight over the head. The sword stops about midway down his torso. He heaves a belabored groan and falls backward off the blade, crumping to an immobile heap. Meanwhile, the severed head sticks out its tongue, pushing at the dirt to spin itself so it can see me. His headless body wheels around in my general direction and staggers closer while face-plant woman pushes herself upright.

A pair of skinny men in flannel shirts and jeans lurch up to a brief sprint, forcing me to dodge to my right—straight into the pounding fist of a seven-footer. He wallops me in the chest so hard I'm flat on my back and sliding before I feel any pain.

Before I can sit up, Mindy runs by, jumps over me, and swings a huge shovel at the big guy. The metal part comes down on his head with enough force to liquefy it and send a spray of gore everywhere. Nice dress woman pounces on me, but I raise the trash can lid in time to catch her by the chest. I end up nose to nose with a zombie and her snapping teeth just inches from my skin.

Evidently, these guys didn't get the memo that I'm already undead.

Wait. I'm not anymore. Argh. No wonder they're coming after me. I have body heat again—and, according to Kingsley, a human-like scent as well. In fact, with Elizabeth—and the darkness that came with her—now gone, one could argue that I've never been more fully alive. Nothing possesses me and my soul fully radiates its powerful life force.

At this distance, I glare into her eyes... and *don't* see the flickering flame, merely a faint glow. That confirms it. No dark master. Mindy's flame was on the small side, too. Could that mean she doesn't have one either? Or maybe she got one like Danny, not quite out of dark master school. Or maybe something not human at all? It doesn't make sense for any of them to want to jump into a supernatural monster anymore now that Elizabeth has the 'keys to their jail' so to speak. At least, until or unless the Alchemists manage to repair the Void.

Unless whatever was inside her had never been bound to the Void... which means, it could escape at will. So what could it be?

Years ago, on an island in the Pacific Northwest, I came across a demon who could body hop via the bloodline of a cursed family. Was this similar? Maybe. But now, whatever it was, wasn't so much hopping... as spreading, expanding, growing.

Grunting, I fling my left arm up, hurling her to the side before rolling to my feet. She tumbles over onto her back, so I take a stepping swing like a one-handed golfer and slice her head in half at the ears. She goes still. Okay, that does the trick.

I turn toward Mindy to tell her that we need to destroy their brains—not simply cut their heads off—but hold my tongue, watching in curious horror as she pounds her shovel down on top of the head I cut off before. It bursts like a watermelon under a sledgehammer, and the headless body it once belonged to falls over, dead.

The next few minutes become a blur of moaning, flailing limbs. I feel somewhere between an extra on the set of *Braveheart* and a character from one of Anthony's games. Every so often, I forget myself and take a swing of opportunity, uselessly cutting off an arm or stabbing someone in the chest. As viscerally satisfying as it might be for a fan of sword combat to ram it to the hilt in these creatures, it's functionally worthless. Nothing even slows them down but obliterating the brain. Well, okay, hacking off a leg literally slows them down, but not what I meant.

A few intermittent gunshots go off back in the

town, but I've got too many problems around me to worry about it. I'm insanely grateful that I'm immune to their bite since I'd have to fly or teleport to get away from the crowd at this point. Only my supernatural speed is keeping my ass intact. These guys may be slow on their feet, but their punches are far from sluggish. My trash can shield has knuckle dents to prove it.

With a loud moan, a red-haired guy with no skin left on his face—but both eyeballs still in their sockets—lines me up for a haymaker. A little too into character, I raise the 'shield' to block, but his meaty fist bends the upper half of the lid back like aluminum foil and continues into my jaw.

I stop sliding about fifteen feet later, unsure if my jawbone is simply dislocated or shattered.

Oh, that smarts.

Stupid lid. I drop it and grab my face. Oh, bonus points. It's dislocated *and* broken. Last time my jaw broke, it took a day or two to heal. Over the past few years, I started healing faster. Let's hope my new and improved self heals faster still.

"Sam?" yells Mindy. "You okay?"

No point even trying to talk at the moment. She wouldn't understand me.

I roll over onto my back and spring to my feet, trying to push my jaw back in place with my left hand while swinging the sword at flailing limbs coming at me from all angles. A sharp *crack* shakes my entire skull as the bone sets and begins to knit. Ow. I think mending hurt more than the break. On the plus side, I can feel it healing... and quickly.

Mindy spins around with a two-handed shovel swing, right into the face of a crawling zombie. Although the shovel head emits a dull, fleshy *clank,* her swing doesn't stop or even hesitate. All I'm going to say about that is blunt force decapitation generates a significant amount of fluid spatter. The eyeballs probably land a mile or two out in the desert.... Damn that girl is strong.

I'm about to ask how the hell that shovel is surviving when I notice... it didn't. That hit broke the handle into a primitive spear. The metal end is stuck like a dagger into the chest of another zombie about twenty feet away, who doesn't appear to notice it. So... Mindy does the natural thing for a twenty-year-old college co-ed turned zombie: she bashes their heads in. Every hit snaps off a little more wood. After five dead zombies, her weapon has shrunk to the size of a Billy club and stops getting smaller.

I throw myself back into the fray, aiming for heads and trying to cleave the skulls in half rather than decapitating them. More gunshots come from the town along with people shouting commands to run or duck as well as screams of fear.

No, not quite fear.

Terror.

When the woman with the leg that won't stay attached finally reaches the scene of battle, I almost feel bad for killing her—again—but I can't let her hurt people... or create more of her kind. This one's evidently been in the ground a while as she mostly resembles an Egyptian mummy. Dark brown, withered, no eyes. Ugh. That's eerie. As soon as she falls again, I pounce and stab the Devil Killer into the back of her skull, pinning her to the dirt for a few seconds before wrenching the sword loose with a crunching twist.

"This is kinda fun in a morbidly terrifying way," says Mindy. "Better than Tae Bo."

"Hon," I say, while swiping the blade at a pair of zombies walking shoulder to shoulder (and cutting both their heads in half with one swing), "you don't need to exercise anymore."

The two guys I sliced fall to their knees at the same time, and teeter over sideways.

"Oh, yeah." She kicks a guy in the groin with enough force to drive her foot up to the base of his ribcage… then winds up hopping on her left leg with her right foot stuck in his torso. "Oh, eww! That's so nasty!"

I don't even have *cajones* and the sight of that makes me pause in sympathetic agony. In fact, I think two of the male zombies groaned a little louder.

The one she kicked reaches for me, moaning and trying to drag itself after me like it doesn't even realize it's impaled on her leg. Mindy yanks her foot back and falls on her butt. The zombie staggers at me, but I thrust the sword out, stabbing it in the face. By the time its weight drives its head down the blade until the hilt touches its cheeks, its animating force has gone.

"This is truly disgusting," I mutter, while flinging the body to the side. "And why did you kick it in the balls?"

"Umm. Sorry. Instinct." She frowns at her slime-covered leg. "I won't do that again."

Two stragglers lope toward me, the last of the fifty-some-odd shamblers in the main group.

"Sam, is it weird that I kinda feel bad hurting them?" asks Mindy. "Like I'm betraying my friends."

I leap at the one on the left, swinging a diagonal downstroke through his head before spinning, grabbing the sword in both hands, and chopping the other zombie clear in half from skull to crotch. The severed edges smolder and smoke from little fires left in the Devil Killer's wake.

"Whoa. You totally *'Voltron-ed'* that one."

"Huh?" I ask.

"My friends and I used to watch Japanese cartoons a lot. There's this one, where a giant robot always fights giant monsters. Almost every single episode ends with him cutting his enemy in half like that, straight down the middle."

"Oh. Never heard of it." I survey the street and landscape... bodies everywhere, though none of them are moving. "Well, that wasn't *too* bad. Either these things aren't anywhere near as tough as you, or this sword is epic, as Anthony would say."

"You can poke me in the arm if you wanna test it." Mindy holds her arm out. "It won't kill me or leave like a permanent wound, will it?"

"Umm. Well... this sword can kill *anything*, but I think it still needs to deliver a mortal blow. A slice to the arm wouldn't kill."

"Those little zombies were kinda squishy." She waves what's left of the shovel handle at me.

"Yeah, but you've got to be one of the strongest magical beings I've ever seen."

"Really?" she blinks in awe, evidently proud of herself.

"In terms of raw physical strength, yeah. Though, ancient vampires are about on par with you."

"Except they're gone now."

I shake my head. "Not all dark masters escaped the confines of the physical body." I had proof of that with Kingsley and Fang. Not to mention, Fang's blood bar still attracted vamps of all shapes and sizes and ages, though his business had decreased significantly.

"Enough with the damn dark masters," groans Mindy. "Stab me, dammit. Let's see what happens."

I raise the Devil Killer and prod it somewhat reluctantly into her right forearm. The tip pokes through her tough exterior like butter. But other than a faint wisp of smoke, it didn't appear to do much. I note the distinct lack of blood.

"That didn't even hurt much. Burned a little," she says. "Try harder. Interest of science and all that."

After a brief hesitation over the idea of trying to

harm a person I've been working to help—and come to like—I jab the blade at her forearm again with about the same force I used on the zombies. That time, the point leaves a roughly two-inch slice in her skin along with a lot more smoke.

"Ow." She examines the wound. "It hurt, but not as much as I figured being stabbed with a sword would hurt… and, look, it's closing. But yeah, that thing could definitely kill me. I wouldn't stand a chance against it."

I nod, figuring as much. The Devil Killer was no joke.

"Oh, Mindy?"

"Hmm?" She tilts her head, all innocence.

I put an arm around her shoulder and pull her close. "If you summon another wave of zombies, you're grounded."

She throws her head back and laughs. "Sorry… I didn't mean to start the apocalypse. It just kinda happened."

"Ugh. We have to contain this somehow. If they bite someone and we don't notice, or one of them wanders out of town…"

"Maybe if we play Nickelback loud enough they'll all explode."

I chuckle. "If only it would be that easy."

More gunfire comes from town.

"That's our cue. Let's go."

Chapter Thirty
The Battle of Canelo

Canelo is the sort of place that makes other small towns feel good about themselves.

It's effing tiny.

I have half a mind to 'call it in,' but the last thing I need is for the CIA or NSA to get wind of it and make everyone here vanish to keep public awareness down. And they'd surely take Mindy 'in for testing.' I can't do that to her.

The government would also probably try to weaponize her, and then *they* would initiate the zombie apocalypse. Yeah, no. This stays here. We run toward the nearest sound of moaning, darting over open scrubland, a small dirt road, and up a tiny hill to the backyard area of a house trailer. Three rotting corpses are pounding on the back door while a fourth, a little old dead woman, ambles around toward the front.

"I got granny," says Mindy, running after the elder lady.

Someone inside the house screams. The back door opens an inch and slams again, suggesting there's a person inside physically holding it closed. Crap. No lock? Yeah, we're definitely not in California anymore.

"Hey, maggots!" I shout.

The three zombies spin toward the sound of my voice. Since there's nothing between us, they abandon the door to come after me. They're quite a bit faster than the ones in the main group, but that only puts them at 'slow human.' I chop down into the head of the one in the middle while the other two both lunge at me, trying to bite. Flesh sizzles wherever the blade touches them.

While grabbing the left one by the throat, I brace the handle of the sword at the neck of the other, holding them back… barely. They're nowhere near Mindy's strength, but they *are* stronger than me by a hair. Trying to hold back two of them at once forces me to yield ground, though I'm honestly not sure why I'm so worried about being bitten.

Mindy grabs the old woman's shoulder and pulls her around, I presume to confirm she's a zombie before bashing her head in. When they make eye contact, it's almost as if time stops for them—not me though. The two crush inward, their teeth worrisomely close to my face.

Since I'm holding back the woman's head with

the hilt of the Devil Killer, I retreat to the left, letting her surge forward while twisting away and yanking the blade across her throat. Putrid black ooze seeps from the stump of a neck as her head falls back and lands in the dirt with a *thump.* I end up behind the other zombie and chop into the back of his skull.

When I look up, the old woman zombie is tottering off beyond the gate and heading for the road. Strangely, Mindy stands near the corner of the house, watching her.

Blam!

She jumps back and shouts, "Ow! Dammit, Dad!"

"Ah, crap," yells Art. He hurries into view.

"Oh, shit that burns." Mindy swipes at her chest like someone just spilled hot soup on her. I don't see any blood at least.

"Uhh, sorry, hon. Thought you were one of them."

"Cripes, Dad. You shot me. And look, you blasted Kermit's face off." She looks down and picks at a three-inch hole in the middle of the shirt where the frog's head used to be. The T-shirt still covers her sensitive bits, but it's got hillbilly air conditioning. "Oh, whoa." Mindy plucks something off her chest and holds it up.

Looks a bit like a nickel.

Art stares at me.

I hurry over. Seems the buckshot flattened on impact with her chest. Which makes my sword all the more impressive; after all, there's no way I stabbed her as hard as the shotgun hit her, yet the pellets didn't break skin. Then again, knives go through Kevlar that laughs off pistol bullets… so who knows. Maybe a high-powered rifle could penetrate.

And damn, I need to stop thinking about this kid as a creature in need of testing.

"What happened with grandma?" I ask. "And by the way, Art, you should be shooting them in the head, not the body."

"Yeah, I know. I'm a little jumpy. I fired before thinking."

"Umm." Mindy spins to face me, looking confused. "I had the weirdest feeling she'd do what I told her to do, so I sent her back to the graveyard."

More gunshots go off in the distance.

I say, "Okay, this is going to sound a bit strange, but trust me."

Mindy nods.

"I think you somehow called them. To some degree, you probably have control of them. Remember when you told me you could see your dog buried behind the house?"

"Yeah."

"What?" asks Art.

"She can sense dead things underground," I say before staring into her eyes again. "Can you feel where the zombies are around town?"

Mindy closes her eyes. "Wow… yeah. I think I do. There's one almost to Fort H."

"Oh, hell." Art shakes his head. "This ain't gonna go over well with the neighbors."

"I can handle the neighbors," I say to him, then look at Mindy. "Try commanding them to go back to the graveyard. No, better yet, send them to where we took out that first huge group."

Mindy nods, closes her eyes.

A few minutes later, moans come from the distance along with a lot of scuffing footsteps. A few minutes after that, maybe another twenty or so zombies stumble into view, all heading down the street, toward Mindy's house.

"Well, it seems like she's controlling them," says Art.

"Yeah." Mindy smiles, opening her eyes. "It's kinda like a video game. I think about a place and they all go there. Kinda like having minions."

I chuckle. "Technically, you *do* have minions. That's why they never attacked you."

"Oh." Mindy nods. "That makes sense."

"So she can control them?" asks Art. "If this ever happens again, she could simply round them up before they hurt anyone?"

"Now that she knows she can do it, yeah." I bite my lip so I don't add 'if she wants to.' I'm sure she'll want to as long as Mindy remains Mindy.

"Good. That means we don't need to lock her in at night." Art smiles.

"You'd need a much tougher house for that to even work," I mutter. I think back to Kingsley's cell in his basement. Then again, his turnings were predictable. Mindy hearing voices might be a continuous thing, not just regulated to nighttime. No, she was going to have to learn how to lock *it* up in her mind. Whatever *it* was.

Mindy mimes wiping sweat from her brow. "So… now what?"

"You send them back to that spot. Art, do you have any gasoline in a can?"

"Yeah. Good idea." He trots off.

"Come with me. Let's move them a little closer to the graveyard for the bonfire." I head in that direction, the sword still out and ready in case one of them gets any fancy ideas about where to put its hands. Mindy is, after all, new at this and might slip.

"What's the plan, Sam?" asks Mindy.

"You're going to drag any zombies that the people in town managed to kill to a staging area near the graveyard where we're going to burn the remains. Meanwhile, I'm going to make sure the neighbors don't all wind up in a mental institution or talking to the *National Enquirer*."

It takes us about an hour to collect corpses, which Mindy heaves into the back of Art's truck. Her father had managed to blast the heads off six, and a few other locals bagged another thirteen or so. While Mindy and her father head off to the site of our first annual Burning Zombie Festival—I think we're going to skip the forty-foot-tall wicker figure this year—I work on the memories of nine freaked-out locals. It's easier to alter a memory than outright erase it, plus there could be more people who heard gunfire but didn't see zombies. The idea of coyotes or even chupacabra comes to mind, but I don't want to start a panic and cause the deaths of innocent animals, so I do the most logical thing I can think of.

Grey aliens.

Hey, Roswell, right?

I figure if any of them have the balls to tell anyone they saw (and shot at) grey aliens, they'll be laughed at. Perhaps claims of zombies would trigger laughter, too, but I don't want to take the risk that documentation of zombies catches on. Plus, I want the dark masters to know their plan, thus far, has failed.

***

We gather at the spot where the disinterred remains of about ninety people lay upon the ground.

Since Mindy couldn't figure out any way to release the animating force she spewed into the zombies, Art used his own off switch: the shotgun. After systematically shooting the remaining undead, Mindy and I stack the bodies into a pile then retreat to a safe distance. Art douses them with gasoline from a red plastic can, then lights off a bonfire.

Fire is *not* an immortal's friend, especially not a vampire's. Being even this close to a sudden bloom of flames the size of a box truck would have once drawn an involuntary hiss out of me, but doesn't…

now just a typical human flinch. Mindy cringes as well. I imagine it wouldn't do nice things to her either.

"Whoa," she whispers, pointing at the blaze. "Why did that scare the shit out of me?"

"Because it can actually hurt you."

"Oh. Duh. That was kind of a stupid question, wasn't it?"

"There are no stupid questions when it comes to this shit."

Art wanders over to us, the gas can dangling from two fingers. "If we don't burn them, will they get back up?"

"No," says Mindy. "The head shots released whatever dark energy was in them. They're just rotting corpses now. Still, best to cremate them, unless we want to spend the next six weeks re-burying them."

We are silent, watching the crackling flames. The superheated bones and glowing, grinning skulls repulse me. Back in the day—hell just a few weeks ago—such a sight might have intrigued me. I knew for damn well sure it had intrigued Elizabeth. Her darkness had definitely seeped into every aspect of my life.

Mindy, I note, is looking a bit forlorn, her somewhat milky eyes aglow. "Sorry for waking you guys up," she whispers.

"Eh, it's okay. At least you're safe," says Art.

"No, I was talking to them." Mindy points at the former zombies. "But I'm sorrier for waking you and Mom up."

"Well, then. I guess we're all gonna have to cope with a learning curve. Maybe you *should* move back in here and commute. Would be nice to see you... and keep an eye on you."

I step in… because that's what moms do. "If nothing else, having her parents to help will make her unusual diet a little easier to keep hidden. She can probably get away with eating raw meat or cow brains twice a week... and if she does it at home, who would be the wiser?" I turn to her. "Mindy, you might be able to ride out the rest of the school year in Tucson and lead a somewhat normal life."

Mindy whines. "But I feel bad leaving Natalie and Alisha stuck with the rent, but I also really wanna go home. But there's still the issue of commuting. No car."

"Well," says Art. "Maybe if Miss Moon here can help convince your bosses to take you back on, and you're not needin' to pay rent anymore, you can save up enough for a beater that'll do the job. Guess your mother and I don't rightly need to worry so much about you being hurt in a wreck."

Mindy hugs him, choked up. "I'm already… never mind. I'm gonna be around for a long time."

We stand there a while watching the fire burn down.

"So is that going to happen again?" asks Mindy. "Like, I randomly zone out and barf up the apocalypse?"

I chuckle. "I'm not sure. Now that you know

what the voice means, I think you can control it… but I'll have to get back to you on the rest. If nothing else, I can teach you how to suppress the voice. There are some techniques that should work for you."

Of course, I also had the diamond medallion, which restores an immortal back to a mortal, and release the dark master within. Perhaps it would be best used on her now that I no longer needed it. That is, of course, if it worked on her. At the time, it had been created to be used by vampires... and maybe werewolves. Whatever was inside of Mindy was obviously different, which might nullify the magic of the diamond medallion. Looks like I had yet another question to ask the Alchemist... if I could just find him.

"Aren't you an occult specialist?" asks Art.

I'm not sure if I really qualify as one of those, but compared to anyone in this town, I am… so I don't feel like a total liar when I say, "Yeah. But, zombies—real zombies—are kinda new. Vampires are another story."

"Vampires?"

Oops, I strike his memory of that last line. Mindy giggles, then lapses into silence. "I can feel its anger and disappointment in me. It thinks I turned on my brothers and sisters... my friends. It wants me to do better next time."

"Sweet Jesus," says Art.

I take her hand. "I think your training begins now."

Chapter Thirty-One
The Scion of Grief

My phone pings with a text.

I pull it out and find a message from Allison that says 'Duck, Sam!'

What the hell is she doing awake at damn near four in the morning? Oh, right. She's hosting her radio show—

Wait? Duck!?

"Gah!" I fling myself at Mindy and Art, tackling them to the ground.

"Oof!" yells Art.

"Ugh, what was that for?" asks Mindy.

The instant I open my mouth, the pyre of bodies explodes in a shower of flaming gooey bits that zoom away in all directions like meteors. A deep, growling roar comes from inside the inferno. I raise an arm to shield my eyes from the glare and heat, wind whipping my hair at my face. The curtain of flames parts to reveal a tall, somewhat humanoid figure with shiny coal-black skin. Great bat-like wings spread out from its back, fluttering in the wind like leather flags. Four horns sprout from the top of its bald head, the outer pair sticking two feet straight up, the inner pair a quarter of that length and curved forward. A huge, vertical mouth runs up the center of its otherwise featureless face, lined with elongated needle-like teeth.

Two glowing red eyes—in its chest where it ought to have nipples—fixate on me.

"Be right back. Gotta tell my wife her mother's here," mutters Art.

"*Dad*," says Mindy, adding a sigh. "Gran isn't *that* bad."

"Not ta you." He chuckles. "So, Miss Occult Expert. What the hell is that? And should I be shitting my pants or laughing?"

"Demon," I say, as the thing throws its head back and grows another foot or two. "And I'm leaning more toward shitting your pants." I step in front of Art and Mindy, raising the black sword. "You two probably ought to go back to the house now. Not a lot you're going to be able to do out here but get hurt."

"Discretion and valor, some such thing like that. I get it." He takes a step backward. "C'mon Min."

His daughter shakes her head. "I gotta help her."

"Girl, you—"

"Art, your daughter's strong enough to hit this

thing over the head with a pickup truck. I guess I wouldn't mind the help."

"And," says Mindy, adding a hint of snarl. "It's payback time."

I glance at her, raising an eyebrow.

"*This* is the one that made me a zombie."

"How do you know that?" I ask, a little stunned.

"It told me. It's talking in my head now."

"Are you sure that's the demon talking and not your dark master?" I mutter.

Art hoofs it for the house.

"Yeah. Way different voice. I think the one in my head is human—or was human. He's speaking to me now. Sam, they are working with the demons."

"The dark masters?"

"Yes."

"Listen to me, Mindy. Do not let him take you over. This is important."

"I know, Sam. I'm only repeating what he says, I promise. I'm still me."

"He says the dark masters didn't have access to enough power—at least not from the Void—to create the monsters we call zombies. The Void is without magic, as ordained by the vile alchemists. His words, not mine. Prior to losing the war centuries ago, the dark masters infected a number of human slaves with the darkest of black magicks... that is, that which would taint their blood and leave a doorway open to them. From the Void, dark masters can slip into their human hosts and, ideally, take over. Additionally, the dark magick could be transferred through the tainted blood. The dark masters were, at first, what we call vampires, for only the clever and most advanced made the transition. Next came the werewolves and their many close cousins. Finally, came the lumbering monsters... sparked to life by the lesser of the masters, although these would barely be called acolytes. Mistress knew the day was nigh of the coming collapse of the Void prison. Her ingenious centuries-long plan had finally come to fruition... thanks in large part to you, Sam. But there was still one more step... one that involved distracting the alchemists, one that involved sowing fear into mankind, one that involved laying the groundwork to command thousands, if not millions of soldiers... whatever it took to win the war against the so-called light warriors. But to command that kind of an army took far more power than we could ever summon... or control."

"Demons," I said.

"He says the demons were needed to create the magick necessary for the zombies. There is something... let me see if I can explain, Sam. He says the demons and dark masters needed to wait for that popping moment... that is, the moment the Universe itself would aid in the creation of something, even something as vile as zombies."

"And that popping occurred, when, two weeks ago?"

"No. He says two years ago. Once the Universe

itself was behind the creation of these things, everything started falling into place, including summoning the Red Rider to the West Coast. It was no accident that the witch eater was in your own backyard, Sam." Mindy pauses, shakes her head. "Witch eater, really?"

I nod. "Long story."

Mindy looks like she wants to ask more about that, but I suspect the voice in her head is persistent. She continues: "And with the destruction of the Red Rider, enough force—enough magical force—was released to break down the Void. Almost simultaneously, the plan to invoke the zombies, was put into place. We are pleased with our choice... and we are pleased with the magic behind the waking of the walkers. We are not pleased at their subsequent destruction."

"Are you a dark master?" I asked, knowing with certainty that Mindy was going to have to shove him back down deep, lest she risk him taking a foothold in her psyche.

"Of course, I am, Sam Moon. An altruistic one, you could say. Rather than escape like my greedy brothers and sisters, I stayed on to fulfill the plan. I am needed, after all, to give life to your undead friend."

"And where does the demon come in?"

"The vile blackness is all him... and his magic. He was injected directly into her, as was I, during her testing. Think of that needle pinprick the equivalent of a vampire bite. And think of the serum as magical, rather than scientific."

"Okay, enough with you," I said. "Mindy, mentally imagine shoving him down into the deepest hole."

"He doesn't want to go."

"Of course not. Force him into it."

"Trying."

"Try harder."

"I am, Sam. I think he's in the hole. He's screaming at me."

"Good, now imagine the biggest hulkiest rock you can imagine, and throw it on top of the hole."

"Okay, there done. He's quiet now. And I don't think hulkiest is a word."

"Well, it should be."

"Enough talk," says the demon, shifting its nipple-eyes to me. Vertical pupils like those of a cat widen.

Okay, that's too messed up.

My surroundings blur into a whirl of color and re-form. I'm no longer out in the Arizona desert, but some gothic graveyard in a rainy, temperate area. Probably Eastern Europe based on the buildings.

"You're fighting a losing battle," says a reasonably normal sounding male voice, though I appear to be alone.

"Oh, I'm pretty sure I'm not."

A man in a black cloak with a mantle, little round sunglasses, and a top hat emerges from the shadows between two mausoleums. He's not terribly tall, only about my height, but has a severe look to his features that still makes him come off as intimidating despite being dressed like an actor from the set of *Les Mis*. The way he carries himself, the energy burning in his eyes is somehow familiar despite me never having seen this man before. We stare at each other for a moment before a thought occurs to me. I've heard the voice before… Cornelius. Dracula's dark master.

"He will be reunited with her. No matter what you do," says the pleasant male voice behind me.

"No shit. Containing her isn't my problem anymore." I snarl and try to raise a mental wall, shielding myself from this demon's mental assault. Cornelius wouldn't refer to himself in third person. That's not really him.

The European graveyard disappears, replaced with my bedroom back in Fullerton. I'm standing near the door, while Danny and another version of me are going at it hot and heavy. Based on his hairstyle and age, I think we're in the process of making Anthony.

"Your life is over, Samantha Moon," says the silky voice. "Your time is finished."

"In case you missed a memo somewhere, you are a demon, numbnuts. You have nothing to do with dark masters."

"They will usher in a new age of misery upon humanity… and that, I wish to watch and savor."

In a flash of light, the scenery changes again. I'm on the beach, standing beside myself. Other-me relaxes on a folding lounge chair in a bikini.

"You used to adore the sun."

I tap my foot. "We made up. I can go to the beach if I want to now. Get the hell out of my head."

A rushing noise draws my attention to the left. Danny, in bright red swim trunks, holds two-year-old Anthony up to eye level, exhaling a stream of black vapor, which draws into my son's mouth and nostrils. Rather than struggle or protest, Anthony breathes deep, welcoming it.

"You are fighting a doomed battle against her. Everything you do is futile. Everything you cherish dies or changes. Your *beloved* husband is going to corrupt him. It has already started. Warrior of Light —Hah!—you are painfully naïve."

Infuriated at this arrogant silky voice, I spin, swinging the Devil Killer at empty air. False-me's hair flutters in the breeze of the blade going over her head, but she doesn't react. "You lie! Danny's a wretch. He's weak. He has no power over my son."

"Oh, how you fool yourself, Sam. Your precious son is already lost to you. Why do you think he is so responsible and sweet? What fifteen-year-old boy is *that* well-behaved? He deceives so you do not suspect the truth."

"Liar!" I roar.

With every ounce of willpower I can summon, I turn my power inward, trying to force this thing out of my head. I stagger away from the beach chair, slashing wildly at nothing. Every random person I hit with the blade merely disappears.

"Out!" I scream. "Get out of my thoughts!"

The demon voice laughs.

"Daniel is slowly twisting your son's mind. Even Anthony does not realize he will become a scourge upon the Earth. That blade in your hand is the only thing that will be able to stop him. Will you be able to do it, Samantha Moon? Will you kill your son to protect the entire world?"

Tears stream out of my eyes at the mere thought, but I have to cling to the knowledge that this is a demon trying to break me. It lies. Anthony is not evil. Danny is a shit, but he's Walmart made-in-China evil. He doesn't have the power to do anything like that. My son trusts him, but I also know as much as a bastard Danny was to me, in his twisted way, he thought he was protecting the kids. He wouldn't hurt them. He wouldn't corrupt them. Not intentionally.

"I hate you!" shrieks Tammy.

I look up, spinning right as my seventeen-year-old daughter lunges at me. The beach is gone. I'm back in Arizona beside the bonfire of bodies. She slaps me across the face hard enough to knock me over.

"You're such a bitch!" shrieks Tammy. "What kind of mother gets turned into a vampire and stays around her family? I'm a goddamned *freak* because of you. And look what you did to Ant! You murdered him when he was only six! And you made him into a mega-freak too!"

"Sam?" asks Mindy, her voice nearby but also

distant. "You okay?"

I scramble to my feet as Tammy runs in again, her black hair mostly covering her face like that girl from *The Ring*. She catches me with a right hook, then a left jab, then another right cross that sends me stumbling to the side. Instinctively, I recover my balance and bring the blade up to defend myself—but it's Tammy. I can't strike her.

"Tam Tam, you—"

"Don't call me that!" shrieks Tammy. "I'm not a goddamned child anymore."

I dive out of the way when she lunges again, backpedaling out of her reach. She may be a ridiculous telepath, but she's no faster than a normal teenager. "Calm down, Tammy. What are you even doing here?"

She laughs. "Wow, you're so damn easy to manipulate." Her sinister smile fades to an innocent look of contemplation. "I suppose I really should have listened to you after all. We went to Las Vegas anyway. You were right. I shouldn't have gone. I died in a car accident. Veronica was high and swerved in front of a big rig on our way home."

My heart almost shatters. "No…"

"Sam?" asks Mindy. "What are you doing?"

"So, anyway… the demons got me." Tammy rolls her eyes. "Guess living with a vampiric monster stained my soul or something. Better enjoy these next few minutes, 'cause they're the last you'll ever see of me. At least until you have to identify my body… if they can even find the Ziploc bag they scooped it into."

"No..." I shudder with grief.

"There's nothing left for you, Mom. Anthony's going to become some supreme evil, and I'm already gone. Might as well help Elizabeth and these damn zombies... and just say fuck it."

I stare down at the dead weight of the Devil Killer hanging in my limp hand. The idea of Tammy being dead repeats again and again in my thoughts. It's all I can think about. For as long as she's lived, I've done everything I can to protect her, and now... she's... dead...

I picture her four-year-old face staring up at me with pure worry and concern that day I first saw myself disappear from a mirror. The day I almost bit her. She had no idea what kind of monster I'd become, and I don't think she'd have cared back then. I was Mom. She worried about her mother. Maybe this Tammy is right. I shouldn't have subjected my innocent daughter to being around a creature like me.

I sob, lost to regret and grief.

Tammy grins, her eyes sparkling in victory.

Victory?

My tears slow to a stop. It wouldn't matter how furious Tammy was with me, that little girl who cuddled by my side after I'd been shot, the same kid who thought simply being next to me would make my pain stop, would never take such *delight* in causing me grief.

Tammy chuckles, shaking her head. "You're

such a loser, Mom."

A faint snarl escapes my throat. I pounce at her, tackling her over backward. She goes wide-eyed, struggling to push me away, but she's only a mortal. I'm a vampiric monster. Tammy's arrogant swagger collapses into a pitiful whimpering plea.

"Mom… stop. You're scaring me."

I press the flat of the Devil Killer against her forehead. It burns on contact, sizzling and spewing smoke.

"Get out of my mind, demon! You are not my daughter!"

She screams.

"Out!" I press harder. Small fires start on Tammy's face.

Again, she screams, but the shrill howl of a teenage girl in agony pitch-shifts down into the dreadful bellow of a demon.

Something comes out of nowhere and crashes into the side of my head. For an instant, I'm weightless.

Then everything explodes into white energy.

Chapter Thirty-Two
Stoned

I find myself staring up at a starry night sky, motes of fire and ash drifting by above me.

The scent of burning carrion adds a putrescent note to the wind. Hmm. I'm flat on my back listening to faint squealing noises emanating from my cheek as the bones begin knitting back together. Something walloped me pretty hard.

Crap. Demon.

I spring up into a somersault, not a full second before a big clawed hand pounds the dirt where I'd been.

"Sam," shouts Mindy. "What are you doing?"

"Trying not to die," I yell.

"No, I mean you were just staring at that *thing*."

I roll to my feet and turn toward it, gripping the sword in both hands—but it's on me too fast. I abort my attempt to swing and again somersault to avoid a sideways slash. It stumbles from the force it poured into the attack, catches its balance, and wheels around to growl at me. Its entire head splits open down the middle as it roars from a sideways mouth, blasting me with the leaf blower from hell. The brief gale is painfully hot and powerful enough to knock me back a few steps.

Mindy runs at it from the side and hammers her fist into its chest. Both tennis-ball-sized nipple eyes shift toward her. She draws back her hand to hit it again, but it palms her face like a schoolyard bully and shoves her over onto her back.

Taking advantage of the distraction, I run in with a slash. It pivots to the side, causing the blade to glance off its torso with a *clank.* Damn. Armored chitin. It rears back to slash at me; I avoid its attack by hurling myself into a backflip. Mindy leaps in an attempt to tackle the demon, but winds up grabbing it around the thighs and carrying it only a few steps. Its massive wings flap, holding it upright. As soon as she sets it down, it plucks her off and casually tosses her aside as if throwing a too-small fish back to the stream.

She lands on her chest with an *oof* and slides a half dozen feet.

It whirls at me with a left handed rake; I slash into its attack, parrying and drawing black blood. The demon growls and tries to grab me with its other hand. I dart to the side, hacking at its armored wrist to little effect. It launches itself into a flurry of claw swipes, and for a moment, we duck and avoid each other. The few times I penetrate its defenses, my blade bounces off it. Twice, Mindy runs in, and twice it throws her aside like an annoying child.

Evidently, she *is* its pet project and it doesn't want to ruin her yet. Ugh. If this thing survives, it's going to be a big ass problem. Both for her, and likely humanity in general. Our stalemate ends when it nails me with a wing bash I don't expect. The hit doesn't hurt—much—but it does throw me fifteen feet to a chest-first landing on hard-packed dirt.

Okay, *that* hurt.

I sit up, spitting out dirt. I'm going about this all wrong. Why am I trying to make *new* holes in armor that I'm clearly not strong enough to punch new holes in?

My inner alarm is going nuts, which means the sucker is just behind me.

Sensing it at the perfect distance, I spring up and spin around with a two-handed thrust, plunging the Devil Killer straight into its left nipple-eye. The blade pierces with ease, sliding a good eighteen inches deep before the tip hits the inside of its back armor and stops. Bubbling, smoking lime-green foam wells up from the wound. It raises its head and lets out a horrible cry of anguish at the sky.

The demon swoons, staggering away from me, its giant vertical lips flapping with a belabored groan. My sword doesn't want to come loose, dragging me after the thing. Refusing to let this monster disarm me, unintentional as it may be, I jump up and mule kick it in the chest with both feet while pulling at the sword. The weapon tears loose, syrupy black ooze gushing from the empty socket. I fall flat to the ground on my back, gawking at the deflated eyeball stuck three quarters of the way down the sword. Steam wafts from a thick tarlike substance coating the part of the blade that had been inside.

Its remaining eye widens in terror, fixating on me. The demon can't seem to quite stand up to its full height anymore, and clutches its left arm curled up close to the wound.

"Oh, you finally realize what I'm holding, huh?" I smile.

"*Zhat vorxha!*" snarls the demon in an inhumanly deep voice.

"Whatever you just called me, back atcha."

It whirls away, heading for the pyre—probably hoping to jump back down its hole to hell before I can finish it off. A quick dash puts me in front of it. I manage to sink a few inches of sword into a seam between armor plates on its gut before it slaps me aside.

Wow. I'm getting really sick of eating dirt.

Before it can get all the way past me, I lunge up to my knees and slash at its ankle. The superficial cut makes it stumble, but doesn't stop it. Damn. If this thing gets away, we're not going to be rid of it for a long damn time. I doubt it would be arrogant enough to show itself in person again after having a good taste of this sword.

I unfurl my wings and power up in a flap-leap, arcing about fifteen feet into the air. Screaming a war cry, I grab the sword inverted in both hands like a giant dagger and swoop down onto its back, my feet on either shoulder, and stab the Devil Killer down into its hide. The force of my hit knocks the demon over onto its face.

Yes. Payback time!

"How's that dirt taste, shithead?"

It groans as I wrench the blade with a half twist and yank it loose.

One of its wings coils around me, the claw barb at the joint hooking my shoulder. I let out an involuntary scream of pain as it flings me to the ground on my side with a huge bleeding hole in my left arm.

Enraged, the demon drags itself upright and whirls to face me. It stomps on my sword, pinning it to the dirt, then laughs at me when I discover I lack the strength to pull it clear.

Mindy lets out a war shout worthy of a Viking shield-maiden.

I look up in astonishment a split second before a broken-off gravestone comes down on top of the demon's human-shaped head with a wet, meaty *splat.* The next thing I know, I'm covered in boiling hot black ooze.

When I manage to peel my eyes back open, the demon's tottering there, headless. Well, I *think* it's headless. She might've pounded its skull down into its intestines for all I know. Or maybe it simply exploded. If the amount of scalding hot demon blood everywhere is any indication, its head detonated. Mindy huffs like she's out of breath, still clinging to a two-by-three-foot tombstone that's at least four inches thick. She's brandishing it like a styrofoam Halloween decoration.

"Holy shit," I mutter.

The demon collapses to the ground, the rest of its body rapidly melting into a small lake of black, steaming ooze that seeps into the dirt.

"Yay!" Mindy waves the stone slab over her head and shouts, "What do *you* want on your Tombstone!"

"Ugh." I'm not sure if I'm groaning at that pun or the sensation of being covered in hot slime.

"Yay! I got it," cheers Mindy, tossing the lump of granite aside. It hits the ground with a *thud* that jars my bones.

"Damn, you're kinda strong." I push myself up to sit. "But, you actually didn't kill it. You only sent it back to… wherever they go. It's not dead." I hold up the black sword. "Only this can truly kill it."

"Oh." Her enthusiasm dies. She slouches. "Sorry. Oops."

"Damn, you have a hell of an arm."

A geyser of black ichor erupts from beneath me, launching me ten feet in the air. The spraying liquid coalesces into the shape of the demon, its right hand clamped around my chest. Flowing ooze begins to harden again into armor plates.

"Oh, screw you," I groan.

I swipe the sword at the semiliquid forearm holding me up. Above the slash, the limb disintegrates to smoke. As I start to fall, I whirl the Devil Killer around and chop at the base of its neck, tearing a rent down into its torso to the midway point. Its outer layer hardens once again into demonic armor, leaving me hanging by my grip on the blade, my feet a good twelve inches off the ground.

The demon emits a gurgling noise, part growl of anger, part death rattle.

My sword wobbles, then stabs itself six inches deeper in.

"Whoa, what the heck? Did Azrael give me a sentient weapon? Is this blade thirsty for demon blood?"

It keeps trying to burrow deeper all on its own, and slices downward another half a foot. The demon's entire body explodes into a dark mist, revealing Mindy holding the tip of the sword, which had stuck out its back.

She'd pulled the blade in and down, evidently the last little distance needed to hit the heart. Both of us drip with black slime like we went swimming in Tar Lake.

"Nice assist. Thanks."

"Awesome. Now is it dead?"

I glance at the dissipating fog and vanishing bones. "Yeah. *Very* dead."

Chapter Thirty-Three
The Morning After

One moment I'm scraping burned bodies and demon bits into a hole, the next thing I know, I'm on a bed staring at the ceiling.

It takes me a few seconds for the disorientation to clear from my head, and I recognize the Hogans' guest bedroom. Except for my shoes, I'm still fully dressed, but wrapped in an old sheet and set on top of the covers. The instant I try to move, I realize why: everything is sticky.

"Ugh," I mutter and sit up.

My hair sticks to the bedspread, but peels away with minimum pain. The shirt I'm wearing feels like it's been affixed to me with wallpaper glue, and it's gone crusty in parts. Yeah… I'm going to need a forever shower.

I sit there surrounded by funk for a few minutes,

not quite sure I want to know what it would feel like if I tried to move. Why the hell do demons *always* have to die in a shower of blood? Mindy pokes her nose in, sees me awake, and enters carrying a white plastic jug. She's changed into a cute pink sweater with white kittens on it and sweat pants.

"Hey. If you wanna use the shower, I can loan you something to wear while the washing machine chews on your clothes." She looks me over and winces. "Can I get you blood or something? My little brother works on a farm."

"I don't do the blood thing anymore."

"Yeah, I know. Just trying to make a stupid joke."

I chuckle. "I never liked having to drink blood before anyway. Something… major happened to me not long ago and I changed. So… What happened? How did I wind up back here?"

"You just passed out while we were cleaning up all the demon bits. Guess you were exhausted."

"Ugh." I rub my forehead, almost at the point where I can't hold back the urge to drain energy from people. "Yeah."

"It's okay. I told my parents you were just tired. And, my dad *did* see the demon. Don't worry, they're not going to tell anyone. They don't want to wind up in the hospital with padded walls."

I exhale, nodding. Yeah, that story would go over well. All they'd have to say is 'nipple eyeballs' and they'd be fitted for a strait jacket.

Mindy fills me in on how she and her father

managed to scrape the cemetery back into passable shape. A couple days of wind should erase the dark spot where the zombie bonfire had been; then again, few come this way anyway. I wince-walk to the bathroom. It feels like I've been dipped in molten plastic, which hardened into an annoyingly tight, adhesive bodysuit. Mindy follows me in, but I'm beyond caring at this point—and I might need her strength to get out of this outfit.

Piece by piece, I peel my clothes off. Yeah, there's some skin tears as the 'glue' tugs at me.

Fortunately, the vampire who made me had awesome timing. He got me right after I shaved my legs and certain other areas. So I have a minimum of body hair that'll never grow back. At the moment, that's a *real* advantage… as this dried demon blood would've ripped everything out by the roots. It's worse than wax. Since Mindy didn't warn me about that effect, I imagine she changed and cleaned up before it dried. Lucky dog.

My skin looks like a critical failure at purple tie-dye. Not an inch of me is the color I should be, except my face since I'd managed to wipe that off before passing out.

"Cool. I'll throw your things in the machine. Be right back with something you can borrow 'til the wash is done."

I rub my jeans between two fingers. It's somewhere between sticky and armored. "I'm not sure this *can* be washed. Are you sure?"

"Yeah, my mom has this detergent from like the

sixties. It'll eat anything, even demon blood."

"Now there's a marketing slogan."

Laughing, Mindy heads out and shuts the door.

A few minutes into my shower, Mindy pops back in long enough to drop off some clothes. It takes a surprisingly long time to scrub dried demon blood off my skin. It's so thick and stubborn it basically counts as wearing something. Fortunately, they have one of those horrid yellow pumice soaps on the shelf in addition to the normal stuff, probably for Art since he works with his hands... but it does the trick. I use up way too much shampoo, but eventually think I'm back to normal. A hint of residual stickiness remains in my hair, but it's got to be in my head. Just to be sure, I wash it a fourth time.

I hop out, dry off, and put on the offered T-shirt and jeans. Only, the jeans fall straight off me. Guess they're Louise's. Not that she's fat. She's the size I probably should be at this age, while I'm still curvy in the hips, I'm even leaner now than I had been when a bloodsucker. Guess there's not a lot of calories in mental energy. Still, I only need to put up with the borrowed pants for about two hours. I can't say I'm surprised at the lack of loaner underwear—that's a little too personal to borrow, but it feels super bizarre to go commando in someone else's house.

With a hand on the waist to hold the jeans up, I head out of the bathroom and find the Hogans gathered in the kitchen around the table.

"Fit okay?" asks Mindy

"Little loose, but I'll deal." I sit.

"Thank you for helping out with that… situation," says Art, swaying in his seat. He looks like he got only an hour of sleep.

"Not a problem." I lean my elbows on the table.

"Are you hungry?" asks Louise. "I could whip up some eggs or something, even if it is noon."

"That sounds great," I say, and tap into some of her overabundance of energy... just enough to clear my head. I leave Art out of it. The poor guy doesn't have an ounce of energy to spare.

Mindy turns to me as her mother breaks a couple of eggs over what appears to be a non-stick skillet. "So, Sam… I've been talking to my parents most of the morning. They're adjusting to what happened, and are being super supportive. I'm gonna try and make a go of having as normal an existence as I can. Umm. We were worried though. What *was* that black blob that came out of me?"

Her parents fidget and look at me like I'm some kind of guru of all things FUBAR.

"Well… based on some other supernatural creatures I've had a"—I wink at Mindy—"lot of experience with, it may be essentially a 'power' of yours that you can do whenever you want to. Though, I wouldn't advise using it. Those minor zombies are likely quite contagious and no matter your reason for summoning them, it runs the risk of getting out of control. Remember, just one such creature can cause a major outbreak."

"Yeah. Like bacteria multiplying." She nods. "It's kind of a lame superpower, right? I can't even use it because I might accidentally apocalypse the world."

"Apocalypse isn't a verb, sweetie," says Louise.

Art and I crack up.

Someone outside screams. Momentarily forgetting my oversized jeans, I leap to my feet. My vampiric reflexes have saved my ass numerous times over the past thirteen years. In this moment, they literally save my ass—from exposure. I manage to grab the jeans before they fall more than an inch or two, and run barefoot to the front door. At the *crack* of a gunshot, I dash outside. Mindy and her parents follow close behind.

Maybe a quarter mile away to the right, the next nearest house, I spot a man with a shotgun standing on a dirt road near two bodies. One's completely still in a white dress, the other's also a fan of the flannel-and-jeans thing, and he's still twitching. The guy with the gun is almost as pale as Mindy, shaking and sweating.

He looks up at me as I jog over to stand beside him, gazing down at the remains of a woman of indeterminate age. She's clearly a zombie, and between the shotgun blast to the face and severe decay, it's anyone's guess how old she was at the time of death. The guy lying next to her looks a few years into his thirties, and has a gushing human bite wound on the side of his neck. He's still alive, but bleeding out rather rapidly despite clamping his hand over the injury. A shiver runs down my back as the scene is a little too close to home for me. Though, my neck wound had been quite a bit bigger.

"What the shit is this?" asks the man with the shotgun. "Am I hallucinating or is that a goddamn zombie? It came outta nowhere and jumped on Lenny. Bit him sure as shit."

Lenny gurgles, reaching up toward us. Given the amount of blood already on the dirt, he's a lost cause. Maybe if a medical helicopter had already been parked right here ready to go, he'd have a chance… Talos, of course, could do it. His powerful wings could hit ungodly speeds. Except there was a problem here. A major one. Already, I could see Lenny's aura shrinking in on itself. I'm fairly certain the man was turning as we spoke.

And yeah, I wind up fixating on the gore, but *don't* find myself licking my lips. In fact, I'm not the least bit hungry at the sight of blood… even repulsed.

"What happened?" asks Mindy in a too-apologetic tone.

I give her a 'wait a sec' hand, and face Shotgun Boy. "Zombie? Nah. There's no such thing. You didn't see anything at all."

The man stares into space for a few seconds, then walks off like we don't even exist.

Lenny gurgles and flops lifeless. Something light and shimmery slips free from the man, and moves toward another bright and shiny mass at the corner of my vision, something I can't quite see, but know is there.

"Oh, shit…" Mindy covers her mouth and starts crying. "I know that guy. Never really talked to him much though. He's like twelve years older than me. Lives on the other side of town in the southeast."

I prod the rotting woman with my toe. "Looks like we missed one."

"Sorry." My young friend cringes. "I think she was trapped in a well or pit or something. When I commanded them all back to the cemetery, she didn't go anywhere. Looked like she was buried way underground already so I didn't pay her any mind."

"Guess she figured out how to climb."

"Lenny feels funny to me, Sam. He's turning, like right now."

I sigh and pull the Devil Killer.

"I can't look." Mindy averts her eyes.

One chop into Lenny's head severs the top at the level of the eyes. Half a brain and the skull cap wobbles around like a hubcap falling off a tire.

I squat beside him to keep my jeans from falling off, and wipe the blade on Lenny's shirt. "Yeah, he turned."

Mindy nods. "I felt him starting to wake up again. Just didn't want to watch you kill someone I knew… well, sorta knew." She wipes her tears. "Umm, did I kick him off the circle of life, too?"

"No, that's the dark master thing. This is more like black magick jumping into dead meat and making it move around."

She nods. "Umm. Am I contagious, or is it just the other ones?"

I glance over at her. "Not sure. You should probably try to avoid randomly biting people."

Mindy laughs. "Yeah, well. I wasn't planning to. Just curious."

"So what are you going to do?"

"Help you burn these bodies."

"No, I mean long term."

"Probably move back in with my parents after this school year's over. I don't want to leave my roommates high and dry, but come summer, I think it'll be better if I'm in a remote place after dark. Plus my parents can help me with the whole special diet issue. If Natalie or Alisha find brains in the fridge, that'll be hard to explain."

"Yeah. Good call, but you're still going to have to figure out how to keep a low profile for the rest of the school year."

"I'll manage. I can eat raw beef or chicken until I return home."

I tug at the jeans, and motion to the bodies. "I'm not going to be much help at the moment with one hand. These jeans are going to fall off me if I let go of them."

Mindy chuckles. "It's okay. I'll take care of it. It's my mess." She hugs me. "Thank you so much for helping me. I'm still not sure if I should be crying my eyes out over being dead or happy I have superpowers."

"I know the feeling. Haven't quite made up my mind yet on that one either."

She grins. "Guess you're going home once your clothes are dry."

"Yeah. I need to get back."

"Right. Is it okay if I call you if something weird happens or I have questions? I mean, Lenny here was technically murdered by a zombie. Someone's going to come looking for him."

I look at her. "If they do, let me know, and I can pop in real quick and redirect the inquiry. Also, practice your own telepathy slash mind control. The dark master within you is a powerful one. Undoubtedly, the thing still has a few tricks up its sleeve."

"I can just use him like that?"

"In a weird way, you're kind of one now. What's his is yours, and vice versa."

"So creepy, but okay."

I smile. "You also probably should light a gasoline fire here on the blood. Just in case it's contagious, too."

"Ick. All right."

I glance up at the clouds. Zombies. Go figure. Never imagined that happening. Then again, when I first became a vampire, I never thought I'd be able to see a daytime sky again.

The world is a weird place.

Chapter Thirty-Four
The End of the World

Four hours into the ride home, the guy on the radio cuts in with a news bulletin about a zombie outbreak in El Paso.

Oh shit. Here we go. I bonk my head on the wheel a few times while chanting, "Please be idiots on bath salts. Please be idiots on bath salts."

The DJ and his buddy make fun of it for a little while before moving on to rip on Kanye for saying something about being a proud non-reader of books. Now I remember why I rarely listen to actual radio. Too many commercials and chatter. I plug in the cord to my iPod and hit random. The Momvan's too old to support an Mp3 player, so I need to plug it into an AUX port via a headphone wire. Guns 'N Roses *'Welcome to the Jungle'* comes up. Gee, how apropos.

When I check the news on my cell a few hours later, I learn that the zombie outbreak in El Paso was only a prank. Let's hope it stays that way.

I get bored on the drive. How bored? I start daydreaming about stupid shit like trying to make the Momvan into a vampire so it won't grow old and fall apart. If I changed my van into an undead, it would develop sentience and start talking to me… sort of like a suburban family version of *Knight Rider*. Would it pounce on other cars and suck the oil out of their engines?

Ugh. Yeah. I'm. That. Bored.

At least I don't have to stop for a bathroom break. I do, however, need a stop for gas. Out of habit and needing a flavor in my mouth other than demon blood, I grab coffee. Nothing like gas station java to wake you up—or strip paint. The guy behind the counter's wearing a shirt with the name Cletus above the pocket. Seriously. The dude's name is Cletus. I look around to make sure I haven't stumbled into a USA Up All Night zombie movie. Ugh. I'm going to be paranoid for the next few years.

Nothing unusual happens and I make my way back to the van, pay for the gas, and keep on driving while sipping coffee. It tastes like burnt disappointment and sadness, but it's better than the horror that had been lingering on my tongue since that thing's head exploded right in front of me.

Yay for time zones. I arrive home a little after eight, gaining an hour. By this time, I'm so bored and fried from hours of staring at road with no one to talk to, I consider a vampire on a jet plane flying west. If they experienced perpetual night, would they ever sleep? Is vampire sleep based on Earth's rotation or an internal timer? If the sun never rises where they are, would they ever become tired?

Wow. Yeah, I'm out of it.

An unfamiliar forest-green car that looks all shiny and new sits on the street in front of the house. Tammy, her hands full of grocery bags, is halfway across the front yard to the door when I pull into the driveway. Another, rather slim, girl with long pale blonde hair behind the car pulls a few more bags out of the trunk and hurries after her. I park, cut the engine, and hop out, folding my arms in surprise at finding my daughter being so… domestic.

The girl trots up behind her and smiles at me. As soon as there's no car blocking most of my view, I realize *he's* not a girl at all.

The boy is amazingly cute, with striking emerald eyes. For a second, looking at him leaves me stuck in a mental warp trying to comprehend his presence. I've never seen a boy—or anyone really —that beautiful. He's slim, but toned and athletic… enough to notice under his Zelda T-shirt and cargo shorts. He doesn't have any hair on his legs either, which is kinda weird. But maybe he's a swimmer. I think Tammy once said something about the boys on the swim team shaving to reduce drag in the water.

I'm dangerously close to staring at him for too

long, so I force myself to look away.

"Hey, Mom." Tammy holds up the bags. "I'd hug you, but my hands are full."

"Not a problem." I glance at the car—a Tesla—and blink. Oy. Not only does he have supermodel looks, he's got rich parents. Something's not right here. Not that I don't think my daughter's pretty enough to catch the interest of a cute boy, but he's throwing off 'too good to be true' vibes like mad. "Who's this?"

"Hello, Mrs. Moon," says the boy. "I'm Kai."

"We weren't sure when you were coming back. I hope you don't mind. Kai was going to cook dinner for us… me and Anthony."

"Miss is fine." I smile and lock stares with him… and whoa. He doesn't have an aura, nor can I see into his thoughts.

We migrate inside and I help put groceries away. Since Kai doesn't know where anything belongs, he focuses on cold stuff going to the fridge and leaves the cans and everything else to us.

Once the groceries are packed away, I fold my arms and fix him with a stare part overprotective mom, part curious. "Okay, Kai. Out with it. What sort of freak are you?"

"Mom!" yells Tammy, her face reddening. "Why is he a freak? Because he's interested in me?" She catches herself, no doubt looking into my head, and seeing what I'm seeing. "Oh. Umm. Sorry. Yeah."

The boy scratches his head. "You weren't

kidding when you said your mom was interesting."

"That's not an answer," I say.

"Sorry, Miss Moon. I'm no threat to you or Tammy."

I step closer and give him a once over... then the twice over. Okay, he's on the short side for a boy, roughly the same height as Tammy, which just so happens to be my height. Nearly nose to nose with him, I stare into his eyes, hunting for the telltale glow of a dark master. It's absent, but there *is* something. Soft greenish light lingers in there the same way the fire of possession would. Normal people wouldn't be able to see this glow... at least, I don't think.

Kai fidgets, but doesn't appear frightened of me. When I lean back, he casts a sidelong glance at Tammy.

"She knows," mutters Tammy. "I didn't tell her. She can see it. Or rather *can't* see your thoughts."

"He's something supernatural," I say. "Question is, what?"

"Mom's a little overprotective," says Anthony from the doorway.

"A *little*?" asks Tammy.

Kai chuckles. "From the few scraps you've told me, it sounds like she has every reason to be." He turns his gaze back to me with a warm smile and brushes his fingers through the hair on the side of his head. When his hand passes over his ear, I catch a brief glimpse of a point before it magically fades back to normal roundness.

Well, that's new. He's a fey? Elf?

Not that new, Mom, says Tammy's voice in my head. *He's like a thousand years old, but don't freak out, please? He's basically seventeen, I swear. Just like every other boy in school. Well, not exactly like them, but he's forever young at heart.*

Is that a new phrase for you, young lady? We will talk about this.

Yeah, yeah. And holy shit. Zombies? Seriously!? As soon as she hits the memory of me peeling off the blood-soaked clothes, she squirms and makes a face like she stepped barefoot in cat vomit. My daughter has seen some shit as they say, but that feeling would make anyone wince.

"I'll tell you about it later." I rub the bridge of my nose. "Give me a few. I need to change. Been stuck in the same outfit for days."

She nods. Kai sets about the task of cooking dinner. I'm about to consider it impressive that a boy his age can (and wants to) cook, but then I remember how old Tammy said he is. For a moment, I almost protest, but then again, I am dating a werewolf. All things considered, I suppose 'elf' is reasonably tame for this family. As long as he's functionally equivalent to seventeen, I'll deal. Plus, my daughter is just a few months shy of eighteen. I guess then she can do anything she wants. Of course, the rules of normal humans don't exactly relate to things like us.

The kids start discussing school as I walk out, a conversation that sounds remarkably out of place between them due to its mundanity. A potent telepath and an elf are standing in my kitchen discussing a Social Studies paper they have to write.

Go figure.

When I reach my bedroom, I stop short and stare at the ceiling, relieved that I managed to forestall a zombie apocalypse.

A few seconds later, it hits me.

Crap! My daughter has a boyfriend.

It *is* the end of the world.

The End

DEAD MOON

To be continued in:
Dragon World
*Vampire for Hire #18
Coming soon!*

About J.R. Rain:

J.R. Rain is an ex-private investigator who now writes full-time. He lives in a small house on a small island with his small dog, Sadie. Please visit him at www.jrrain.com.

About Matthew S. Cox:

Originally from South Amboy NJ, **Matthew S. Cox** has been creating science fiction and fantasy worlds for most of his reasoning life. Since 1996, he has developed the "Divergent Fates" world, in which Division Zero, Virtual Immortality, The Awakened Series, The Harmony Paradox, and the Daughter of Mars series take place.

Matthew is an avid gamer, a recovered WoW addict, Gamemaster for two custom systems, and a fan of anime, British humour, and intellectual science fiction that questions the nature of reality, life, and what happens after it.

He is also fond of cats.

Please find him at: www.matthewcoxbooks.com

Printed in Great Britain
by Amazon